For Greg

A NEW DAWN

Light slowly seeps into the early spring sky, but the town of Jeremiah is still asleep and dreaming. Its curtains and blinds are closed, its doors all locked. The streets and the sidewalks are empty and silent. Which is not to say that no one stirs. A solitary dog trots purposefully through the centre of town. A cat sleeping in the window of the barber's shop opens its eyes, stretches and yawns. A light goes on in the apartment over the hardware store. And, just outside the town limits, two figures suddenly appear, as if they've materialized out of the thinnest air. And perhaps they have, for they certainly look like no one else in Jeremiah.

The young man is dressed in sharply creased beige slacks and a dark green blazer with a cornflower in the buttonhole. He wears a tie. The young woman is dressed in worn, vintage jeans and a T-shirt with the portrait of Frida Kahlo with a monkey peering over her shoulder on it. Her hair is peacock blue. His is dark, but a little too long and parted in the middle. They are Otto Wasserbach and Remedios Cienfuegos y Mendoza. The rising sun bounces off the mirror polish of Otto's shoes and makes the tiny silver stars in Remedios' nose and ears shine. Except that they both look to be the same, indeterminate age, they are so dissimilar that it's difficult to believe they're actually together.

'Well, here we are!' says Otto with the brightness of a cheerleader urging on a losing team. And, in case his companion hasn't seen the large metal sign at the side of the road, reads, 'Welcome to

Jeremiah—Population 7068.' A small frown creases his perfect features. 'It really should be seven thousand and seventy, now.' Otto is something of a pedant.

His companion, however, is not. 'Show a little mercy, will you? We're not moving in. We're just visiting. Temporarily.'

Temporarily but indefinitely.

'We don't know how long we'll be here,' corrects Otto. 'It may be for quite a while.'

Remedios groans. Suffering Samaria, she certainly hopes not.

'Oh, I don't know . . .' Otto gazes into the distance to the tree-lined main street with its raised sidewalk and attractive storefronts, the windows gleaming, the awnings folded up for the night. The dog is just disappearing around the Methodist church. 'It doesn't seem so bad,' he says. He brushes something from the sleeve of his jacket. 'It looks rather pleasant, if you ask me.' A real, old-fashioned town.

Remedios rolls her eyes. 'Well, I didn't ask you,' she snaps. 'And if you ask *me*, what it looks like is a very long day in the desert.' Probably buried up to your neck.

'No, it doesn't. It's peaceful and it's attractive.' As sunlight falls over Otto, he almost seems to glow. 'Far from the cares and tears of the world . . .'

'Spare me.' Remedios is still snapping. 'You sound like a psalm.'

'And you sound like a doubter.' Which is something she's going to have to get over. Challenging situations demand a positive attitude, and the current situation—he and she working together—is nothing if not a challenge. Otto

2

AWAY FOR
THE WEEKEND

Dyan Sheldon

PLUS

First published in Great Britain in 2011 by
Walker Books Ltd
This Large Print edition published 2012
by AudioGO Ltd
by arrangement with
Walker Books Ltd

ISBN: 978 1445 886251

British Library Cataloguing in Publication Data available

Printed and bound in Great Britain by
MPG Books Group Limited

gestures to the thickly forested slopes that loom up around them. 'What about those mountains, Remedios? And those trees! They're glorious.' He takes a deep breath. 'Just smell that air.' He smiles and the morning brightens perceptibly. Locationwise, this is the best assignment he's had in centuries. 'You know, I do believe I'm going to like it here. I believe I'm going to like it very much.'

Remedios scowls and the sky dims. 'Well, I'm not.' She isn't that interested in trees and mountains, or even in peace. She'd much rather be on the *Titanic*. With plenty to do. 'What are we supposed to accomplish *here*?' Her gesture doesn't take in the inspiring landscape, just the pristine, well-ordered road on which they stand. 'They don't even have litter.'

Otto's sigh is as soft as the beating of a butterfly's wings. 'You know what we're supposed to do here, Remedios. It was made extremely clear.' He might add 'again', but doesn't. 'We're here to guard and guide.'

'Guard and guide . . .' parrots Remedios in a childish voice. 'What are we? FBI agents? Boy Scouts? Cops?'

But they are, of course, none of those things.

'No, Remedios,' answers Otto in his patient, literal way, 'we're angels. We—'

'For the love of Lachish, Otto, I do know we're angels.' She's been one for millennia. And a very good one, too, even if she has to say so herself—which, at this point in time, she apparently does. 'It was a rhetorical question.'

'I know that,' says Otto—who didn't. 'But you don't seem to understand that guarding and guiding are what we're meant to do. That's our job.

3

We have rules.'

Remedios makes a face. Ten Commandments for mankin', but a hundred rules for divine beings.

'And t' e primary rule,' Otto goes on, 'is that we help, r rture and support. We can influence, but we'r not supposed to interfere.'

Remedios makes a so-what? face. It's not as if 'ney can't interfere. They have powers a magician can only dream of—from being able to do a thing by simply thinking it to turning back floods or armies; from shifting shape to stopping time.

'But we can't use our powers willy-nilly,' says Otto. 'We can't just alter the course of human events.'

This, of course, is a dig at Remedios. Remedios isn't too keen on guarding and guiding. She sees herself as part of the life force, not as a celestial policeman, and is easily drawn into people's lives and problems. No matter how complex or difficult. No matter how impossible to solve. If she were a plumber and not an angel, she would rather try to mend the hole in a dam than fix a leaking radiator. Over the centuries, Remedios has ministered at thousands of wars, accidents and disasters, started revolts and uprisings, and stopped purges and pogroms. For her, ending up in Jeremiah is like moving from Paris to an asteroid. But, of course, she is not here by choice. She is here because of her very long history of doing more than she has to— or more than anyone wants her to. God may have infinite wisdom, but that doesn't mean that He also has infinite patience. In her last mission, Remedios went too far, even for her. She was supposed to help the residents of an English village in their fight to stop the government demolishing their houses for another runway, and instead she lead them in a demonstration that shut down one of the busiest airports in the world for ninety-six hours. She is here to learn self-control. There are to be no more grand gestures or dramatic interventions. No more getting carried away. No more sticking her nose into things that don't concern her. Forget the flood; just fix the leak. *There are no small problems*, she was coldly informed, *only small angels*.

'Oh, don't you go putting all the blame on me.' Remedios has finally stopped snapping and is snarling instead. 'Let's not forget that you're here because you messed up, too.'

'I didn't mess up.' Otto certainly never brought global air travel to a standstill. He never even started a very small revolution. 'I just tend to be a little disconnected.'

'Yeah, right,' says Remedios. 'I heard it's more like Absent Without Leave.'

Otto's problem is the opposite of Remedios'. Otto is an angel who likes order. That, he believes, is his job: to create and maintain order. Not to carry messages between Earth and Heaven like a mailman: the seraphic express. And definitely not to shake the box.

Remedios, however, likes chaos. Energy, matter, heat and space. Colliding planets and shooting stars. A soupy swamp one day and a green-blue world teeming with life the next. Bam, whizz, pop, fizz—that's what Remedios likes; to mix things up and see what happens.

Otto prefers to know what will happen. He sees safety in systems. Miraculous Methusela, there are only Ten Commandments; think how much better the world would be if people actually followed

5

them.

So, while Remedios can't stop herself from getting involved with humans, Otto likes to keep his distance. He much prefers other species. You know where you stand with killer whales; but people are much more difficult to deal with. They complain a lot about Acts of God, but if you ask Otto, it's the Acts of Man that cause most of the trouble. When people aren't being irrational, they're being deceitful. Or treacherous. Or greedy. Or violent. And if they're not actually dangerous, they're probably totally useless. No wonder the world is filled with so much unhappiness and suffering. Otto doesn't mind straightening out a misunderstanding or giving someone a shove in the right direction (indeed, he not only offers sound financial advice, he's extremely good at finding lost things), but when he's asked to intervene in a real crisis, he never quite succeeds. Suffering and cruelty, injustice and hypocrisy, thievery and opportunism—all these things upset him so much that he winds up paralysed by depression. The incident that led to Otto being in Jeremiah is a perfect example. He was sent into a combat zone to sway hearts and minds, and instead was so horrified by what he saw that he simply disappeared. It was days before he was finally found on a remote Scottish island, surrounded by sheep. No wonder he likes Jeremiah; on the Richter scale of misery, Jeremiah never goes above one.

'Remedios, I really don't want to discuss this any more. This is a new beginning for both of us.' Do well here, and who knows how they might be rewarded. Otto has dreams of being assigned to the Andes, so close to the sky that he walks in clouds.

'Let's just do the job we've come to do.'

'It's not a job,' she gripes. 'It's more like a hobby.' Knitting while the world cries out for hope and help. 'Besides, I'd much rather work alone.'

'And I wouldn't?'

But that, of course, is not the deal. The deal is that they work together. Partners. A team. Her habit of acting first and thinking later balanced by his habit of thinking first and not acting at all. Together, goes the reasoning, they make one perfect angel.

A car passes them, and then another.

'We'd better get a move on.' Otto points not towards the town, but to the north. 'We don't want to get there after everyone else.'

Remedios' day just got worse. Glory Hallelujah, the school! She forgot about the school. As a further challenge—or downsizing—they've been stationed at the high school.

'I don't see why we can't look after—'

'Don't start again,' says Otto. 'You know what you were told: there are no small problems, only small angels.' And with that he sets off up the road on the right.

Shuffling behind him, Remedios glances back at the town sign. *Welcome to Jeremiah*, it says. *Population 7070*.

TWO, POSSIBLY THREE, OF THOSE
IRONIES FOR WHICH LIFE IS FAMOUS

It is a beautiful day in Jeremiah. The sky is clear and blue, the sun is big and bright, and there is a breeze as gentle as Heaven's breath. It's a breeze that carries not just the chemical smells of civilization but the scents of forest, sea and desert as well; not just the electric noises of human occupation but also the timeless singing of the world. This is the kind of day that makes you want to climb a tree, run through a shower of blossoms, paddle in the breaking waves—or just sit on a hillside, listening to the planet going about its business. A day to make you glad to be alive. Yippee! Though it has to be said that there is no particular *joie de vivre* in room 07W of Jeremiah High on this particular afternoon. This is the last class on a Friday. Everyone wants the day to end.

No one wants the day to end more than Gabriela Menz. Gabriela glances at her watch and then looks back to the front of the room, where Mr Sturgess is finally finishing off a lesson so long and boring that even by his standards it should win a prize. Geesh. The bell's going to go in about two minutes, and he's still writing. (Gabriela is not writing, because she knows she can get one of the boys to photocopy his notes for her—as per usual.) Gabriela's sigh is as soft as cashmere. Just because she doesn't have to get to another class doesn't mean she isn't in a hurry. She happens to be in a really big hurry. Her mother's picking her up to take her to the airport, and Gabriela has to change and reapply her make-up before she goes out to the car. Mrs Menz gets totally unreasonable about being kept waiting (just possibly because it happens so often), which means that if Gabriela wants to talk to Mr Sturgess she'd better do it now. Even though he has his back to her, Gabriela raises one slender arm, the gold rings and bracelets shining against her tanned skin. 'Mr Sturgess?' she calls. 'Mr Sturgess? Can I ask you something really quick? It's really important.'

Edward Sturgess' sigh is not as soft as cashmere, it's as sharp as a snapping twig. He's been teaching a long time. So long, in fact, that if it were any other voice interrupting him like this, he would ignore that voice and continue writing. If the voice persisted (as these voices always do) he would slowly swivel around with a sarcastic look on his face and ask what's so important that it couldn't wait a few minutes. Isn't it obvious that he's trying to get this on the board before the bell rings and they all stampede for the door like a herd of frightened cattle? 'This had better be good,' he'd say. 'At the very least, I hope God's just warned you that the world's about to end.'

But it isn't any other voice that's interrupting him. It's the voice of Gabriela Menz. Which, compared to the whining, whingeing and carping of most of his students, is like the sound made by tiny, hand-blown glass bells ringing across the secret mountain pass that leads to a hidden kingdom on an impossibly beautiful day.

'What is it, Gabriela?' He turns round, and she is gazing at him with her usual warm, open smile—her face radiant with youth and cosmetics. And confidence. Gabriela is a girl who always expects to be indulged, and is rarely disappointed. She was one of those babies everyone fussed over, and now she is well on her way to being one of those women for whom doors automatically open and seats instantly empty. She lowers her arm and her nails flash in the sunlight as if someone let loose a flutter of hot-pink butterflies. There is something

9

almost angelic about Gabriela Menz—something that makes it nigh on impossible to be annoyed with her, even when she's actually being incredibly annoying. When, for example, she's late for class because she had to touch up her eyeliner or change her socks. Or, as another example, when she won't wait till class is over to talk to him because she wants to touch up her eyeliner or change her socks before she goes home.

Good Lord, thinks Edward Sturgess. *Listen to me! What if it's something important? What if someone's terminally ill . . . Or, God forbid, dead . . .*

He frowns in concern. 'I hope everything's OK at home, Gabriela. If—'

'Oh yeah, yeah, yeah.' More brilliant butterflies shimmer in the air around her. 'It's not anything *bad*, Mr Sturgess. It's something really good.'

'Oh, right . . . something really good . . .' Well, that's a relief.

'See, the thing is, I'm a finalist in this really major fashion competition?'

Of course. He might have guessed. Fashion. Well, it wouldn't be chess.

There's a congratulatory rattle of applause from the girls (except for Beth Beeby who stares blankly ahead with the constipated look on her face that means she's worrying about something). The boys whistle and cheer, and someone shouts out, 'Way to go, Gab.'

Gabriela beams, pushing back a wayward strand of hair, pleased yet modest. When the display of support dies down, she picks up where she left off. 'You know, to discover the designers of the future?' Given the way he dresses, Gabriela isn't sure that this is something Mr Sturgess can

10

understand, but she gives him a hopeful smile. 'So anyway, this weekend they announce the winners at a big presentation. In LA. They're putting us up at this totally fabulous hotel, The Xanadu? And there's going to be a real fashion show where they model our clothes, and we're meeting designers and retailers and all kinds of professionals, and we're visiting this hot studio.' She pauses, briefly, for air. 'It's going to be awesome.'

'Well, congratulations, Gabriela. That's—'

'So you see, Mr Sturgess, I'm like not going to be able to do the homework for Monday. You know, because I'm going to be so busy?'

'I see.' Gabriela is far from stupid, but she is pretty much the poster child for lazy. Mr Sturgess doubts that she's ever read one of the assigned books from cover to cover. (Assuming, that is, that she's ever read more than the cover.) She looks up plots and critiques on the Internet, and watches the movies. And she is possibly the least motivated student he has ever taught. Gabriela has less interest in her academic subjects than a leopard has in playing the harpsichord, and the only reason she does as well as she does is because she gets everybody else to help her. Especially the boys. There was a time when it was the Three Rs that were important, but all that Gabriela cares about are the Three Cs—Cosmetics, Clothes and Celebrity. He suspects that if coming to classes didn't give her the opportunity to wear a different outfit every day, she would never show up. In this, however, Edward Sturgess is being slightly unfair. He would be surprised to learn that while it's true that Gabriela has never read an entire assigned novel, she has read over a dozen books on the

11

history of fashion. The simple fact is that Gabriela doesn't want to clutter her mind with unnecessary information. She thinks of her brain as being like a closet—a large walk-in, floor-to-ceiling closet, but a closet nonetheless. To pack it with things she'll never have any use for (things, for example, like calculus, the string theory, the works of William Faulkner) would be like filling your closet with bathing suits, sandals and sundresses when you live in Alaska. 'Well . . . I certainly don't want to appear churlish . . . '

Churlish is not a word found in Gabriela's closet, but it doesn't sound good. 'Oh please, Mr Sturgess . . .' She doesn't actually clasp her hands in prayer but she somehow gives the impression that she does. 'All my other teachers are letting me have an extension.'

Of course they are. Mr Sturgess isn't the only one who finds it hard to use the 'N' word around Gabriela Menz.

'Well, if all your other teachers are giving you extra time—' He breaks off as, out of the corner of his eye, he sees another hand—this one pale and unadorned, the fingernails resembling not exotic butterflies but a field attacked by locusts—tentatively raised just above head level. 'Yes, Beth?' Beth Beeby is more or less the anti-Gabriela Menz. If motivation were money, Beth would be a billionaire. She is not just the best student in his class, but the best student in every class she has. Hardworking, conscientious, punctual and diligent. If she were a railroad, every train would always be on time. Beth is the girl most likely to succeed—and, he thinks, cynically if automatically, drop dead by thirty-five. 'Don't tell me you want an extension,

12

too?'

That'll be the day they turn hell into an ice rink.

Everybody's laughing too much for Edward Sturgess to hear the sound of skates hastily being strapped on to cloven hooves.

*   *   *

Until now, it had never occurred to Beth to ask any of her teachers to let her hand her homework in late, even though, remarkably enough, she, too, is going away for an extremely busy and very important weekend. Beth doesn't make excuses. Excuses, she believes, are for losers and underachievers. Beth always gets her work in on time no matter what—even if she's ill, even if the electricity has been turned off again— and is used to staying up half the night, finally falling asleep still fully dressed with her head on her desk. Why should this weekend be any different? Every minute of it has been planned by the organizers—from the welcome dinner tonight to the presentation on Sunday—but that should still leave plenty of time for homework. According to the letter she received, the nights are free for socializing and relaxing, neither of which Beth does. Of course she has friends and they do things together (go to a museum, a play, a movie, a classical concert or a special exhibit), and last summer she went to a camp for gifted teens for a very long month—but that's not what most people mean by socializing or relaxing. They mean parties and barbecues and ball games and things like that. Beth hasn't been to a party since she was five (she threw up on one of the house plants because of the

13

stress of playing musical chairs and had to be sent home). She doesn't even relax when she's asleep.

When Gabriela asked Mr Sturgess for a special dispensation just to go to a *fashion* weekend, Beth could hardly believe what she was hearing. A fashion weekend? Was she serious? Yes, apparently she was. And Gabriela doesn't think a fashion weekend's frivolous? Good grief, it practically defines frivolity! Though Beth is fairly certain that Gabriela does nothing but talk about clothes every day of her life, the idea of going all the way to Los Angeles to do that for an entire weekend is nothing short of ludicrous. With all the problems there are in the world, it makes fiddling while Rome turns to charcoal seem like responsible behaviour. People are starving, wars are raging and the planet is dying—but Gabriela Menz's greatest ambition is to make sure we don't run out of handbags or shoes. It was then that Beth started feeling worried. Should she ask for an extension, too? She's already close to vibrating with anxiety about the weekend. In case it doesn't go well. In case she doesn't win. In case the other contestants are more sophisticated and knowledgeable about popular culture than she is— like last summer's gifted campers. She can already feel a migraine simmering like a brew of newts' eyes, frogs' toes and adders' forks in a cauldron behind her forehead. It couldn't hurt to take some of the pressure off, could it? She can still take her book bag, but if it turns out that she doesn't have time or she gets one of her attacks and has to go to bed, then at least she'll know that she won't be penalized if her homework's incomplete. Beth has been known to cry inconsolably over an A-. Though

14

at the moment what she feels is that she may be sick. It's all the tension and anticipation. She won't be able to wait until everyone leaves to ask Mr Sturgess privately, as she normally would. She has to get to the girls' room. Quickly.

And so Beth cautiously raises her hand.

'Yes, Beth?' Mr Sturgess looks over. He smiles. Kindly. 'Don't tell me you want an extension, too?'

'Well . . . I . . . Uh . . .' She can feel the blood racing to her face. She probably looks like a tomato. A tomato with glasses. And a pimple on its chin. 'I . . . Uh . . . I'm really sorry, but I—'

'Excuse me?' He leans towards her. Even though Beth always sits in the front row so people can't turn around to look at her if she says something, she speaks so softly that it's never easy to hear her if there's anybody else breathing in the room. 'What did you say?'

'I just . . . I'm sorry it's late notice, but I—'

Mr Sturgess sits down on the edge of his desk so that he's almost in front of her. 'Excuse me?' She seems to be apologizing. So, no change there. 'What are you apologizing for, Beth?'

'I'm not, I just . . .' Even if she can't see them, she knows that the whole class is looking at her now. 'I . . . I'm sorry but I . . .' She takes a deep breath and rushes on. 'I would like an extension. Please. If that's all right. I'm a finalist and I'm going away for the weekend, too.' And then, for some stupid reason and illustrating the truth of the statement that life is famous for its ironic coincidences, she adds, 'To Los Angeles. To The Xanadu.'

'*You?*' Mr Sturgess' smile starts to slide from his face. He used to think Beth had an older brother whose clothes were handed down to her. He can't remember ever seeing her in a skirt, let alone anything with a must-have label. 'You're a finalist in the fashion competition?'

The laughter is good-natured but still she couldn't get any redder if the Queen of Hearts had her painted. Her cheeks feel as if they may pop.

'No, no . . . I'm sorry . . . No, I'm not . . . No. Not fashion.' As the racket in the room increases, Beth's voice decreases. 'Writing,' she whispers. 'It's the Tomorrow's Writers Today National Competition.' Beth has been shortlisted for fiction. 'It's this—'

Edward Sturgess waves a hand at the rest of the class. 'Simmer down, guys . . . Simmer down!' He can tell this is something he should be interested in, but he can't hear what it is. 'Let's show—' *Let's show Beth a little respect here*, was what he was going to say, but the end-of-period bell and the ensuing noisy bolt for freedom cuts him off. When he turns back to Beth she is already out of her chair and moving fast. 'Beth?' he calls. 'Beth! Yeah, sure. Of course you can have extra time.' He watches her charge through the door. He has no idea if she heard him or not.

*   *   *

A solitary figure, dressed in jungle combat trousers and a souvenir T-shirt from a rock concert that happened over fifty years ago, sits on one end of the bank of sinks in the first-floor girls' room (west wing). Unusually for someone at Jeremiah High, her hair is not only peacock blue but woven into dozens of tiny braids. It is also unusual for a

16

Jeremiah student to have no reflection in the wall of mirrors on either side of the room, of course, but it is normal for an angel in invisible mode. Which Remedios is. She's having a break, enjoying the silence and reading the local paper she picked up in the staffroom. The *Jeremiah Crier* is unlikely to take any interest from the Dead Sea Scrolls, that's for sure. This issue contains a long article about the town budget. Another about raising money to restore the bandstand in the park. A recipe for low-fat cheesecake. Advice on fitting a new window. A photo collage of the elementary school's fair. An interview with 101-year-old Mrs Celeste Rubins who remembers when the trolley car ran between Jeremiah and East Jeremiah. A piece entitled: Youngsters Plant Trees. Advertisements for classes in tennis, golf, yoga, Pilates, kung fu, t'ai chi, scrapbooking, weaving, salsa, jewellery-making, a diet club, a walking group, Alcoholics Anonymous, baking and cooking. A photograph of three small children dressed as polar bears for the Earth Day celebration. The scores for the bridge club. The results of the county bowling tournament. Three birth announcements, two obituaries and a book review. Remedios sighs. The town of Jeremiah may be as exciting as cold mush, but next to the world of the high school it's a two-day royal banquet with minstrels.

Remedios yawns, and leans her head against the hand dryer. This is only the end of her third week here and although she's still, as it were, finding her wings, she couldn't be more bored if she were walking across mudflats on crutches. Not that the teenagers of Jeremiah don't have problems—they do have problems (to hear them talk, they

17

have more problems than Noah)—but they are no more than petty worries and everyday anguish and despair. They should try living through the sacking of Rome or the Blitzkrieg if they want a real problem.

The last bell of the day rings and Remedios lets loose another sigh. *Where,* she wonders, *are the innocent and lost souls who really need my help?*

The door opens and Beth Beeby hurls herself into the girls' room, miraculously managing to look both flushed and eerily green at the same time. Beth, of course, is no stranger to anxiety— it's the most constant companion she has—but her nervousness about the weekend surpasses anything she's experienced before. She desperately wants to win in the way that only a girl who is depressed by getting an A- rather than an A can; but at the same time winning means that she will have to do even better in the future—publish a novel before she's twenty-five, be profiled in *The New York Times,* win the Pulitzer Prize. Great expectations, of course, open the door to great disappointments.

Remedios watches Beth clasp a hand to her mouth and run to the end stall. Because Remedios often comes in here to avoid the tedium of hearing the same lectures and conversations over and over, she has seen Beth before. Sometimes Beth simply hides in the end stall reading a book, but sometimes she comes here to vomit or weep. This afternoon, it seems, she's come to do both.

The door opens again and Gabriela Menz glides in like an image on a screen, her book bag and handbag held over one shoulder and a suit bag in her other hand.

Gabriela is also a familiar face; the first-floor

girls' room (west wing) is practically her office.

Since Remedios isn't visible at the moment, Gabriela is oblivious to her presence, but she's equally oblivious to Beth's retching and sobbing in the corner stall. She dumps her stuff on the counter opposite the sinks and hooks the suit bag over the door of the nearest stall. While she changes out of her school clothes into her going-away-for-the-weekend clothes, Gabriela is thinking not about her mother, out in the parking lot, tapping the steering wheel and checking the time every few minutes, but about the next two days.

There are three reasons why Remedios doesn't normally bother listening to thoughts: it requires a lot of concentration; most of the time they're way less interesting than you might imagine; and if there are more than a few people around it's like listening to 97 TV channels at the same time. Now, however, she sits up, leaning forward, and tunes in. Gabriela doesn't have to worry about homework . . . blahblahblah . . . she can't wait to get to LA . . . blahblahblah . . . OMG that dikey girl, the brainy one, whatever her name is . . . she's going to be in LA, too, *in the same hotel* . . . like, really, what are the chances? blahblahblah . . . shopping . . . shopping . . . blahblahblah . . .

Other girls come and go—hurrying in and hurrying out again, eager to be away from school until Monday—but not Beth or Gabriela. Beth stays in her stall, sick with stress and nerves. Gabriela dresses with even more care than usual—changing everything from her shoes to her accessories—and then stays planted in front of the mirrors, redoing her make-up. She examines every inch of her face, peering and pulling and pouting—

19

touching up and then touching up again—until she's finally satisfied that the only thing that could make her look better would be plastic surgery. They'll both be lucky not to miss their flight.

But Remedios doesn't leave, either. She stays on the counter, her arms around her legs and her chin on her knees. She closes her eyes. Remedios has enormous empathy for humans, but even she sometimes finds it hard to feel compassion for a species that makes so much misery for itself. Now would be a good example. Listening to the muffled sounds of Beth's distress while watching Gabriela paint her face with the same care Leonardo took when painting Lisa del Giocondo in Florence that time, Remedios is struck anew by the strange ways humans find to occupy themselves—and how inventive they are when it comes to creating unhappiness. God gives them a miraculous planet of heartbreaking beauty—and what do they do? They do their best to destroy it. They pollute the air and land and oceans; they blow up mountains, dry up rivers and turn forests into deserts.

They don't treat themselves any better. They murder, they rape, they lie, they cheat, they steal and they bomb each other to Kingdom Come. They waste their time accumulating possessions, as though they're either planning to live for ever or take their golf carts and jewellery with them when they go. They worry about things that are a lot less important than a tree frog. Things like not having a certain handbag or a certain car; not being thin enough or pretty enough; not knowing more than anyone else about the history of Hungarian cinema or pop music; not having a big house; whether or not two celebrities they will never meet are really breaking up. Remedios stares at Gabriela's reflection in the mirror. Different as Gabriela and Beth are, each believes that she has to be, in her own way, flawless; that happiness comes not from the miracle of life itself, but from how you look or how much you know.

What was that poet's name? Remedios frowns. She can see him as clearly as she sees Gabriela fiddling with her eyebrows. They used to enjoy arguing about the meaning of life. He could get a little maudlin, especially after a couple of pints of ale, but he was clever and he wasn't a bad writer. 'What fools these mortals be . . . '—that was one of his. 'What fools these mortals be . . .' *Tell me about it*, thinks Remedios. She couldn't agree more. People should embrace life, not fear or hate it. God knows it's over quickly enough.

Finished at last, Gabriela checks her clothes one last time for specks of dirt and fluff. Meanwhile, in the corner stall, Beth is getting herself together, too, and starting to worry that her mother, waiting to drive her to the airport, will be worried that something has happened to her.

If you two had seen half the things I've seen you'd really have something to worry about, thinks Remedios. And it is now that she gets her idea. It is technically against the rules, of course, and it certainly isn't going to make the Earth a better place. But she was told to work on a micro, not a macro level. Those were the instructions—they were very clear—and this is as micro as you can get. *There are no small problems, only small angels . . .* Remedios smiles. Surely she can't get into trouble for doing as she was told.

As satisfied with her appearance as she's ever

21

likely to be, Gabriela scoops up her things and sashays off to find her mother. A few seconds later, Beth emerges, splashes cold water on her face and also leaves. Remedios is right behind her.

Otto, of course, is waiting in the hallway. If Remedios had a shadow, it wouldn't follow her more closely than Otto does. As always, the sight of Otto is one that, if she had a heart, would make it sink like a three-tonne block of steel thrown into a lake. Getting to know him over the last few weeks has done nothing to improve her opinion of him. In her opinion, Otto Wasserbach is a prime example of a person who doesn't know how to enjoy himself. The fact that they are saddled with one another can be considered another of life's famous ironies. As always, he is fussily and formally dressed, looking more like a trainee accountant than either a high school student or a divine messenger.

'I knew you had to be in there!' says Otto. Accusingly. 'I've been waiting for over twenty minutes. You were supposed to be in world history.'

'I couldn't take it. It was so inaccurate it was painful.'

'You're not supposed to do whatever you want whenever you want to do it, you know. If you say you're going to be somewhere, I expect you to be there.' Otto peers at her disapprovingly over the top of his glasses. 'We're working together. Partners? Remember?'

And how could she forget? 'For now. Remember?' Just because a partnership is made in Heaven doesn't mean you have to like it.

'*For the foreseeable future,*' Otto corrects.

'Right. Well, maybe you'd better keep your

22

girdle on and just get used to waiting for me now and then,' says Remedios. 'I mean, what's a few minutes here and there? It's not like we're going to run out of time.'

'We have to make plans, Remedios. We haven't decided what we're doing for the next two days.'

'Well, I know what *I'm* doing.' The smile returns to Remedios' face. 'I'm going away for the weekend.'

'Away?' Otto likes Jeremiah. Tucked into the woods, it's peaceful and homey and not a lot happens here. He has no desire to leave. 'Away where?'

Remedios watches Beth go down the corridor. 'LA.'

'LA?' Otto has never been to LA but he knows that it isn't peaceful or homey and that a lot happens there—a good percentage of it bad. 'Why LA?'

'It is the city of angels, you know.'

'Not literally. It was originally *Nuestra Señora de los Angeles*.' If you told Otto the sky is blue, he'd tell you the exact shade. 'It was just another mission town. They didn't name them because they were filled with angels and saints.' Seeing that Remedios has stopped listening, he adds, 'Anyway, we're supposed to stay here.'

'Where does it say that?' demands Remedios. 'Nobody told me that. We go where *they* go . . .' The bowling alley . . . the pizza place . . . the mall . . . 'Isn't that the deal?'

'But I don't want to go to LA,' bleats Otto.

'So stay here.' As if. It would take more than a miracle for her to be allowed to go to LA by herself.

'You know I can't do that,' says Otto.

Remedios is already walking away. 'So come.'

WELCOME TO LA!

Beth was so worried about the weekend that she forgot to worry about the flight. When she got to the airport, rather than being at least half an hour early as she is for most things, she was exactly on time—so that, what with checking in and answering questions and taking off her shoes, it wasn't until she sat down and buckled her seat belt that she started to panic. She'd only flown twice before and never without her mother beside her, holding the airsick bag in one hand and the emergency-landing instructions in the other. As a result, she spent the entire journey with her head on her knees, trying not to throw up and afraid to even glance out of the window in case she saw the wing snapping off.

As soon as they landed Beth turned on her phone (she'd been afraid to leave it on in case it interfered with the aircraft's electrics and caused a crash), put on her headset (so she doesn't radiate her brain) and called her mother to tell her that she'd arrived in more or less one piece. Shaky but determined, she managed to stagger off the plane, make her way out of the airport and find the hotel bus. The other passengers were several prosperous-looking businessmen, three less-prosperous-looking middle-aged couples on vacation and one teenage girl wearing a batik dashiki.

The girl smiled as though they'd already met. 'You're in the writing competition?'

Beth nodded.

'Me too.' She held out her hand. 'I'm Delila.'

'Delila Greaves?' Beth sat down next to her. 'I'm your room-mate. It said in the letter. Beth. Beth Beeby.'

'Well, how's that for luck?' laughed Delila.

Delila Greaves has been shortlisted in the category of poetry. She's written a series of poems about heroic, and largely forgotten, women in American history. She's nearly six-feet tall, loud and outgoing, and about as far from most people's idea of a poet as Tokyo is from Black Kettle, Wyoming. Delila Greaves comes from Brooklyn and isn't fazed by any of the things that send Beth running for the painkillers.

'Really?' said Beth. 'You're not stressed out?'

'About what?' asked Delila.

Where was Beth supposed to start? There are some people who enjoy competition. It fires them up, stirs their imaginations and whets their minds. They don't care about prizes; it's the game itself that matters. Beth, however, is not one of those people. Who sold the most cookies in the school's book drive? Who got the highest marks in the maths test? Whose geography project was the longest? Whose plant grew the fastest? Whose goldfish lived the longest? Whose science project was the most complex? Whose macaroni necklace was the neatest? This is a girl who can't do a crossword without turning it into a competitive sport. For Beth, the game barely exists; it's the prize that matters. *If you don't win, you lose. If you don't think you can win, don't play.* Which is why this weekend is the stress equivalent of a nuclear bomb.

'Well, you know,' Beth muttered. 'Everything.'

Delila laughed. 'You're kidding, right?'

But Beth, of course, was not kidding.

'Relax, girl. Just flow with the go.' Delila patted her knee in an almost maternal way. 'They're giving us a free weekend in LA, so no matter what happens, we're ahead of the game. I don't see anything to worry about.'

'You don't?'

Delila doesn't. Not the competition; not the other contestants; not even the congestion, pollution and vibrating brightness of the city cause her a second of anxiety.

'You know what they say,' said Delila. 'Que será, será.'

Beth looked at her feet. 'I don't believe in fate,' she whispered.

Delila patted her knee again. 'Well, you'd sure better hope, then, that fate doesn't believe in you.'

But despite the sanguine presence of Delila, Beth's stress got even worse when they pulled up in front of the hotel, a Churrigueresque confection of pale stucco and faintly tinted glass that stands out against its more mundane neighbours like a castle set down in a development of summer bungalows.

Delila, of course, didn't so much as blink. 'Hot dang!' she laughed. 'Will you look at this temple to Mammon! I've always wondered how the other one percent live.'

As arresting as it is on the outside, The Xanadu is even more impressive (or, alternatively, more terrifying) on the inside. The rooms are small and understated but elegant, and come with all the amenities its guests expect (music system, iPod dock, Wi-Fi, large-screen TV and mood-lighting). Should you want to leave your room, the hotel has three pools, a sauna and a health and fitness room, complete with personal trainers and yoga instructors, hot tubs and a jacuzzi; three restaurants, a bistro, a coffee house, two bars, several stores, a beauty salon and a laundry.

Beth has never seen anything like The Xanadu, and rather wishes that she weren't seeing it now. The one time Beth and her mother stayed in a hotel, it was a motel and they snuck their cat Charley into their room in Beth's backpack. Beth wouldn't try to sneak a gerbil into a place like this. She's so afraid that she'll break something or spill something that she can barely move. If she had any fingernails left, she'd have chewed them all down to the quick before she got out of the elevator. And what if her mother is right about the allergies? Lillian Beeby (who has excelled at nothing in life so much as being afraid of it) has impressed on Beth that she not only has to fear things like migraines, nervous rashes and being so anxious that she sits on her glasses again, but the possibility that she might be allergic to the hotel itself.

'These fancy hotels are all recycled air and synthetics,' her mother is saying now—almost as though she hasn't said it before. 'Didn't I tell you that when Mrs Panki stayed in Toronto that time, she was allergic to the carpet? Her head puffed up like one of those blimps. She thought she was going to die.'

Beth doesn't want to think of Mrs Panki and her head like a blimp. 'I really have to go now, Mom. I have to unpack before supper. I'll call you later.' And she disconnects before Lillian can think of something else that could go wrong. Beth pulls off the headset and drops it and the phone on her bed, and starts to remove things from her bag.

Delila lies on the other twin, eating a bag of barbecue chips and watching Beth put her things away with the curiosity of an anthropologist studying a lost tribe. 'Johnson says it's blood money,' she says at last, continuing a conversation that was interrupted by Lillian Beeby's third and most recent phone call. Johnson is Delila's grandfather. Delila has lived with her grandparents since she was two because her mother is unreliable. 'Johnson's some kind of anarchist now. It makes him argumentative like you wouldn't believe.'

Beth stares at her precisely folded clothes, systematically arranged by size and function. She was expecting a dresser—for all the things that don't go on hangers—but there's only a desk and the small table between the beds. How can things stay unwrinkled if she has to root around in her suitcase every time she needs to change her socks?

'Anyway, Johnson says these big corporations exploit everybody. The people who work for them . . . their customers . . . the planet. And then they run a contest like this to show how much they care about regular folk and education and stuff like that, but really all they care about's money,' Delila goes on, though it's obvious that Beth has more important things on her mind than corporate greed and planetary degradation. 'But I said, "Listen up, old man. If they want to give your granddaughter a big scholarship to go to college, then that's fine by me. So long as they wipe the blood off it first."'

Beth shuts her case, carries it across the possibly infected carpet, opens the closet and sets it down on the stand. There are already several items of clothing hanging from the rail. Like the clothes Delila's wearing, these are so bright they could stop traffic in a tunnel on a starless night. Beth puts her own things—including a dress bought especially for the occasion—on the opposite side.

'Hey, how much stuff did you bring, girl?' Delila props herself on one elbow, scattering tiny crumbs laced with artificial flavourings and salt into the air. 'We're only here till Sunday, you know.'

Beth looks over her shoulder. 'Well, I . . . Not that much really . . .' Just everything she needs to survive the next two days. 'I have an outfit for tonight and for tomorrow . . . And, you know, back-ups in case the weather changes.' Even when she doesn't think she has anything to apologize for, Beth sounds apologetic. 'And another outfit for the presentation ceremony on Sunday, and I brought a jacket in case it gets cold . . .' She shuts the closet, deciding not to mention the raincoat in case it rains and the sweater and flannel pyjamas in case it gets *really* cold. Neither snow, nor rain, nor a sudden heat wave will catch Beth Beeby unprepared.

'What's in there?' Delila points at the bags Beth has put on the desk.

'Oh, you know . . .' The smell of mesquite is making her feel slightly nauseous; the sight of the chip crumbs makes her think of her mother, who disapproves of eating on beds because it attracts insects. 'My toiletries and vitamins and supplements and—'

'Vitamins and supplements?' Delila has a laugh like a bear hug. 'What are you supplementing? The whole west coast?'

Beth is looking at Delila's smile, but she is hearing her mother at the airport. *Now you're sure*

29

you have everything, honey? You're sure you haven't forgotten anything? Toothbrush? Floss? Spare glasses? Inhaler? Painkillers? Anti-depressants? Beta blockers? Eyewash? Earplugs? Sleeping pills? Water? The cream for your eczema? Aunt Joyce isn't that far away, you know. So if you need anything . . .

'Well, not *just* vitamins . . .' Beth opens the largest of the bags and starts removing jars and bottles. 'My mom, you know, she kind of worries a little.'

'A *little?*' Delila sits up, her eyes on the display Beth is setting up. It looks like it belongs in the window of a drugstore. 'You call *that* a little? What do you call a blizzard? A snow flurry? Man, about the only thing your Mom's left out is the inflatable raft in case there's a flood.'

Beth straightens out the last bottle, making sure it's perfectly aligned with the others. 'My mother doesn't think it'll rain that much. She's more worried about earthquakes.'

'My grandma's just the opposite,' says Delila. 'She says she's had so much trouble in her life, she's stopped worrying altogether. What's the point? Bad luck's like cockroaches, no matter what you do it always comes back. And anyway, she figures we all have angels looking out for us.'

'Angels?' Beth has enough to worry about in the observable world without involving other dimensions.

'Yeah, you know, hanging around to keep an eye on things.'

'It doesn't seem to me that they're doing a very good job,' says Beth.

'You don't know . . .' Delila shrugs. 'Maybe things would be even worse if they weren't around.

30

Think about that.'

'Well, my mom definitely doesn't believe in angels.' If Lillian Beeby had an angel, she'd be fretting about it getting its wings caught in something. 'My mom says you can never be too careful.' When her mother dies, those words are going to be etched on her gravestone:

Lillian Beeby 1975–20??
You can never be too careful . . .

'Man, it staggers me that you finalled with a short story,' laughs Delila. 'I would've bet anything you specialized in Prophecies of Doom!'

*   *   *

Gabriela enjoyed the flight to Los Angeles so much that you might think she and Beth had travelled on different planes. And they might as well have. Gabriela was the last passenger to board, and by that time Beth already had her eyes closed and her head on her knees. While Beth went over emergency procedures in her mind and tried not to be sick, Gabriela chatted to the people sitting on either side of her, telling them all about the contest and the weekend, and receiving their wishes of good luck in return. Forty minutes before they landed, while Beth was just beginning to believe that the plane wasn't going to crash and resumed worrying about the weekend itself, Gabriela took over one of the toilets to repair any damage done to her clothes and make-up by the journey, only coming out when the stewardess banged on the door to tell her to return to her seat for landing.

And now here she is at one of the most glamorous hotels in a city of glamour. And so do

31

dreams come true.

'Can you believe it, Gab? Why is this happening to me *now*?' Lucinda drops a handful of accessories back on her bed and turns her attention to the hillock of clothes on the chair beside it. Lucinda Abbot is Gabriela's room-mate for the weekend. Unlike Gabriela, who is showing the composure of the heir to the throne at the christening of an ocean liner, Lucinda's nerves are jangling like a box of bells on the back of a pickup going over rough terrain. Some day, Lucinda hopes to be as at home in the world of exclusive hotels and luxury cars as a moose in the forest, but that day is far in the future. At the moment, all she wants is to look as if she comes from somewhere stratospherically sophisticated and not a small town in Maine. 'I know I packed it. I would never bring that green skirt and not bring the belt that goes with it, too. I don't want to look like a total hick!'

Gabriela, who is kneeling in front of the tiny table between the beds like a supplicant at an altar, keeps her eyes on her reflection. 'This room's way too small.' This is less a statement of fact than a complaint. After all, even Paradise had its serpents. 'I know The Xanadu's supposed to be the last word in cool and everything. But, really, there are cells bigger than this room.'

'Oh, but this is still a really awesome place,' says Lucinda. 'I mean, celebrities and billionaires and people like that stay here all the time—I heard Galatea—'

'Galatea?' Gabriela makes a discouraging sound. 'You can bet your last pair of boots that if Galatea stayed here, she wasn't in this room.' Gabriela, who is adding individual lashes to her own with

32

the precision of a surgeon changing the valve of a heart, drops another into place. 'She'd be in a big suite, Lucinda. I mean, look at this place! Galatea wouldn't even be able to get her hand luggage in here. You can hardly move.'

This is a slight exaggeration. You can move, but not easily or far. For although this room is identical to the one Beth and Delila are in—but on a different floor and in a different colour—it is so crowded that getting from the balcony to the bathroom is something of a trek, even for girls who follow a regular programme of exercise and have been on diets since the age of twelve. The information that Gabriela has left out, however, is that all the things that crowd the room belong to her and Lucinda. Each girl brought with her one very large suitcase crammed with clothes, a medium-sized suitcase packed with indispensable appliances, a smaller suitcase full of shoes, and a metal make-up case. Gabriela, as we know, has put her mirror where the lamp and hotel phone used to be. Lucinda's is on top of the desk. Also on the desk are a box of heated curlers, curling irons, hair straighteners, three hairdryers (one bonnet and two hand), two manicure-pedicure kits, two facial saunas and the two cosmetic cases. The hanging toiletry bags are hanging—one on the back of the bathroom door and one on the closet door; some of their clothes are stuffed in the closet and the rest are piled on the chairs and the floor for lack of anywhere else for them to be.

'You can't find anything either. At least I can't.' Lucinda sighs. 'What am I going to do? I had it all planned to wear the green tonight. This throws everything off.' She stares at the green skirt appraisingly. 'Maybe it's not that bad. Do you think I should risk wearing it without the belt?'

'Are you nuts?' Gabriela watches herself blink in the mirrors. 'Weren't you in the limo with me?' All six contestants were picked up from the airport by a Cadillac Escalade driven by a character actor named Ru Morgenstern. By the end of the drive it was clear that, as well as having impeccable taste and knowing more about fashion than Einstein knew about physics, the other girls are competitive in a scorched-earth-policy kind of way. 'Those girls are going to look like they just stepped off the runway in Milan tonight. First impressions, Lucinda. We never met Taffeta Mackenzie before. We can't be flawed, or those girls'll make us look like major losers.'

'But there isn't time to start all over!' Lucinda's wail is directed at her phone whose luminous face is suggesting that it agrees with the old saying about time flying faster than a jet. 'If I change my outfit, I'll have to redo my make-up and my hair.'

Gabriela shakes her head again, frowning critically at her reflection. 'What do you think?' she asks. 'Do I look too much like Bambi?'

Despite her own personal problems, Lucinda climbs across the bed and peers over Gabriela's shoulder. 'No,' she says after a few seconds of scrutiny. 'No, I think you look great. Sort of romantic and innocent, but knowing and doomed at the same time.'

'Thanks.' Gabriela sits back on her heels and smiles. 'It's really a big relief to have somebody who can give me an intelligent opinion. My family is just so useless. If I want someone to tell me the truth about how I look, I have to send a photo to my friends. And, you know, sometimes they're in the middle of something else and by the time they answer it's way too late. So most of the time I have to shop twice. Go once and try everything on and take pictures of myself, and then go back again after I've decided what I looked best in.'

'You don't have to tell me,' says Lucinda. 'I have the exact same problem.'

Gabriela rises gracefully to her feet. 'Right,' she says. 'Now, let's decide what you're wearing tonight. I may even have something that'll set off that skirt. Don't you worry. The two of us are going to make the others wish they wanted to be plumbers.' They both laugh. 'We're definitely the team to beat!'

*   *   *

Otto stares out of the tiny window. Glumly. 'I can't believe I let you talk me into this.' Otto doesn't like to fly. Which, of course, is one of the reasons Remedios insisted. She was hoping she would lose him at the airport. That he would chicken out at the last minute or mistakenly get on the wrong plane. The other reason they had to fly was because Remedios wanted to be on the same plane as Gabriela and Beth, in order to put her plan into operation effortlessly, efficiently and quickly—so that it would be done before Otto even knew what it was. But he managed to dither so much that they missed the girls' flight, and then he stuck to her like a leech. 'I hate this. Why couldn't we just *be* there? Why do we have to take a plane?'

'Because, unlike you, I've always enjoyed flying machines. Even when they were made of muslin and wood.'

He shudders at the thought.

'And besides, Otto, you didn't have to come with me. You could have met me at the hotel.' Remedios doesn't lift her gaze from the magazine she's reading. 'It was your choice.'

Some choice. Get on a plane or run the risk of not seeing Remedios for days.

Remedios finally looks up and gives him the kind of smile many painters have associated with the gentle plucking of the strings of a harp. 'Besides, I thought it would get us into the spirit of things. I thought this would be more fun.'

'And that's another thing. Why do we have to fully materialize. Why—'

'Because I thought it would be more fun, too, that's why.' There's no way she's going to Los Angeles disguised as air.

'Well, it's not fun.' It's a mistake to think that the cherubic nature is always sweet. 'Bailing out a sinking ship with a teaspoon in a monsoon would be more fun than this.'

'I don't know what you're getting so worked up about.' She leans closer so her mouth is near his ear. 'What's the big deal? So what if we crash? It's not like you're going to die, Otto.'

'That's not the point, Remedios.'

That's not the point, Remedios, she silently echoes. He really should be an accountant and not a holy helper. 'Well, what is the point?'

'The point is that this is one of the most insane things humans ever came up with!' This is what he means about people; they never leave things alone. 'Soaring around in the sky like birds. Doesn't it occur to them that they would've been born with

36

wings if they were meant to fly?'

'Heavenly hosts, get a grip on yourself. We haven't even left the ground yet.'

'And I'm not planning to.' He suddenly unsnaps his seat belt. 'I'm getting off.'

'You can't. We're on the runway. We're about to take off.'

He straightens the sleeve of his jacket. 'I can stop it.'

'And I can stop you stopping it.'

Otto's smile is more suggestive of Biblical droughts than heavenly choirs. 'That could take quite a while.'

The smile is not returned. 'I thought we were supposed to be on the same team. Partners.'

'If we're partners, then I think I have a right to know what you're planning, Remedios.' He taps the buckle of his seat belt. 'That is, unless you want to sit in this plane for the rest of the day. It's not going to look too good if you bring another airport to a standstill.'

She stifles a sigh. 'What makes you think I have a plan?'

'Oh, you have a plan.' Even on so short an acquaintance, Otto has learned that Remedios always has a plan; they're just rarely any good. 'And I'm giving you to the count of three to tell me what it is.'

The engines kick in as the plane starts down the runway.

'One . . . Two . . . Three . . .'

And so, as they gather speed, Remedios tells Otto that all she intends to do is make sure that Beth and Gabriela win their competitions. Beth needs the confidence and Gabriela needs the challenge. 'That's it,' says Remedios. 'They're probably both going to win anyway, I just want to guarantee it. I'm not going to do anything excessive. I'm really just going as insurance.'

Take offs and landings are usually the most stressful parts of air travel, and this is certainly true for Otto. He is, at the moment, in no state to think too deeply or argue too intensely. 'That's it?' he says. 'You're sure?' Usually Remedios shimmers ever so slightly when she's lying. 'You're telling me the truth?'

With a shudder and a bang, the plane lurches into the air and Otto closes his eyes.

Remedios smiles. 'Of course I'm telling you the truth.'

THE WEEKEND BEGINS BETTER THAN IT MEANS TO PROCEED

Gabriela and Lucinda's competition is being run by The City of Angels College of Fashion and Design. The founder and president of the college, Taffeta Mackenzie, was once one of the most famous and highly paid models on the international scene. When it was time to step elegantly off the runway and away from the camera, not only did she start her own studio—the iconic Madagascar—she also decided to use her connections and contacts to open a school, which is now one of the most successful design schools in the country. Tonight's dinner is for the finalists to meet her and some of her senior staff, but it is also for her to meet them. She didn't get to be where she is today by letting anyone else control things—not even fate. Which means that, though it may not be strictly ethical, Taffeta will only hand over first prize to someone she is behind two hundred percent. This is not a business that runs on sentiment.

'I'm so nervous,' Lucinda is saying as she and Gabriela near the entrance of the most upmarket of the hotel's restaurants. She tugs at her skirt and pats her hair. 'Do you think she'll know that I come from the boonies?'

'She knows where you come from, Luce. She's seen your application.' Gabriela stops and puts an arm around her. 'Stop worrying. You look terrific.'

'But Taffeta Mackenzie . . .' Lucinda takes a deep breath. 'I mean . . . she's practically a legend. What if she doesn't like us?'

'Oh, please . . .' Their reflections shimmer in the immaculate glass doors. What's not to like? 'We're finalists. That means she already likes us.' Gabriela winks. 'We just have to make sure that she likes us the best.' The doors open silently as they reach them. 'Look straight ahead and smile like you're filled with inner serenity,' Gabriela orders, and they glide through.

At a table in the farthest corner of the room they see Taffeta (unmistakable in a floral-print, stretch-satin dress that only she could have designed), her colleagues (simply but elegantly turned out) and the other finalists—Nicki, Isla, Hattie and Paulette—all of them, as Gabriela predicted, dressed to seriously injure if not actually kill (but in an oh-so-last-week kind of way).

'Oh my God!' Lucinda squeezes Gabriela's hand as if she were the last drop of toothpaste in the tube. 'We're late. Everybody's here already. Taffeta will think we're unreliable. Now what do we do?'

'We're not late.' Gabriela wouldn't think twice about keeping the President waiting while she gets her hair right, but she'd rather go bald than be late for Taffeta Mackenzie. 'They're all early.' Hoping to score points and make her and Lucinda look bad. 'Didn't I tell you we can't even blink around them? They're like hungry lions. Show any sign of weakness and you're dinner.'

'Oh, no . . .' moans Lucinda. 'I don't know if I'm up to this. Those girls are way more sophisticated than I—'

'You have nothing to worry about.' Gabriela straightens her shoulders and raises her chin. 'You're with me.'

As if Gabriela's movements have sent a signal across the room, Taffeta glances at the watch on her wrist and then looks over at the door. Eight on the dot. Ignoring the fact that Nicki is talking to her, she waves, her smile of approval moving from Lucinda to Gabriela and settling on her like a laser.

'Oh my God!' breathes Lucinda. 'Look at Taffeta's face. She's happy to see us!'

Gabriela returns Taffeta's smile. 'What did I tell you?' Her lips barely move as she talks. 'Come on, let's show the competition how to schmooze.'

Lucinda beside her, Gabriela moves slowly towards the table, confident and cool, all the while hearing the presenter's voice in her head: *And now here comes Gabriela Menz, wearing a dress she designed and made herself—a simple silk sheath in tropical fruit over matching lace leggings with a beaded, spider-web scarf and pearl-grey wedges.*

Taffeta rises to greet them. 'I'm Taffeta Mackenzie. Lucinda Abbot, right?' She extends her hand. 'And you must be Gabriela Menz.' Her eyes move down the simple silk sheath in tropical fruit. 'I recognize your style.'

Though the other contestants keep smiling, glances move between them like fleas between dogs, suddenly aware that if Taffeta Mackenzie has a favourite, it isn't one of them.

Taffeta introduces her colleagues—her deputy, the Dean of Students, the head of Admissions, the Careers Advisor. 'And I believe you girls have already met?' She gestures vaguely at the others, as if she's already forgotten their names.

'Yeah, we came from the airport together,' says Nicki.

Hattie and Isla nod.

Paulette, whose smile looks as if a stiff wind would crack it, says, 'Wow, that's an awesome dress, Gabriela.' She wrinkles her nose. 'But, you know, it looks kind of familiar. Would I have seen it somewhere?'

Gabriela has no trouble recognizing a challenge when she hears one. *So it's going to be like that, is it?* 'Well, I don't know . . .' Her smile could only be sweeter if it were carved out of sugar. 'Do you watch a lot of old movies?'

'Old movies? You mean like from the nineties or something?'

'No, older.' Gabriela lets the scarf fall off her shoulder. 'I got the idea for this dress from this movie I watched that was made in the thirties. It was in black and white! Can you believe it? No colour! Anyway, the woman who ends up ruining her life, she had this incredible negligee.'

Hattie gives an embarrassed laugh, though not, of course, for herself. 'Isn't that just like *copying*?'

41

'I didn't copy it,' says Gabriela. 'I was inspired. I changed everything about it—the length, the material, the fall of the skirt—all I kept was its essence.'

Taffeta touches her shoulder. 'That's the kind of creativity I like to see. That's what real art is all about.' She removes her Hermes Birkin from the chair beside hers. 'Why don't you sit next to me?'

Gabriela's night goes on from there, rising as effortlessly and brightly as a helium balloon. She can't remember ever enjoying herself more. It's like every fantasy she's ever had come true. Gabriela loves her friends—her friends are great—but though they like to shop and wear clothes as much as the next girl, they do have other interests. They don't look at the shell of a tortoise and think: wow, that pattern would look great on a coat. They don't look at a dress in a movie or in a store window and think: drop the neckline, make it longer, add ties and only wear it with ankle boots. She's never been with so many people with the same interests— and with the same passion. They talk; they laugh; they share thoughts and ideas on everything from tatted collars and tailored skirts to strapless bras and open-toed shoes. Taffeta has a million stories about Hollywood, LA and the fashion industry, and drops celebrity names the way a waiter roller skating on ice drops dishes. Even Nicki, Paulette, Hattie and Isla warm up as the night goes on. Still guarded but not as prickly, they no longer want to push Gabriela down the nearest laundry chute; they just want to be her.

By the time Taffeta says that they'd all better get their beauty sleep since they have a big day tomorrow, the restaurant is almost empty.

'That was awesome,' Lucinda whispers as she and Gabriela follow the others out. 'That was totally awesome. And Taffeta really, really likes you.'

Gabriela, too happy to speak, just smiles. This is so definitely her lucky day.

But, as things will turn out, tomorrow not so much.

*　　*　　*

The dinner for the Tomorrow's Writers Today group is being held in one of the hotel's smaller function rooms on the main floor. There are five categories in the competition—fiction, non-fiction, journalism, poetry and drama—and four contestants shortlisted in each category. Tonight's event brings together all the contestants for the first time, as well as representatives from the corporate sponsors, all dressed like the President attending a summit and wearing the same kind of all-purpose smiles.

Beth and Delila are ten minutes early, but already there are people sitting at all four tables. They stop in the doorway for a few seconds so that Beth, who of course is sorry she couldn't reply immediately, can answer the text her mother sent her while they were coming downstairs.

'Shoosh, man, will you look at them?' Delila sees no need to whisper. 'I feel like I'm in court, there are so many suits.'

Beth, having assured her mother that she'll double-check about nuts, looks up. Delila's right about the suits. Indeed, the only people—male or female, judge, student or waiter—who aren't wearing one are Delila (who is wearing a turquoise, orange, light green and yellow tunic over orange cotton trousers) and Beth (who is wearing her new grey dress).

But the sight of all these suits doesn't make Beth think that she's in court. It makes her think that the other contestants are all here for their college interviews—with Harvard, Princeton or Yale. And, from the look of them, that they're bound to get their first choices.

'You think I should go back and change?' whispers Beth. She doesn't want to stand out. *Ooh, who's the girl who didn't dress for dinner?* 'Maybe I'm too casual.'

'Too casual?' Delila gives her a you-really-take-the-last-piece-of-cake look out of the corner of her eyes. 'You look like a pilgrim. All you need's a white handkerchief on your head.'

'I have a skirt and blazer my mom got me for my grandmother's funeral.' That might be better. It almost looks like a suit. 'I cou—'

'Listen,' says Delila. 'You have got to stop worrying like you do. It's not really conducive to your mental health—or mine.' She shakes her head. 'Man, I'm surprised you ever leave the house in case an air conditioner lands on your head.'

It's falling pianos that Beth usually worries about.

'Here's the rule,' Delila tells her. 'You don't worry about nothing until it happens. *After* you break your leg—that's when you start worrying about how you're going to climb Mount Everest on crutches. Not before.'

'I can't help it if I have a sensitive nature.'

'Sensitive nature, my Aunt Winnie's goitre,' says

44

Delila, eloquent as only a poet can be. 'What you have is a sensitive mother.'

Beth's phone makes the grunting sound that means it's getting another message from her sensitive mother.

'And as for that instrument of torture . . .' Delila glares at the small, black rectangle in her room-mate's hand. If Delila had magical powers, Beth would be holding a handful of ash. 'You don't want to be rude, do you? Sitting there texting your mom in the middle of supper.'

The last thing Beth wants is to be rude.

'Right,' says Delila. 'So put it on vibrate and put it away.'

Born to take orders, Beth does as she's told.

They've been seated at table 4, with Professor Cybelline Gryck, a leading authority on the Norse sagas. Professor Gryck is the chief organizer of both the competition and the weekend.

At the sight of the group at table 4, Beth's temperature drops and her stomach clenches tighter than a miser's fist around a nugget of gold. 'I'm getting a bad feeling,' she whispers to Delila. One of the reasons for this bad feeling is Professor Gryck herself, of course. She is a tall, large-boned woman whose stern and rather formal appearance intimidates Beth, suggesting as it does that she'd take off points if you forgot to cross a 't' or dot an 'i'. Another reason is the three girls with her, all of whom, even from across the room, exude the confidence of dictators. Forget the interviews, they all look as if they're already at Harvard and are attending a sorority mixer. They certainly don't look as if they go to high schools—not like the one that Beth attends anyway.

Delila continues to pull her forward. '*You* have a bad feeling? So what else is new? The stars come out at night?'

Professor Gryck and the girls are in earnest conversation—nodding and gesticulating and no doubt reinventing postmodern literary theory—but, as if they're not just brilliant but psychic as well, all four heads turn to look at Beth and Delila while they are still several yards away. Professor Gryck waves graciously, but the girls look Beth up and down with smiles as thin as piano wire and noses pointed towards the ceiling—as if they can tell that her mother is a cleaner; that Beth has never read Proust; that she has deodorizers in her shoes.

If she were alone, Beth would probably apologize and excuse herself to go the ladies' room, to deep breathe and try to think of a few really clever things to say before she returned to the table. (Either that or simply sob and throw up.) But she is not alone, of course. She is with Delila Greaves. Delila doesn't care how thin the smiles are or how high the noses. Henry VIII couldn't intimidate Delila. As her grandfather Johnson would say, those girls are going to be just as dead as Delila when the time comes, so what's to be so arrogant about? She gives them a big you-can-have-the-leftovers grin. She repeats everybody's name in her let's-make-sure-they-hear-me-in-Bel-Air voice—Esmeralda . . . Aricely . . . Jayne—asks them where they're from and what they write, and shakes their hands as if she's glad to meet them. Somehow, when they're ready to take their seats, Beth is sitting between Delila and Professor Gryck.

Beth doesn't want to sit next to Professor Gryck, who makes her feel even more nervous than people in authority usually do. She'd rather take her chances with Jayne, the playwright, Aricely the poet, or Esmeralda the non-fiction writer. She's going to have to go to the restroom. And very quickly. She pushes back her chair, and knocks her fork to the floor.

'I'm sorry,' Beth mumbles to no one in particular, and bends down to retrieve it at the same moment as Professor Gryck. 'I'm so sorry.' There doesn't seem to be any blood on the professor, but she touches her own forehead just to make sure. 'I really am sorry. I—'

'So you're Beth Beeby,' says Professor Gryck. 'I was hoping I'd bump into you—though not, perhaps, literally.' Even her smile looks serious. 'I wanted to tell you how much I enjoyed your story.'

The phone in Beth's pocket starts to vibrate as the bad feeling starts to go away. 'You did?'

'Immensely. I couldn't help thinking of Don Delillo. Would he happen to be an influence?'

And that's how the evening begins. They talk about writers they admire, novels they love, poems that have inspired them, their favourite books when they were children. Beth's love of writing being greater than her fear of failure or falling short, she manages to hold her own against Aricely, Esmeralda and Jayne, all of whom seem to have swallowed whole libraries and committed them to memory. The only person who mentions names that Beth has never heard of is Delila, but that's all right because none of the others have heard of the names she mentions either.

'Diane di Prima?' says Aricely. 'John Trudell? Are you sure they're poets?'

'Sure as I am that you're sitting there telling me

47

that they aren't,' says Delila.

It happens that Professor Gryck, too, suffers from allergies and agrees that if there is even the slightest chance that Beth's meal has been contaminated with nuts it should be sent back. When Beth has a sneezing fit (probably because of something the napkins were washed in), Professor Gryck asks the waiter to bring her paper napkins from the bar. When Beth feels a twinge over her right eye, Professor Gryck fishes a box of painkillers from her bag.

After the meal, Professor Gryck gives a welcoming speech and introduces the men who have come on behalf of the sponsors—a company that makes sports clothes, a soda company and a company that has made cheap hamburgers more globally accessible than water. 'There was a time,' says Professor Gryck, 'when international corporations wanted to teach the world to sing, but now they're far more interested in getting it to read and write.' Everyone claps.

By the time the evening ends, Beth has enjoyed herself so much that it isn't until they're walking to the elevators that she remembers Lillian Beeby, sitting at home thinking of things that might be going wrong.

'I'd better call my mother.' Beth slows down to get out her phone. 'Tell her what a good time I had.'

'What did I say?' says Delila. 'There's nothing to worry about.'

But this, unfortunately, isn't quite true.

*   *   *

It's late. In many parts of the world, this is the hour when people who are out go home, and people who are at home go to bed. But not in Los Angeles, of course. Here, the night is bright not with a million stars but a million lights, most of them in colours never seen on a rainbow, the streets busy and the roads busier. Which means that there are plenty of heads to turn as the candy-apple-red sports car weaves almost miraculously through traffic at a speed that should (but doesn't) have several patrol cars behind it, sirens screaming. Not only is it a vintage model rarely seen even in Hollywood, but although it isn't raining its wipers sweep back and forth (because no one knows how to turn them off) and something that once grew in someone's front yard is caught in the grill.

As eye-catching as the car are its occupants. A young man dressed rather like a CIA agent in pre-revolution Havana in a white linen suit, Panama hat and dark glasses despite the hour, sits rigidly in the passenger seat, his legs stretched out in the 'braking' position; his hands gripping the dashboard like bryozoans glued to the side of a rock. Driving (for lack of a better word) is a young woman wearing farmer's overalls and a feather boa that keeps slapping her companion in the face. He is handsome in what an artist might describe as a classical way; her ethereal beauty is oddly heightened by her bright blue hair and the silver stud shaped like a star in her nose. Both of them are talking at once, but they aren't having a conversation. The young man is praying rather fervently and the young woman is singing a song of welcome to California—loudly but off-key. The car makes a sudden, heart-halting turn onto Sunset

49

Boulevard.

'Hallelujah!' cries Remedios. 'We're almost there! Was that an awesome ride, or what?'

'Awesome isn't really the way I'd describe it,' says Otto. Frightening. Terrifying. Perilous. Undoubtedly largely illegal. 'It was even worse than the plane.'

And considerably longer.

Remedios isn't listening to Otto. She has already learned how to turn his voice into background noise—like the sounds of traffic and aircraft overhead and the constant twenty-first-century electronic hum. Not listening to Otto makes everything so much easier. She looks around with a happy smile. 'I know it's been a few years and everything, but I can't believe how much this place has changed since the last time I was here.' The last time Remedios was here was over two hundred years ago. There were no lights or cars or sprawling communities or freeways then, of course. The floodplain was still covered with woods; the woods were filled with bears and deer; and the chapel was about to be built on the plaza. The fact that so much has changed in the intervening years is one of the reasons it's taken them so long to get from the airport to the hotel. That and nearly being hit by a bus, the incident at the gas station, and then that woman getting so hysterical over a few uprooted weeds. 'I can't wait to see the sights,' she says.

Otto can. Even this brief an acquaintance with the city has made him think that several other places where he was very unhappy may not have been so bad after all. Otto, who has yet to let go of the dashboard, says, 'I want to go home.'

'And where would that be?' Remedios squints

50

through the windscreen, looking for the hotel. It should be coming up on the right. Or possibly the left.

'Jeremiah, Remedios. Where do you think?'

'But we just got here. We haven't even checked in yet.'

'And we're not going to,' says Otto. 'I don't know how I let you convince me that this was a reasonable idea. I should have stopped you right from the start. I insist that we leave. Immediately.'

'But why?'

'Why?' His voice is almost the same pitch as the screech of brakes behind them as Remedios makes a last-second turn into the driveway of The Hotel Xanadu on what seems to be only part of one wheel. 'You're asking me *why*?'

'Yes, I am. We are allowed to go away for the weekend. Especially on business.' They slip into the line of cars waiting to be parked. 'This is one of the most exciting places in the world, Otto.' Unlike Jeremiah where the most exciting thing to happen in the last year was when the mailbox outside the post office was struck by lightning. She gives him a playful nudge. It's like poking a brick wall. 'We're going to have fun!'

'No, we're not. We're going to get into trouble, that's what we're going to do. Gargantuan trouble.' Trouble, undoubtedly, of Biblical proportions. 'This is going to be a disaster, Remedios, and you know it. We're not supposed to meddle like this. The rules are very clear about that.'

Remedios makes her mouth very small. *Rules are for fools*. 'There are precedents.'

'Yes, but most of those precedents were set by you.' Otto makes his mouth very hard. 'And in any case, my understanding is that those were matters of global importance. These girls' problems aren't in the same league at all.' Though it's likely that they will be after Remedios is through with them.

'There are no small problems, only small angels,' parrots Remedios.

'Remedios, that's not the point. The point is that it's not up to us to decide who wins or loses these contests. That's not part of our brief.'

Remedios groans. She doesn't have time for this. By now, both girls have long finished eating, and soon they'll be going back to their rooms. This is her chance—possibly the only one she'll get—to do what she's really come to do. 'It'll be fine. I told you. The chances are they'll both win without my help.'

'Then there's no reason for us to be here, is there?'

She groans again. 'Yes, Otto, there is. In ca—'

'No, Remedios, not in case they don't win.' He shakes his head. 'That's interfering. That's precisely what I'm supposed to be here to prevent.'

'If you spent any time in the girls' toilets, Otto, and heard poor Beth sobbing and vomiting you'd be more sympathetic.'

'Remedios, please.' What a thought! 'And in any case, I'm certain you've never heard Gabriela crying or being sick.'

'Of course not. It's different for Gabriela. Gabriela's problem is that everything's too easy for her. She needs to really have to push—' Remedios breaks off as she accidentally honks the horn and squirts water on the windscreen.

Several people look over. Otto flinches. It's a miracle he has any nerves left.

'Then what you should be doing is guiding them to a better mental state, not fixing the competitions,' he says.

Suffering seraphim, how is she supposed to accomplish anything with Mr No-you-can't around? No wonder she's had to resort to deceit. Her voice takes on a tone of regret. 'I knew I should never have told you.'

'Oh, no, telling me your plan is the only thing you've done right so far.' He lifts his sunglasses so she can see the look of stern disapproval he's giving her. 'You had to tell me. And I have to stop you. This isn't as bad as what you pulled in Haiti, Constantinople, Tenochtitlan, medieval Cologne and all those other places, Remedios, but I still can't allow it.' Before she knows what's happening, he reaches over and snatches the keys from the ignition and holds them outside his door. 'I'm not discussing this any more. I've made up my mind. We're going back to Jeremiah.'

Not if she can help it. The time has come for even more deceit. She has no choice. 'I am just trying to help the girls, Otto. Isn't that what we're supposed to do?'

'Not like this.'

She gives a sigh of defeat. 'Isn't there anything I can say to persuade you?'

'No. No, there is not.' Unused to victory, he feels almost sorry for her. 'I blame myself. I shouldn't have let it get this far.'

She shakes her head. Sadly. 'No, you were right. It's all my fault. It's just that I really feel for them. Especially poor Beth.'

'I know. Beth does have a hard time.' He has to resist the urge to pat her knee. 'But we have to go by the book.'

'Okay. From now on, we go by the book.' She sighs again. 'So what do you want to do?'

'I want to go back to Jeremiah and forget the whole thing. Put it behind us.'

'You know, you look really tired.' Remedios' voice is gentle, her smile full of concern. 'It was probably that flight. And that was my fault, too.'

He's not used to her being nice to him, it makes him feel generous towards her. 'I'll be fine. I just need a little time to recuperate.'

'Hey, I have an idea.' Remedios sounds as if she's surprised herself. 'It's already late. Why don't we stay here for the night?' She gives him another concerned smile. 'Then we can make an early start in the morning.'

He lifts the glasses again to peer at her. 'This isn't one of your tricks, is it?'

'Otto! I wouldn't trick you.'

'Yes, you would. I have been warned, you know.'

'OK, OK. So maybe in the past I've been a little flexible with the truth now and then. But I'm not messing with your head now. It's been a stressful trip. And it is very tiring dealing with a body. And we do have a very nice suite booked.'

He is tired. And it has definitely been a stressful trip. 'All right, but you're not going off on your own. I want to know where you are every second. Every fraction of a second.'

'It'll be like we're handcuffed together.' Remedios lifts herself out of the car as the valet approaches. She points to Otto. 'He has the keys.'

If the desk clerk thinks there is anything unusual about the couple booked into the El Dorado Suite, she doesn't show it. She is courteous and

54

friendly. She hopes they enjoy their stay. She hopes everything is to their satisfaction. She asks three times if they're sure they don't need help with their bags. She hands back Remedios' platinum credit card with a smile. 'If there's anything I or anyone else on the staff can do for you, Ms Mendoza, please don't hesitate to ask.'

Remedios says she won't.

'Maybe we should have asked for help,' Otto grumbles as they make their way to the elevators. 'I don't know why you brought so much luggage.'

'So we look like tourists, of course. You can't come to a joint like this without luggage.' She takes a step back as the elevator doors open and people get out.

Otto steps inside, but when he turns around she is still in the foyer.

'Remedios!'

'I left my wallet at the desk!' She makes a what-can-you-do? gesture. 'I'll just go and get it. I'll be right behind you.'

'You'd better be,' says Otto as the doors slide together. 'I'll be counting the minutes.'

As Otto's elevator starts to ascend, the descending elevator suddenly stops on the seventh floor. Remedios looks down the hallway. There are quite a few people coming towards the elevators. And among them, of course, are Beth, talking to her mother and not really looking where she's going, and Gabriela, glancing at her reflection in a mirror she's passing.

By the time the girls reach Remedios, the second elevator has finally arrived and its doors are about to open. Although she's been waiting there the longest, Remedios is the last to get in, taking a

55

place between Gabriela and Beth, both of whom are absorbed in themselves. As the doors silently shut, she allows herself a small but self-satisfied smile.

The truth is Remedios never planned to fix the competitions. That was simply something she told Otto to distract him from what she really intended. She would have made a good conman. Which shell is the pea under? That one? That one? Why, no, it's under here!

What she always intended was to put Beth in Gabriela's body, and Gabriela in Beth's. She doesn't give a feather whether or not the girls win or lose their competitions. What she wants is for them to look at the world and themselves from a different point of view.

The elevator rises very slowly, but only one of its passengers notices. Timing is everything. She could make the switch and have them realize what happened in a matter of seconds, but for it to do them any good they have to be kept isolated. She doesn't want them joining forces or making a fuss. And she especially doesn't want them joining forces or making a fuss when Otto's around. The last thing she needs is for him to discover what she's really up to. It's better if the girls don't realize what's happened until they wake up in the morning—by which time Remedios and Otto will have gone from the hotel, and he won't have any idea of what they've left behind.

On the top floor, Otto has finally given up trying to unlock their suite with the electronic key and, with a glance over his shoulder to make certain no one is watching, simply wills the door to open itself. And as the second elevator stops on Beth's floor,

Remedios lightly touches both her and Gabriela, and simply wills them to swap.

Being an angel definitely has many advantages over being a magician.

THERE ARE SOME THINGS FOR WHICH YOU JUST CAN'T PLAN

When Gabriela first opens her eyes, she has a moment of not knowing where she is. This is something that happens to most of us when we sleep away from home. *This isn't my room. The window's in the wrong place. There shouldn't be a door over there.* But then, as the fog of sleep clears, Gabriela remembers where she is. She's in LA. In the hotel. About to have one of the best weekends of her life. And—if last night is anything to go by—about to take the first step in her career as a fashion designer to the stars. If she were in a musical and not in the bed next to Lucinda Abbot, she'd probably start singing.

And then, slowly coming fully awake, Gabriela notices something odd. She sniffs. The room doesn't smell. That is it smells, faintly, of soap, cleaners and detergent and The Xanadu's air freshener of choice, *California Dreaming*—but it doesn't smell of her. The innocent but alluring scent of her perfume. The wildflowers fragrance of her hair. The slightly sweet aroma of her night cream. She sniffs again. It doesn't smell like Lucinda, who favours something sharper and more avant-garde, either.

This is when Gabriela finally looks over at the

figure in the next bed. It isn't Lucinda Abbot. Even with the curtains drawn she can see that. It is someone so completely different from Lucinda that she might be from another species. Someone much larger. Someone whose hair just happens, like a tangle of string. Someone who probably thinks Dolce & Gabbana is a brand of ice cream and who wouldn't know a Dior suit if it had a sign on it. Someone who sleeps in a New York Giants jersey.

This, of course, is not something that happens to most of us when we sleep away from home, and Gabriela refuses to believe that it's happening to her. She closes her eyes, counts very slowly to ten, and then, even more slowly, opens them again. The next bed still contains a lump of a girl, her mouth open and drool dripping down her chin. It is an interesting fact of human behaviour that if a person really doesn't want to believe something, she won't. You go back to where you left the car and it isn't there, so you spend the next hour walking around, looking for it in case it decided to park itself somewhere else. Your boyfriend says he doesn't want to see you any more and you ask him what he wants to do on Saturday night. You find yourself in a hotel room with someone you never saw before and you decide you must have forgotten something fairly crucial about the night before.

Gabriela closes her eyes again, trying to remember everything that happened last night. She and Lucinda went downstairs. They sat with Taffeta Mackenzie. They had a great time. Better than great. It was like Heaven, if Heaven were located on the ground floor of The Hotel Xanadu. She was feeling really wiped out by the time they got back to the room, but she figured that was because of all the excitement and the travel and everything. In fact, she was so tired that she actually skipped her beauty routine, and was under the covers in a matter of minutes. She fell asleep as soon as her head touched the pillow. That's the whole ensemble. They had dinner; Taffeta said the car would pick them up at nine o'clock sharp; they came back to the room; she was feeling so totally exhausted she almost nodded off while brushing her teeth; she went to bed. Which means that when she opens her eyes the next bed will be occupied by Lucinda Abbot, not some girl who looks as if she plays professional ice hockey.

Because it is not Lucinda that she sees when she opens her eyes again, Gabriela sits up with her heart pounding. And for the first time notices that she isn't wearing her good ivory-silk pyjamas with the maroon piping and the mother-of-pearl buttons (copied from another old movie), which is what she should be wearing. Not a pair of cheap flannel pants in a fake tartan and a T-shirt advertising some museum—the kind of outfit guaranteed to raise her from the dead should anyone be demented enough to bury her in it. It's as she's looking at the T-shirt that Gabriela notices her hands. They're not tanned. Not only are they not tanned, the nails are unpolished and chewed so far down that her fingertips look like the tops of very thin sausages. She pulls one foot out from under the blanket. Most of us would agree that the foot is not the most beautiful part of the human body, but this, without a doubt, is the ugliest foot she's ever seen. Bony. Calloused. The nails like something you'd find on a rhino. There's no tiny rose tattooed on the ankle; no gold chain encircling it; just—*God help me,* she thinks, and, holding her breath, slowly raises the hem of the flannels. She has the hairy leg of a boy. Or a spider. The only reason she doesn't scream is because she doesn't want to wake the Incredible Hulk in the next bed.

Gabriela's eyes move slowly around the room. There's nothing piled on the furniture. There's nothing to stop you from crossing the floor without having to jump from bed to bed. The closet door is open. Two small suitcases (generic) and two backpacks (old) sit on the shelf. A few items of gauche clothing hang at one end of the rail, and a few items that haven't been fashionable outside of Eastern Europe for at least sixty years at the other. Four pairs of shoes (cheap and boring) have been arranged on the floor, separated by two laptops in plain black cases (also generic). Everything that she'd expect from someone who sleeps in flannel pants and someone who shares a room with her.

Don't panic, she tells herself. *There's got to be some explanation.*

Gabriela takes long, deep breaths to calm herself. This is like the dream she had where she found herself at this major holiday party in Hollywood and everybody who was anybody was there—it was A-list all the way—and she suddenly realized that she was wearing corduroys. Corduroys! At this totally to-die-for party. Corduroys, those gross-looking rubber shoes people wear on boats and a sweater decorated with a Christmas tree. The Christmas tree lit up. And not only did it light up, the tiny bulbs twinkled too. Her earrings were plastic reindeer. Everybody thought she'd come with the caterers. That she was someone's hick niece they were

60

afraid to leave home alone. One of the guests came over and kindly guided her towards the kitchen. *Honey, I think you're in the wrong room.* The major difference between that dream and now, of course, is that she woke up from the dream.

Well, that's it! It has to be! She hasn't woken up. She's still asleep. That's all this is—a bad dream.

She pinches herself. Hard. She presses her palm into the corner of the bedside table.

This is ridiculous. She has to wake up. Water. She'll splash cold water in her face. Even though she's doing it in a dream, her body may think it's real and wake her up.

Very quietly, Gabriela slips out of bed, carefully stepping over the grubby pair of bunny slippers waiting for someone who isn't here, and tiptoes over the clear, open space of carpet to the bathroom. She turns on the light and steps up to the sink.

Looking back at her from the mirror is a face that is not her face. It is a familiar face. Kind of. Vaguely. She's definitely seen it before—but not on her, of course.

This is when Gabriela finally panics. Still staring at her reflection in disbelief and horror, Gabriela lets out a scream that could curdle steel.

*   *   *

Beth has been having one of her anxiety dreams. Over the years, Beth has created an impressive catalogue of these dreams, covering every possible personal and global disaster and combination of disasters—from being asked in front of the whole school what Shakespeare's first name was and answering 'George' to being on a ship sinking in a horrific storm and missing the last lifeboat because she couldn't find her inhaler.

In tonight's dream, Beth has won the writing competition and is standing on a stage, reading her short story to an audience of hundreds of published writers, distinguished academics and famous intellectuals. Somehow, the fact that this is an audience that values brains over beauty doesn't make her feel any better that her hair is dull and limp, her nose is running, she has a cold sore starting on her bottom lip and the dress she's wearing looks as if she borrowed it from Jane Austen. She knows, in her heart, that even if the audience admires her intelligence, when they look at her what they are thinking is: dog . . . no-go zone . . . about as attractive as foot fungus. In the publicity material written by the organizers, Beth's story is described as 'a sensitive, unsentimental exploration of the realities of teenage life—the confusion and uncertainty, the pressure to conform and the search for personal identity—written with maturity, grace and style.'

In her dream, however, Beth's story is about a sea turtle that is dragged onto the shore and flipped on its back by a fisherman, and only manages to save itself because it cries so much it floats back out to sea—and is written in doggerel. Every time Beth finishes a sentence, a fresh salvo of laughter rolls across the auditorium. The published writers, distinguished academics and famous intellectuals in the audience all know it's doggerel and are doubled over and clutching each other, gasping for air and wiping the tears from their eyes. And yet, though she stammers and whispers and can barely hear herself speak, they hear her. They hear her as if she's shouting in their ears. And even though all she wants to do is run from the podium, she can't seem to stop reading. Professor Gryck is sitting right in front of her in the dream, grimacing and making 'cut it short' gestures, but still Beth reads on. The Nobel-prize-winning poet is laughing so hard he falls off his chair. The country's greatest living novelist has to run from the room. But still Beth keeps going like a runaway horse. And then, out of the corner of her eye, she sees Mr Solman, the head of PR for the major sponsor, coming towards her. He's smiling, but he doesn't look happy. She steps away from the podium. Mr Solman keeps coming. Beth steps away again. Mr Solman moves closer. Move. Step. Move. Step. And then Mr Solman makes a lunge for her. Beth flies through the air like a cartoon character, landing with her face in Professor Gryck's bosom.

Beth wakes up with her stomach clenched, her palms sweating and her face in her pillow. She knows in her head that her dream is only a manifestation of her fears, but in her heart it feels like a premonition. This weekend is going to be a disaster. Even if she wins the competition and the four-year scholarship, she is doomed to be mocked and humiliated.

Oh ye gods of the ancients, she thinks. *Where the heck are you when you're really needed?* Mercury to fly her away . . . Venus to make her beautiful so nobody even listens to what she's saying . . . Pluto to make her invisible . . .

Stop it! she orders herself. *Remember what Delila said! Think positive!*

Beth can see that Delila has a point about her

mother. Sometimes Lillian drives Beth crazy. But that, in turn, makes her feel guilty. Which is how she is feeling now. Maybe she had such a horrible dream because she didn't so much as check her phone once during the entire meal. When she finally did call her mother, Lillian was beside herself with worry. *That's all that dream was*, thinks Beth. *Guilt. For being such an ungrateful daughter.* Promising she'll call her mother right away, Beth lifts her head from her pillow and sits up, ready to face all the day has to offer.

She's wearing somebody else's pyjamas. She touches the fabric. It's silk. Even if Beth owned a pair of real pyjamas with a matching top and bottom and pearl buttons, they wouldn't be made of silk. Silk is so impractical. Not to mention the pupae being boiled alive to make it. She looks around for her own, practical pyjamas—as if, somehow, she changed them in her sleep—but they aren't here. And then something bright pink and shiny catches her eye. It actually takes a few seconds before Beth realizes that the sizzling pink something is on the end of her hands. Impossibly long, perfectly shaped and polished nails. But that isn't possible; it's even less possible than silk pyjamas. And then she notices her hands themselves: long, slender, the colour of café au lait. She's wearing rings. Beth's hands are short, pudgy and pale—and she doesn't wear rings; even gold or silver gives her a rash. She doesn't look any further. Doesn't peer down the front of her pyjamas or examine her feet; she's seen enough. Indeed, Beth is so shocked by what she *has* seen that for once she acts without thinking—and falls out of bed. She looks over to see if the sound of her hitting

64

the floor woke up Delila. But Delila isn't there. In the bed where Delila should be, a girl who could be described as the anti-Delila (thin, blonde and wearing boxer shorts and a camisole, a sleep mask and earplugs) lies curled up on her side, smiling.

Which makes one of them.

Beth's eyes move from the sleeping stranger to the room itself. From what she can see of the furniture (which isn't a lot) it's the same as in the room where she fell asleep; the door, closet and bathroom are all in the same place, too. But the room in which she fell asleep was orderly and neat—and was obviously a temporary lodging. This one looks as if it's the permanent residence of at least half a dozen girls who are always in a hurry. There are things everywhere—more clothes than Beth owns, magazines, bags, shoes, tights, jewellery, scarves, hats and a veritable storeful of small appliances.

Up until this moment, Beth believed that there were no calamities that could befall a person for which she wasn't prepared: disease; accident; random but unkind acts of God and nature; that piano falling from a clear blue sky. But now here is a calamity she never thought of. She stares at the room, her mouth open and a peculiar feeling taking hold of her. Her nerves are numb. How could something like this happen? She has a very clear memory of coming back from dinner with Delila last night. She wasn't feeling well when they got to the room, but she put that down to overexcitement and guilt about ignoring her mother. She was so tired suddenly that she felt as if she had cement in her arteries and veins instead of blood. She said goodnight to her mother, put on her night clothes and got into bed. Delila put on a movie for them to chill out to. Beth was asleep while the titles were still rolling.

Beth goes over the evening again. They went down to dinner; they ate dinner; they came back upstairs; she ended her call to her mother; she got into bed; Delila put a movie on; Beth fell asleep. She must be leaving something out. But what? What is the missing part—the part that explains why she is now standing in a strange room redolent with artificial chemical aromas and not just in some other girl's pyjamas, but, apparently, in someone else's body?

Maybe she's still asleep. She pinches herself hard, but it changes nothing except to bruise her skin.

And then she sees the three-sided, portable mirror on the desk.

Very, very slowly, stepping carefully over the minefield of things strewn over the floor, Beth tiptoes across the room. Even in the grudging light she knows that although the face looking back at her is familiar, it isn't as familiar as it should be. It's the face of that girl in her English class. Gabriela Look-at-me Menz. It's as if she's in that Kafka story *Metamorphosis*. Only instead of being transformed from an unhappy clerk into a grotesque insect, she's been transformed from an anxious overachiever into a prom queen.

This is when Beth starts to cry.

*   *   *

Remedios wakes up smiling. She knows exactly where she is—she is on the sofa of the El Dorado

66

Suite of The Hotel Xanadu. Sunlight melts through the sliding glass doors of the terrace and into the sitting room, so that the debris on the coffee table—the used plates and glasses and uneaten food—is almost illuminated. (Just to keep the record straight, there's also a small bowl and plate on one of the end tables, but those are Otto's and have nothing to do with Remedios.) She is in a very good mood. Never been better. Things may not be turning out the way Gabriela and Beth expected, but they are going exactly as Remedios planned. She gives herself a congratulatory hug. Six days to create the world, and a hundredth of a second to switch Beth into Gabriela's body, and Gabriela into Beth's. And all without Beth, Gabriela or Otto Wasserbach suspecting a thing.

The thought of Otto causes her smile to fade slightly.

She sits up, and realizes that, although she definitely fell asleep watching an old television series that she thought was about angels but was actually about three women detectives, the TV is off, the remote has been neatly placed on top of the programme guide and someone has covered her with a blanket and put a pillow under her head. *Mr Orderly–and–conscientious strikes again.* He went to his room as soon as he'd eaten his holier-than-thou meal of vegetable broth and a wholewheat roll. Heaven forbid Otto should have nachos. Perish the thought that he should eat banana cake with chocolate icing. You'd think there was something satanic about peanut sauce the way he carried on. Remedios squinches her eyes together and makes the face of someone with a coffee bean stuck up her nose. *'I may have a human body right now, but*

67

I don't have to indulge it.' Anyone who has ever met Otto Wasserbach—in any time, in any place—would know exactly whom she's impersonating. He must have come out of his room again to turn off the TV and cover her. Remedios pushes back the blanket with an irritability that might surprise some, but it's helpful to remember that it is saints, not angels, who are known for their patience. Angels are known for avengement and their flaming swords.

Remedios rises slowly, unused to the weight and friction of a body, and as she does she notices the time. She's overslept! What is she, a teenager? By the oracles of Habakkuk, it's almost seven-thirty! She wanted to be on the road by seven, safely out of the way before Gabriela and Beth woke up and discovered the swap, and before there could be any chance of Otto seeing either of them. Not with his eye for detail and his suspicious mind. It could ruin everything. What she wants is to get him out of here and to leave Beth and Gabriela to their own devices. She can switch them back at school on Monday.

But where is Otto? They were going to get up at six. What if he *did*? He always does everything exactly as and when he's supposed to. What if he went downstairs for breakfast? What if, right at this very moment, he's sitting at a table in the restaurant, cutting the crust from his toast and looking at the door as Beth walks in?

Remedios leaps over the coffee table and, her feet barely touching the floor, sprints across the room.

He's lying flat on his back, still as a statue, sound asleep.

68

'Otto! Otto! Get up!' calls Remedios. 'We have to go!'

He doesn't move or mumble.

'Otto!' she shouts. 'Otto, get out of that bed!' She knows he can't be dead, but you'd be forgiven for wondering. 'Otto!' She goes over and yanks off the covers, shaking him by the shoulder. 'Otto! Wake up!'

'What?' He opens his eyes. He was, in fact, having a very pleasant dream. Needless to say, Remedios wasn't in it. 'What's wrong? What have you done now?'

Even though he's no longer asleep, she gives him another shake. 'I haven't done anything. You overslept! We have to get going.'

He glances over at the old-fashioned travel clock on the bedside table. 'It's not that late. What's the hurry?'

'I thought you wanted to get out of here.' Remedios looks and sounds indignantly reasonable. 'I thought you didn't want to spend one more nanosecond in Los Angeles than you had to.'

This was true yesterday, of course; but it is less true now. Comfort is a powerful force. Otto had a very good night's sleep on the orthopedic mattress. The Hotel Xanadu is not so bad. Their suite is cosy and attractive. The wide-screen TV is in the living room, but there is a smaller one in each of the bedrooms on which, he discovered, it is possible to watch nature programmes all night long (which explains why Otto overslept). If you don't look out of the window or sit on the terrace, you can forget that you're right smack in the middle of a sprawling, twenty-first-century city; belching and bleating and complicating life.

'Well, we're here now, aren't we?' asks Otto. Inertia being another powerful force. 'So why hurry? We don't have to check out till noon.' His stomach growls. And that's the other thing. Apparently, he underestimated just how much food a human body needs. More than a cup of broth and a roll. Or even the remains of Remedios' deluxe nachos. He can smell fried potatoes and toasted bagels and strawberry jam. 'I'm going to take a shower, and then I'm going to the restaurant for breakfast.'

Oh, that's terrific. That's great. That's just what she wanted to hear.

'But we can be back in Jeremiah in no time,' argues Remedios. 'You can have breakfast there.'

'You have breakfast there.' He is on his feet now, easing her towards the door. 'I'm eating downstairs.'

'Why don't I just call room service?' Remedios suggests, walking backwards. 'Tell me what you want and it'll be here as soon as you're finished with your shower. Then we won't waste so much time.'

And why, wonders Otto, *would Remedios Cienfuegos y Mendoza worry about wasting my time?* Otto stops so short that if he were a car there would be at least three others piled up behind him. 'You have done something.' Last night when she was being so sympathetic to him he was too exhausted to be wary. But now he's had a good night's sleep and is thinking clearly. 'What did you do?'

Like many of us, Remedios' first reaction when caught out is to lie. 'Nothing. We've been together since we got here. How could I do anything?'

70

This is true. Except for the few minutes it took her to join him in their suite, she hasn't left his side. Nonetheless . . .

'I don't know,' says Otto. 'But I'm not leaving till I find out what it is.'

IT BECOMES APPARENT THAT A CERTAIN AMOUNT OF PERSONAL ADJUSTMENT MAY BE NECESSARY

Lucinda carefully places the tray that's just been delivered on her bed and picks up one of the cups. 'Here. Drink this,' she orders. 'It'll make you feel better.'

Sniffling, Beth wipes the last tears away with her sleeve and obediently grasps the cup, taking a large swallow. She nearly gags. 'What is *that*?' It looks like liquid plant food.

'Double espresso.' Lucinda hands her a napkin. 'I know . . . I know . . . it'll make your teeth beige if you drink too much of it, but I figure just this once it'll be OK. It's good for your nerves.'

Good in what sense? Every nerve Beth has is ringing like an alarm bell. 'I— I'm sorry, but it's so strong.' It's only a guess, of course, but she's fairly certain that it tastes like liquid plant food, too. She wipes coffee from her chin and dabs, futilely, at the stains on the silk pyjama top. 'I don't think I can drink it.'

'Well, do you want my skinny latte?' Lucinda holds out her own cup. 'You should have something. You're pretty frazzled.'

She is that. Frazzled as an overloaded circuit.

71

'No, thank you. It's OK.' She swipes at the last few tears. 'Really. I'm all right now.'

'Are you sure? I've never heard anybody cry like that except in a movie. You know, when all hope is lost.' Because Lucinda has her sleep mask pushed up on her head, she looks as if she has two pairs of eyes that are staring down at Beth—one blankly and one with concern. Her smile is sympathetic. 'You scared me even more than when the bear got into the garbage that time and I thought it was a terrorist or something. I didn't know what was going on when I heard you bawling.'

'I'm so sorry. It must have been awful—' Every time Beth speaks she hears a voice that isn't hers. Compared to that, the bear doesn't sound very scary at all. 'I just . . . I'm really sorry. I didn't mean to wake you up.'

'Oh, that's OK. I had to get up anyway, right?' Lucinda's smile shrugs. 'It's you I'm worried about, Gab. Are you sure you're all right? You're not sick, are you?'

'No.' And whenever she moves her head, a curtain of hair that also isn't hers sways with her. 'I'm not sick.'

'So why were you crying like that? It sounded like you woke up with a pimple as big as Bangor or that somebody stole all our clothes or something. What happened?'

Beth blows her nose on the napkin. Now there's a good question. What's she supposed to say? *I'm really, really sorry, but I woke up in the wrong body and it kind of got my day off to a bad start?*

Lucinda fiddles with her hair. 'Did you have a nightmare? Is that what happened?'

A nightmare. Of course. The number of people

72

skimpy; the dresses look like cummerbunds with minimal straps or sleeves.

When Lucinda comes out from her shower, Beth is still standing more or less where she left her, gazing, transfixed, into the closet as if it might speak to her and tell her what to do there.

'Oh my God, Gab! You haven't even started getting ready!'

'I'm sorry.' Beth looks over her shoulder. 'I didn't order the coffee either.'

Lucinda rolls her eyes. 'You really are acting weird this morning.'

Who's acting?

*   *   *

'What the hell are you screaming like that for, woman?'

Gabriela turns. Standing in the doorway— looming, more like—is a girl who has to be at least six-feet tall, and who is definitely built like a member of the team whose shirt she wears. Not only does her hair stick up all over her head like each strand has a mind of its own, she doesn't shave her legs either and her toenails are more like claws. No polish, needless to say. She is, in her way, an impressive sight, especially with the bedside lamp held menacingly over her head.

It would be stretching it to suggest that the sight of Delila has a calming effect on Gabriela, but it does bring her to her senses rather sharply. 'Who are you supposed to be?' she snaps. 'Xena, Warrior Princess?'

'From the way you were screaming, you sounded like you needed Xena.' The girl lowers the lamp. 'I thought somebody was killing you.'

'I didn't mean to wake you up like that.' Gabriela gives one of her silly-me laughs, but it doesn't sound as charming coming from Beth as it does from someone with a musical voice, sparkling eyes and dimples. 'I just— You know . . . I just had a fright.' Two if you count the sudden appearance of Beth's room-mate.

Delila puts the light back where it belongs. '*You* had a fright? You could've cut my promising young life short by decades carryin' on like that!'

'I said I didn't mean to.'

'Ooooh . . .' Delila makes a well-excuse-*me* face. 'Somebody sure got out of the wrong side of the bed this morning.'

No, just the wrong bed.

Gabriela takes a deep breath and tries again. 'Something scared me, that's all.'

'Oh, I'm sure something scared you, all right.' Delila laughs, though not unkindly. 'So what was it? You suddenly remembered you forgot your malaria medicine? You thought there could be somebody hiding in the shower?' She shakes her finger as if she's tapping something out of a jar. 'I know! You were practising screaming just in case there's some kind of emergency later.'

Gabriela may have shared a class with Beth since they started high school, but all she knows about her is that she's a brain, that she talks so softly the only way you could tell what she's saying would be if you read lips and her name: Beth Beeby (which has occasionally been rhymed with 'creepy'). She knows nothing about the fears and anxieties that follow Beth around like an especially aggressive pack of paparazzi; or about Lillian Beeby, the poet laureate of angst. Which is why she's beginning to think that, on top of everything else, Delila is clinically insane.

'What are you talking about? I was still half asleep, that's all.' Gabriela intends to stalk out of the bathroom, but Delila just stands there, watching her with amusement and blocking the way, so she squeezes past her instead. And then realizes, of course, that there is nowhere to go— just the one small room. A room that seems to be getting smaller by the minute.

'You don't need to get all snippy with me,' says Delila from approximately an inch behind her. 'I was only fooling around. I'm on your side, remember?'

'Right. Of course.' Gabriela gives her a wan smile. 'I don't know what's wrong with me this morning.' At least that much is true.

'Major discombobulation,' judges Delila. 'Don't worry about it. I know you're really stressed out. Last night was OK and everything, but there were moments.' She rolls her eyes in a long-suffering kind of way. 'I swear those preppy types make my butt hurt like I've been sitting on rocks for seventy-two hours. They're so damn full of themselves—' She squashes her lips together and wrinkles her nose as though some unpleasant odour has been let loose in the room. 'Man, if those girls'd dropped any more names the floor would've caved in.'

All Gabriela really registers is the major-discombobulation part. That's putting it mildly, if you ask her. She's like that story about the ugly duckling in reverse. Yesterday she was a beautiful swan and now look at her! Beth Beeby in shades of brown and grey. *Quackquackquack.*

'You're right,' says Gabriela. 'I am really stressed out.' If she were not a resilient young woman but the heaviest duty polyester thread, she would already have snapped. And she's not going to feel less stressed until she gets rid of Xena here. Science may not be Gabriela's best subject, but she does remember that Somebody's Great Law says that two things can't occupy the same space at the same time (which, let's face it, doesn't take a big brain to figure out—anybody who's ever tried to find a place for a couple of new pairs of shoes in her shoe rack could tell you that). Which means that if Gabriela is in Beth's body, then there's a pretty good chance that—as a further example of just how heart-crushingly ironic (and unfair) life can be—Beth is in hers. Which means that she has to talk to Beth. Alone. 'That's why— That's why I think maybe I need some personal time.'

'Personal time?' Many people, hearing such a ridiculous statement, would laugh. Delila folds her arms in front of her, pursing her lips: a warrior princess assessing unfamiliar terrain. 'What's that supposed to mean?'

'You know, that I need some time by myself.'

'Some time by yourself.' Delila cocks her head to one side. '*Today.* Of all the 365 days in the year, this is the one when you want time by yourself?'

Gabriela, accustomed as she is to being agreed with and indulged, not questioned, ignores Delila's sarcastic tone and seeing-through-concrete gaze.

'Yeah, you know . . . I don't really feel up to hanging out with everybody. I think I'll just skip—'

'Skip? Am I suffering from some sudden hearing defect, or are you suggesting that you *skip* today?'

82

'It's not like anyone's going to miss me.' After all, Beth Beeby's been at Jeremiah High School for three years and most of the staff and students don't even know that she's there.

'*I'd* miss you. And you can bet your last printer cartridge that Professor Gryck would miss you, too. And she's not gonna buy that "personal time" dog-dooh, either. You can't skip today. Not one infinitesimal part of it. Not unless you're being hauled off in some vehicle that has a siren.'

'Professor Gryck?' repeats Gabriela.

'Yeah, you know.' Delila's fingers tap against her upper arms. 'She's the one organizing everything? Built like a water tower? You sat next to her at dinner last night and had a big talk about tension headaches.'

Gabriela does her oh-silly-me laugh again. 'Oh *that* Professor Gryck.'

'Yeah, that Professor Gryck. And she's not going to be too happy to find out you came all the way to LA just so you can spend the day in bed.' Delila gives her another scrutinous look. 'What's wrong with you, Beth? I thought you said this was the most important thing that ever happened to you. I thought you said you would've made it here if you had three migraines and body-hives.'

What a difference a day can make.

'Well, I am here. Only now I need some time by myself. It's a lot more stressful than I thought it would be.' Which is certainly true.

'Well, it's not gonna happen.' If Delila were a warrior princess, she would definitely be one who takes no prisoners. 'Santa Claus doesn't sleep through Christmas, and you're not sleeping through the biggest weekend in your life. There's no way I'm letting you lunch it because your nerves are all a-jitter. Your nerves are always a-jitter. Eat an onion and chill out. Because unless they have to put you on life support, you're coming.'

This is insane. Who is this girl to stand there like a prison door? Gabriela not only likes to keep the things in her mental closet limited to what she actually needs, she only deals with them one item at a time. She can't think about what's happened to her and what to do about it *and* deal with whatever it is Beth and the Moving Mountain are doing here.

'Excuse me,' says Gabriela, 'but in case you didn't notice, you aren't my mother.' She may not know who this girl is, but she at least is sure of that much in what seems to be a very uncertain world. 'You can't—' An old-fashioned phone starts to ring—*bringggbringggbringgg*—sounding as if it's coming from under Gabriela's pillow. She looks towards the bed.

'Speak of the devil . . .' mutters Delila. She, too, is looking at Gabriela's bed. 'Tell her you can't talk now.'

Gabriela moves her attention back to Delila. 'Tell who?'

'You know who. Tell her we have to get down to breakfast. Pronto.'

Breakfast? Gabriela hasn't eaten breakfast since she was nine, when she went on her first diet. 'Oh, look, I'll come later. I promise. But I think I'll mis—'

'No, you won't,' corrects Delila. 'We said we'd meet the three witches at eight sharp. Since we seem to be the ones who got stuck with them. The bus isn't leaving till nine-fifteen so that gives you enough time to order stuff and send it back if you

84

think it's been contaminated.'

'The bus?' She should have known. Fashionistas ride in Cadillacs; geeks ride on buses.

'Yeah, the bus. We're having a tour of the cultural highlights of Los Angeles, the Paris of the West Coast. Remember?'

This day's already too long.

'And anyway, you can't miss breakfast. We have the big daddy of big days ahead of us. You don't start a cross-country trip without putting gas in the car, do you?'

Gabriela blinks. Even at her best, she'd have trouble following Delila's conversational style, and she definitely isn't at her best right now.

Delila answers for her. 'Of course you don't.'

Necessity may be the mother of invention, but the mother of inspiration is desperation. 'OK, I agree with that,' says the desperate Gabriela. 'But it's not just gas a car needs, is it? You have to make sure it's got oil and whatever. And you have to wash the windows and vacuum the seats and the floor and give it a wax shine and all that kind of thing . . .'

Delila's hands move to her hips. 'Where is this going, exactly?'

'What I'm saying is, there's more to a car than gas, and there's more to a person than breakfast.' She almost has to shout to be heard over the ringing of the phone, which seems to get louder the longer she ignores it. 'So if I'm coming today, I need time to put on my make-up and—'

'Make-up?' This does make Delila laugh. Almost hysterically. 'What's with you? You're acting freakier than a guy about to change into a werewolf. You don't have any make-up, Beth. All

85

you have is eczema cream.' She points at Gabriela's pillow. 'Now you'd better answer that phone. You know your mom's not going to stop until you do.'

'How do you know it's my mother?'

'Are you kidding?' Delila is still laughing. 'Who else would it be at this time of the morning? I'm just surprised she let you sleep through the night.'

Gabriela retrieves the phone. It's Mom.

She turns her back on Delila's smirk. She takes a deep breath. 'Hi,' she says, sounding brighter than a studio light. 'Mom. What's up?'

'What's up? You mean besides you? At last.' Unlike her daughter, Lillian does not whisper. Indeed, she seems to be under the impression that Beth is actually deaf. 'Do you have any idea how worried I was when you didn't answer? I thought they had to rush you to emergency and you left your phone in your room. It just kept ringing and ringing—'

'I was—'

'Well, you weren't thinking about me. I know you're having fun with all these new people, but you did know I'd be calling.'

'I—'

'You remembered to take your vitamins, I hope.'

'Ye—'

'And what about breakfast? Have you already had your breakfast?'

'No, w—'

'Well, make sure the juice is freshly-squeezed. I know you don't like to ask, Beth, but you really don't want something out of a carton.'

'I—'

'So how did you sleep . . .?'

Lillian Beeby's words are like a waterfall,

86

tumbling forward under their own power and stopping for no one. Why didn't Beth call her first thing this morning . . .? Did Beth have trouble getting to sleep . . .? Did she need any medication . . .? Did she remember to take only half of the yellow pill . . .? Was the mattress too hard . . .? Was the mattress too soft . . .? Was the room too cold . . .? Was the room too hot . . .? Did her room-mate snore . . .? Are her allergies playing-up . . .? Has she thrown up yet . . . .? What is she having for breakfast . . .? What if they don't do poached eggs . . .? What if they don't have wheat-free toast . . .? Has she checked the pollution levels . . .? She did bring the sunblock, didn't she . . .?

Gabriela holds the phone away from her ear. What's wrong with this woman? She barely stops to breathe. All Gabriela wants is to hang up—maybe even make a break for freedom while Delila's getting dressed—but Lillian doesn't give her a chance. Though what she reminds Gabriela of isn't a waterfall; what she reminds her of is her uncle's parrot. He'll talk for hours, on and on and on and on, using every word and phrase he's ever heard again and again and occasionally breaking into song or impersonations of doors closing and timers going off, until finally someone throws the cover over his cage. *My God*, thinks Gabriela, *how am I ever going to shut her up*? No wonder Beth hardly ever says anything in class; she's probably never had the chance to really learn how to speak.

All the time this monologue is going on, Delila thumps around getting dressed, stopping every few minutes to shout things like: *Tell your mom you can't talk too long! Tell your mom you're not dressed yet! Tell your mom everyone's waiting for us! Beth!*

Beth! We're gonna be late! But although Delila's voice is loud enough to be heard in Tuscaloosa, Lillian rolls on.

And while she rolls, Gabriela gets up and looks through Beth's clothes in the closet. If she's going to leave the room, she's going to have to get dressed. There's not exactly a big choice. If everyone were like Beth, the fashion industry would be one factory in Jersey. Grey trousers or a darker grey skirt. A white blouse with a round collar or a white blouse with a bow. One grey dress as stylish as a paper bag. The black shoes or the other black shoes. And that's not even mentioning the underwear she finds neatly folded in Beth's bag. She can hardly bear to touch it. Plain white cotton underwear. Gabriela didn't even know they made stuff like that any more. And then she remembers Beth's legs. What is she supposed to wear to cover *them*? Tights? In April? God help her, if she's hit by a car and rushed to emergency. She'll die of mortification before they get her on the operating table. And Delila is right; there is no make-up. Gabriela, accustomed to checking her appearance with the regularity of a soldier on patrol checking each door and gate, can't believe that somewhere in Beth's extensive collection of bags there isn't at least some lipgloss and an eyeliner pencil. The girl is human, isn't she? Surely she can't go out into the world with naked skin every day? Doesn't she care what people think? But the answers to these questions are obviously: no, yes and no. There are a lot of pills and essential oils, and a bag filled with tubes of ointment for everything from mosquito bites to rashes—as if she were going to the jungle for the weekend, not the coolest city on the continent—but there isn't so much as a stub of pencil or an old tube of lipstick flecked with dust.

Good Lord. If Lillian ever lets her off the phone, she's about to go out in public with no make-up and wearing clothes bought not for what they say about you (trendy, hot, gorgeous, fashion know-it-all) but for how much of your body they cover (all of it).

Her only consolation is that no one will ever know that it's her.

*   *   *

Remedios has been talking incessantly since she and Otto left their suite. Discussing how they slept, asking him how he's adjusting to the human body, commenting on the carpet in the halls and the smoothness of the elevator ride . . . *How awesome is this? You don't even feel like it's moving.* She has read the menu to him, given her opinion on the décor of the restaurant and told a long story about living among the Tongvas before the arrival of the Spaniards, when the Los Angeles area was called Yaa. Through all of this Otto has, at best, only half-listened. He knows Remedios well enough to know that her aim is not to communicate or even entertain, but to distract. And in this, of course, he is two-hundred-percent correct. Every minute spent in the hotel is a minute when Otto may figure out what she's done. She wants to lull (or bore) him into a pliable state where she can get him to leave. She doesn't like the way he keeps looking behind her; she should have sat facing the door. But it hasn't yet occurred to her that Otto is a lot smarter than she has given him credit for.

'You know, I was thinking,' Remedios says now.

89

She stabs another hunk of blueberry pancake with her fork. 'Why don't we drive back to Jeremiah after all? We can take the scenic route. You know, through one of the national parks? All those old-growth trees and majestic mountains . . . '

Otto sips his coffee. 'Does this mean you're planning to leave me in the wilderness?'

'Well, pardon me for trying to do something nice to make up for the plane.' Remedios wipes syrup from her chin. 'I thought you'd enjoy it.' She watches him cut a slice from his bagel—yet another thing about him that annoys her. 'And who knows, Otto. Maybe you'll be able to save somebody who's about to throw themselves into a canyon. That should cheer you up.'

So she's not going to leave him in the wilderness; she's going to leave him up a mountain.

Otto chews the piece of bagel slowly and thoroughly, gazing past her head as though the best movie in the world is being shown on a screen behind it. 'Um . . .' It isn't a movie that he's watching, of course, but Beth. She's seated at a table near the door with several other Tomorrow's Writers Today finalists. Beth looks as she always looks—plain and earnest in her grey slacks and prim white blouse, and as if she's decided to jump from childhood straight into middle age. There's a bowl of fruit salad (barely touched) and one of those foamy coffees (her second) in front of her. The others are all eating and talking, but Beth just pokes at her food and sits there as if she died smiling. Otto cuts another slice of bagel. Like a man a few seconds before discovering that there are sharks in the water, he senses that something's wrong, but he doesn't know what.

Remedios, meanwhile, is shovelling pancakes into her mouth and continuing to talk, her lips stained with berry juice and syrup dribbling towards her chin. 'We might have to go a little out of our way, but I really think it'd be worth it.' Hundreds of miles in each direction out their way. Anything to lure him out of the hotel and away from LA. 'We can see those, what do they call them? You know the ones I mean—those really big, old trees. You like trees.'

'Sequoias . . .' Otto wipes crumbs from his mouth with his napkin.

Across the room, Beth suddenly realizes that one of the girls at her table is calling her name.

'Look! Look at these trees.' Remedios shoves something in front of Otto's face. There are sticky fingerprints on the casing. 'They don't grow trees like this any more.'

She's finally got his attention. 'What is that?' Otto stares down at the screen being held under his nose. On it is a picture of a redwood forest; excepting the smudges of maple syrup, the image is so vivid and sharp you can almost see the leaves rustling and hear the branches groan. 'Is that one of those pad things?'

'Isn't it fantastic?'

'Where in the name of the starry firmament did this come from?'

'A store in the lobby.'

She does it on purpose, he knows that—pretending to misunderstand him. She wants to confuse him, to get him to look in one direction while she does something he won't approve of in the other. 'That's not what I meant and you know it. I meant *why*? Why did you buy that contraption?'

'Because we need it.' Remedios dips the fingers of her free hand in her water glass and dries them on the tablecloth. 'You saw how useless the SatNav in the car was just trying to get here from the airport. But with this we can't possibly get lost. And that's not all. Wait till you see what else it can do.' She starts tapping the printed keyboard. 'Internet . . . email . . . maps . . . directions . . . limitless in—'

'Remedios!' Otto shoves her hand away. 'Heavenly hosts, you're an angel not a teenager.'

'Not right now, Otto. Right now I'm more or less a teenager.' Remedios slips the pad into her bag. 'And anyway, I was just trying to make things pleasant.'

'No, you weren't. You were trying to bamboozle me. But it's not going to work.' He pushes back his chair, so irked by her that he's forgotten he vowed not to leave until he knows what she's done. 'I don't know what you're up to, but we're not going to waste days looking at trees. We're going back to Jeremiah. Now.' That seems to be what she doesn't want, so that's what they'll do. Otto tosses his napkin onto his plate and stands up. 'Now. I'll clear out the room. You take care of the bill.'

'Whatever you say, Otto.' Remedios looks down at the table so that he doesn't see the look on her face. 'You're the boss.' Her smile is so bright that if her plate weren't covered with blueberry-pancake debris, he would see it reflected up at him. *Gotcha again*. Manipulating Otto is as easy as picking a flower. Possibly easier. It's definitely a lot more fun. 'I'll meet you in the lobby.'

Remedios finishes her coffee, and then gets up to go. She is feeling pretty pleased with herself. She has accomplished what she came to do, and she has pulled it off right under the nose of Mr Holier-than-thou. If anything should go wrong, which it won't, she will be safely back in Jeremiah when it does. But pride, as we know, is often one step ahead of a really big fall—a saying that Remedios is about to prove.

She is so full of self-congratulation that as she reaches the door, she almost walks into Otto. He is standing just outside the restaurant, watching a group of girls near the hotel entrance. There are six of them, and each one is more attractive than the next. Make-up flawless. Hair perfect. Clothes to die for (assuming you're a teenage girl). As they peer through the window for a sign of their car, which has been delayed by traffic, they look like a patch of highly cultivated flowers turned towards the sun. They could be models or pop stars. Only one of them isn't smiling as though she's looking at a camera; she's smiling as though she's waiting to be arrested.

'Otto! What are you doing?' Remedios gives him a friendly push. 'I thought you were going to get our stuff from the room. You know, so we can check out?'

'Just wait a minute,' says Otto.

A very large Cadillac is pulling up in front of the building. Shimmering with excitement, the girls start towards the doors, all of them striding forward as if they're on a runway. All, that is, but one. She moves unsteadily, as if she isn't used to heels. And now he can see that she isn't quite as perfectly turned out as the others. Her face is bare of make-up. Her hair is wriggling out of its pins. She gives the impression that she's uncomfortable in her clothes.

'Otto.' Remedios gives him another, less friendly, shove. 'Let's go.'

He holds up one hand. 'Not yet.'

For the love of Lazarus! She doesn't think he's quite figured it out yet, but he will if the girl who's never walked in four-inch heels before stumbles before she gets into the car.

'Otto!' Remedios jerks him around to face her. 'Let's—'

There is a sudden and audible gasp behind her— of horror, or surprise, or both—and then a girl's voice screams, 'Wait!'

Remedios doesn't bother turning round. She knows what she'll see as well as Otto does; she'll see Beth Beeby, as she's never been before, probably with a look of anguish on her face.

'Remedios.' Otto clamps a hand over her wrist. 'I believe you have some explaining to do.'

AND SO THE DAY BEGINS

'This is the first chance I've had. It's been like a sled dog race since we got here—all go-go-go,' Lucinda is saying into her phone as she steps into the hall. 'We're on our way downstairs. The car's picking us up— Of course it's a limo . . . This is Hollywood, remember?' Her laughter bounces down the corridor of identical doors. 'Oh, it's awesome. Totally awesome. I wish you were here. You would die! Really. You can't even imagine. It makes Maine look like it's on another planet. You know, the poor-cousin planet . . .' Lucinda is

94

talking to her best friend back home. 'I know . . . I know, but I really lucked out. My room-mate's the best. She's like a fashion genius. It's awesome. I'd be more nervous than a moose in hunting season if I didn't have her . . . I mean, you should see the other contestants. Man, they are sooo scary . . .'

Lucinda sashays down the hall in a polka-dot skirt that, to the eyes of some, is little more than a ruffle.

Normally, Lucinda's comments about the other contestants would strike as much terror in Beth's heart as a madman with a chainsaw, but she has more to worry about than them at the moment. She's learning how to walk. Teetering on heels like chopsticks, Beth grasps the door frame and looks both ways before following. She wanted to wear the trainers she found at the bottom of Gabriela's bag of shoes (brought in case they played tennis), but Lucinda wouldn't let her. Lucinda said that she gets how edgy and original Gabriela is, but, to be really honest?, even she would look like a hick in them. Apparently, it's better to risk permanent spinal damage than look like a hick.

Beth shuts the door behind her and takes a few tentative steps. Every time she moves, something swings or jingles (earrings, bracelets, the chotskys hanging off her shoes and bag and pinned into her hair). Lucinda walks as if she's crossing a carpet of rose petals being thrown by smiling admirers; Beth walks as if she's in a typhoon and she's crossing a carpet of JELL-O. Right foot, left foot . . . right foot, left foot . . . She doesn't actually hold on to the wall, but she stays close to it—just in case. She gives a silent prayer of thanks when they finally get into the elevator.

Lucinda loses her signal. Finding herself in a phone-free zone, she says, 'I meant that, Gab. I am just *so* glad you're my roomie. I really would feel like I was from another planet if it wasn't for you.'

You may not think that for much longer, thinks Beth. And takes a deep breath as the doors open and they step from the elevator.

There are four girls across the lobby—a blonde, a redhead, a brunette and one with champagne-pink hair—all pretty, all dressed from the kind of magazine that Beth never reads. Indeed, they are so perfectly turned out that they might be mannequins lined up by the front window like palm trees on an oasis. They have obviously been waiting for them, because Beth has barely tottered out of the elevator when they suddenly come to life, smiling and waving. 'Gabriela! Lucinda! Over here!'

Lucinda waves back. Beth can't risk a wave—she'll fall over.

The girls are carrying on as if she and Lucinda are their new best friends, but Beth sees the look in their eyes as they cross the room: they're being scored.

'Lucinda!' shrieks the redhead. 'What an awesome outfit! Nobody'd ever think you come from the backwoods of Maine!'

So at least that's one mystery solved; her room-mate's name is Lucinda.

Lucinda tightens her smile and returns the gush. 'And what about you, Isla? You look fantabulous!' But under her breath mutters, 'For someone who comes from a major urban area teeming with vice and violence.'

For the first time this morning, Beth feels like

laughing, but it's a feeling that passes quickly as the blonde's eyes clamp on her like handcuffs. 'Good Lord, Gabriela!' Her voice is sweet enough to cause toothache. 'What absolutely amazing pants.' And her smile could freeze rock. 'If I didn't know better, I'd think you were wearing pyjamas.'

'They're trousers.' Beth avoids even a glance at Lucinda, though she knows that Lucinda is glancing at her. Lucinda tried to talk her out of wearing the spare pyjama bottoms—the only article of clothing Gabriela owns that comes below the knees (no one will ever accuse *her* of looking like a Pilgrim)—but Beth wouldn't be talked. The shoes are bad enough; she can't stagger around on them *and* spend the day worrying that every time she climbs a staircase some guy is looking up her skirt as well.

'Well, they sure look like pyjamas,' says the blonde. 'My Mom had a pair like that in pearl grey.'

'They're silk,' chimes in Lucinda. 'Pure silk.'

'So were my Mom's.'

'I suppose it's not a bad look, even if people might think you just got out of bed and didn't have time to dress,' muses the brunette, her eyes on Beth's legs. 'Were they inspired by an old movie, too?'

'At least you're not inspired by the sixties,' says Isla, 'or you'd be wearing bell-bottoms.'

Lucinda's laugh flops between them like a dying fish.

'And . . . oh my God!' The girl with the champagne-pink hair and the nose ring leans towards Beth. 'Can I believe my wondering eyes? You're not wearing any make-up! Not a drop!'

Amazingly enough, considering that she's almost paralyzed with tension, Beth can hear Lucinda's

97

words to her friend on the phone. *I'd be more nervous than a moose in hunting season if I didn't have her . . . Man, they are sooo scary . . .* Now she understands what Lucinda meant. She's only known these girls a few minutes and already they're annoying her. She smiles so they can't possibly know just how much. 'It's this really subtle, natural look,' says Beth. 'It's all the rage in Europe. Heavy make-up's considered so *passé*.'

Hattie pretends to yawn. 'And no make-up's considered so primitive here.'

'Practically Neanderthal,' murmurs Isla.

'Oh, you are so funny, Gab!' Lucinda laughs again, turning to the others. 'Don't you think she's just hilarious?'

'That's a joke?' says Nicki. 'That make-up's *passé*?'

'Well, I don't know about hilarious, but you're pretty brave—or insane,' says Isla. 'I mean, it is daylight.'

'The only person who sees me without make-up is my mother,' says Hattie.

Paulette smiles like a movie star who just became the face of a billion-dollar ad campaign. 'I wonder what Taffeta's going to think,' she croons. 'I mean, you saw how she does her face. No one's told her make-up's *passé*.'

'Oh my God, Taffeta!' gasps Lucinda. 'Isn't she just awesome? She was even more impressive than I expected.'

This, at last, is something they can all agree on. Taffeta is definitely awesome. Remember her winter collection? Remember what she wore to the Academy Awards? Remember when she was invited to the White House? Remember the dress she made for that royal wedding? Taffeta proves to be the doorway to other conversations—conversations that have nothing to do with Beth, her naked face or her pyjamas. It gives Beth the small comfort of something for which she can be grateful.

She has no idea what they're talking about. Clothes. Fashion. Names she's never heard of. Things she's never heard of, either. *Colour cues . . . princess seams . . . basque waist . . . placket . . . back yoke . . . ringspun fabric . . . trend boards . . .* But she acts as though she does know. She owes loyal Lucinda that much. When she hears a word she recognizes—'shoe' or 'hemline'—she perks up like a dog who's heard her name. When they laugh, Beth laughs. When they fizz with agreement, she fizzes. When they roll their eyes and groan and sigh because they've spotted someone wearing some outrage against fashion or good dress sense, she rolls and groans and sighs too. But, of course, she has nothing to say, so she says nothing and smiles like a doll.

Everybody looks at them. The men and boys look twice. And not (as you might think) because they can't believe that these girls can stand there, their heels holding them six inches off the ground and their spines pitched forward, wearing so little that it's a miracle they're all not blue and shivering from the air conditioning. They smile at them; they wink. Yesterday, when Beth walked through this lobby she was virtually invisible—bumped into and shoved; hit with someone's golf clubs; trodden on by someone else. But today she is one of the fashionistas, under a spotlight; attracting appreciative smiles, good mornings and hellos.

99

When Lucinda accidentally whacks someone with her bag, the other person apologizes. When Nicki drops her phone, two guys stop to pick it up. The manager passes them with a nod, 'You young ladies have a nice day.' Beth fidgets and tries not to notice. It's like being under constant surveillance. No wonder they spend so much time getting dressed.

Losing the thread of the conversation again, Beth glances towards the entrance to the restaurant. Is Gabriela in there right now? Even if she could get away from her group and hobble all the way to the other side of the lobby before the car comes, she wouldn't. How could she ever stop herself from bursting into tears in front of Professor Gryck and everyone else? But still she keeps glancing over towards the room where she should be. And that's when she finally notices the guy standing just outside the restaurant entrance. There's something peculiar about him. Besides the fact that he looks as if he's just stepped out of a Graham Greene novel. Something not right. It's undoubtedly because of her state of agitation that she thinks so, but he looks faintly luminous. She squints. He really does, as if he's lit from behind. And even though he's wearing sunglasses, Beth suddenly realizes that he's standing there because he's watching her. She couldn't feel his gaze more surely if it had weight and force. Why is he watching her? He could be some Hollywood type, of course. A director. Or an agent. Or a talent scout. It could be that. He's thinking of discovering Gabriela. But he hasn't moved a muscle in minutes; he just stands there like a pillar of light. Maybe he's not a Hollywood type. Maybe he's just a regular, run-of-the-mill pervert. Maybe that's why he's watching her. Can he see her underwear through the silk? She moves her bag to her outside hip.

Nicki says something that makes the others laugh, and although she actually has no idea what it is Nicki said, Beth laughs, too.

Or is it her breasts? Beth's not used to having breasts. Not like these. And if she were, she'd cover them up more than is possible with any of the clothes Gabriela's brought with her. There isn't even a sweater or a jacket in case it gets cold. All Beth could find was a sparkly, tissuey scarf that she's wrapped round her neck, but it doesn't so much cover her breasts as hang off them like an epiphyte from a cliff. She turns slightly, trying to shift them from his field of vision.

She wishes the limo would come. Lucinda keeps giving her what's-wrong-with-you? frowns and Paulette keeps looking over, scrutinizing her, as if there's something different about Gabriela's appearance but she can't put her finger on what. Nicki, Hattie and Isla have all stopped talking long enough to comment on how quiet she is. *You weren't like this last night*. Besides wanting to get away from Mr Peculiar, Beth really would like to sit down. Her muscles are beginning to ache. And her back. She can see the reflection of the man in the hat and the white suit, ghost-like in the window. But she doesn't see the car.

'What I'm really looking forward to is Madagascar,' says Hattie. 'I can't wait to go there.'

The others agree. *Cool . . . Mega . . . Awesome . . . Fabulous . . .*

Madagascar. Unlike famous designers, models, celebrities and terms belonging exclusively to the industry of fashion, Madagascar is actually something with which Beth is familiar. 'Wow, Madagascar,' she says, grateful to be distracted from the man in the suit. 'I'd love to go there. Did you know that they have six different species of baobab? And there are ninety-nine species of lemur that are only found there. It's like a lost world.'

If Beth were paying attention, which she isn't, she might at this moment fully understand the expression 'the silence is deafening'. Her five companions stare at her with varying degrees of incomprehension. Paulette, Hattie, Isla and Nicki's mouths all form Os of surprise. Surprise and sudden understanding. Something has changed; they see weakness where they saw none before. Last night, Gabriela was the obvious leader; today she's not. Today she's barely part of the group. Lucinda's incomprehension is tinged with fear. She doesn't doubt Gabriela for a second—geniuses can be really weird, everybody knows that—but she sees the sharks circling in the water. If Gabriela goes down, Lucinda goes with her. Beth, however, notices none of this.

Nicki takes it upon herself to speak for the group. 'You what?'

'Madagascar,' Beth repeats. 'It's—'

'A joke,' Lucinda cuts in. 'Isn't it, Gab?' She turns to the others. 'You know . . . Madagascar, the country . . .? Madagascar, Taffeta's fashion house . . .?'

'Another joke?' says Paulette. 'Maybe you should be a stand-up comic and not a designer.'

'Look!' yells Lucinda. 'There's the car.'

Thanking God for the Industrial Revolution and

Henry Ford, Beth follows the others outside, and so doesn't see who comes out of the restaurant just then.

*   *   *

Gabriela tried to get away from Delila so she could talk to Beth—oh, how she tried—but Delila, it seems, combines the physique of a quarterback with the dogged determination of one.

As soon as they got to the elevator, Gabriela remembered something she needed that she'd left in the room.

'Silly old me,' she said to Delila. 'You go ahead and I'll catch up.'

Delila refused. 'You're not leaving me alone with the weird sisters, not even for five minutes,' said Delila. 'I'm coming with you.'

When they were almost at the entrance to the restaurant, Gabriela decided that she had to use the ladies' room.

'I'll only be a minute. You go on in.'

Although Delila's arms weren't folded in front of her and she wasn't making her there-are-no-stupid-children-in-my-family face, she sounded as if she were. 'I thought you used the facilities before we left the room.'

'I did. But I have to use them again. You know, it's nerves.'

'I'll go with you,' said Delila. 'I have nerves, too.'

When they finally made it into the restaurant, Gabriela just wanted to pop into the store in the lobby to get a bottle of water for what promised to be a gruelling morning ahead. 'You order for me,' said Gabriela. 'Fruit cup and the largest cappuccino they have. I'll be right back.'

'What's the big rush?' Delila thinks that Beth may be having a mini-breakdown. She's definitely the type. When the woman next door (who is also definitely the type) had her breakdown, she was just going out for a loaf of bread one minute and naked in Rite Aid the next. Nothing like that's happening on her watch. 'You can get it on the way out.'

Gabriela sips her coffee with a sigh. She has only been Beth Beeby for an hour or so, but she's already really tired of it. It's like being a frog or a spider. Or dust. Something no one notices unless it gets in their way or lands on their lunch. Gabriela isn't used to being ignored. She's used to being noticed and admired. If she drops something, someone else picks it up. If she's lugging a lot of stuff down the street, someone will offer to carry it for her. Today she could stagger through the lobby carrying three small children and a German shepherd and no one would so much as step out of her way.

And not only is she stuck behind the invisible shield that is Beth Beeby's body, she is stuck with the geeks. On what should be the most exciting weekend of her life, she's stuck with girls who eat like wolverines and talk like teachers. She takes another sip and lets loose another sigh. If this is the way the rest of her life is going to be, Gabriela will never see eighteen. It isn't worth it.

Delila calls Jayne, Esmeralda and Aricely 'the weird sisters', but Gabriela has already started to think of them as the Bad, the Boring and the Major Pain in the Neck. Which makes Delila the Good.

Jayne is controlling. *I sit there . . . Put that in the*

middle . . . Wouldn't it make more sense to order a pot of tea for all of us . . .? Aricely assumes that everyone enjoys the sound of her voice as much as she does. *Did you know that Mozart . . .? I read this article about Wordsworth . . . When we went to Paris . . .* Esmeralda is always right. *No, that was Martha Gellhorn . . . No, it wasn't in Philadelphia . . . That's not blue, it's aquamarine . . .* All three of them have more opinions than the Supreme Court. If they weren't so irritating, they could put a hyperactive insomniac to sleep.

And that's the other thing. They don't talk about normal, real-life things like clothes and boys; they talk about school things like books and plays. They don't see movies; they watch films. They don't listen to bands; they listen to orchestras. They go to plays, not pop concerts or basketball games.

Gabriela has nothing to say. She thought she did, but she was wrong.

'When you say *musical*,' Jayne said to Gabriela when she tried to get into their conversation on Broadway theatre, 'can I assume that you don't mean opera?'

'I'm talking about the classic existential novel of self-delusion and subjectivity,' Esmeralda informed her with a smile as thin as tulle when she mistakenly thought they were discussing something she knew. 'Not a TV ad for underwear.'

And now, her eyes on Gabriela's fruit salad, Aricely says, 'I can't help it, but that reminds me of the time we went to Costa Rica. Costa Rica is just so amazing. You should see the flora and fauna—I wrote six poems just about the birds. But what I was saying was that while we were there, we visited this pineapple plantation. And ohmygod . . . You haven't tasted pineapple till you've tasted that. And fresh? We had it straight from the field. It was like eating dew.'

Gabriela picks up her fork and stabs at a chunk of pineapple in her bowl. *Of course you did. It was probably reciting a poem while you ate it.*

Jayne's voice, always pitched for command, saves Gabriela from having to reply. 'Are you serious?' she demands. Mercifully, this question is to Delila. 'You've never seen *Jules et Jim*?'

'I don't really watch movies with subtitles.' Delila says this loudly. 'And it's not because I can't read fast enough to catch what they say,' she adds. Also loudly.

'But it's a classic,' says Esmeralda.

Delila breaks a piece of toast in half. 'Coke's a classic, too, but I don't drink that either.'

Aricely, distracted from fresh pineapple, joins in. 'I would've thought that as a poet . . . '

'As a poet,' says Delila, 'I like language. The words are important to me. I don't want to be the prisoner of some bad translation.'

Gabriela allows herself a small smile as she stabs a chunk of banana. *You should think twice before you take on the warrior princess.* Say what you will about Delila—her size, her shape, her hair, her stubbornness, her obvious fondness for bold prints and primary colours—she doesn't let anybody push her around. No matter how hard they may try.

Gabriela carefully balances a cherry on top of the stack of pineapple, while Esmeralda, Aricely and Jayne begin a discussion of world literature. Their voices buzz in the background. She's never been so bored in her life. Not ever. Not even the time she broke her ankle in two places and sat in emergency for four hours with absolutely nothing to do because she'd also totalled her phone when she fell. But at least then the anguish was physical and not mental.

And that's when—unplanned and certainly unprovoked—Gabriela picks up the cherry from on top of the pineapple, and throws it across the table at Jayne.

Jayne hasn't thrown a piece of food since she ate in a highchair, but nature does sometimes override nurture. She automatically hurls her last piece of bagel across the table, hitting Delila. With one hand, Delila wipes cream cheese from the shoulder of her kaftan; with the other she lobs a teabag and gets Aricely right between the eyes.

Professor Gryck can move remarkably quickly for a woman built like a silo, and descends on them like the Day of Judgement. She is horrified and shocked. In all her years of teaching, she has never had anything like this happen. Not ever. Not even close.

'She started it!' Esmeralda points at Gabriela.

'Well?' Professor Gryck glares down at Gabriela. Last night, when they bonded over tension headaches and Beth apologized for everything from knocking her fork to the floor to choking on air, Professor Gryck had assumed that she was going to be the easiest of the group to handle. Shy. Nervous. Afraid not just of her own shadow but everybody else's as well. But now she isn't so sure. This certainly isn't behaviour she expected. 'What do you have to say for yourself?'

'I guess it just kind of slipped,' says Gabriela. 'Or maybe it's all the excitement.'

Professor Gryck's sigh could rock an ocean liner.

'Beth Beeby.' She holds a napkin to her heart as if staunching the flow of disappointment. 'I swear, if I hadn't seen you with my own eyes, I wouldn't believe it. What happened to the lovely, polite, courteous, well-mannered girl I had supper with last night?'

Damned if I know, thinks Gabriela.

As they leave the restaurant, Gabriela suddenly sees Lucinda, looking as if she's just stepped out of an ad for body spray, sashaying out of the doors to where a gleaming black limousine is parked. It's true that one Cadillac Escalade looks pretty much like another, but though Beth's eyesight isn't any better than her taste in clothes, Gabriela recognizes the driver who picked them up from the airport yesterday—6'1", 17" neck, at least a 45" chest, 36–37" sleeve. And then she sees the others—Hattie, Nicki, Isla, Paulette. Her heart stumbles like someone whose stiletto gets caught in a grate. And there—wearing pyjamas and walking with all the grace of a horse in mud—is what looks to be her parents' only child.

'Wait!' she calls, knowing no one will hear her. It's all she can do not to weep.

*　　　*　　　*

As he leaves the restaurant, Otto's attention is caught by the flock of fashionistas by the windows. He slows to a stop, unable to take his eyes off them. Off Gabriela. The feeling that something isn't quite right that he had as he watched Beth mauling her food returns. The longer he watches, the stronger the feeling. Eventually, Remedios comes up behind him, but he ignores her. Suddenly, the girls start to move towards the door, all of them flowing as effortlessly as a river—except, of course, for the one who wobbles as if her ankles are made of rubber, holding on to every wall, door and post she passes like a bewitched mermaid trying to accustom herself to having legs.

'Otto! Let's go!'

But Otto is still watching Gabriela as her fall is broken by a man walking in the opposite direction who opens his arms to catch her even before she topples towards him.

'Otto!' Remedios finally grabs his shoulder to yank him around. 'Let's—'

'Wait!'

It is, of course, not Remedios who cries, 'Wait!' It is Beth Beeby, looking as if the last rescue ship just pulled out without her.

And that is when Otto realizes what Remedios has done. What she'd undoubtedly been planning all along. How could he have believed for even one minute that she intended to fix the contests? Fix the contests? Remedios Cienfuegos y Mendoza? The angel whose specialty is chaos? It would be like the most famous tenor in the world giving up opera to sing at birthday parties.

'Remedios, I believe you have some explaining to do,' says Otto, as he shoves her hand away and turns back to the finalists in the design competition. 'But not now.' The driver of the limo helps the girl Otto now knows to be Beth inside and Otto starts across the room, moving like air. 'Now what I want is the car.'

Although he wasn't actually speaking to her, Remedios answers as she rushes after him. 'The car? But we haven't checked out yet. We—'

'We're not going anywhere.' As he reaches the doors, the red sports car appears at the start of the driveway. 'We're staying here until you put everything back the way it was.' He gazes over his shoulder at her, giving her a look that would send the Devil back to bed. 'Or should I say *everyone*?'

Remedios grimaces with exasperation. This is exactly why she wanted to leave first thing in the morning. She knew he'd be unreasonable if he found out what she'd done. If they'd left when she wanted, they'd be well on their way to the redwood forest by now—and well away from Gabriela and Beth, and Otto standing on his principles like a goat on a mountain ledge, ruining everything. 'You're overreacting.'

'Am I?'

'Yes, you are. Just like in—'

'Baghdad was a special case.'

'I wasn't thinking about Baghdad. I was going to say Egypt. Or Rome. Or Jerusalem. Or—'

'For the love of Peter, Remedios. That's all ancient history.'

She knows more about him than he thought.

'All I'm saying is that you could at least give me a chance to explain why I did it before you get righteous and indignant.'

'All right.' And he stops so abruptly that she passes him and has to turn round. His arms are folded and his face looks like the silence of a stone wall. 'I'm listening like a thousand ears. Explain.'

'I got tired of hearing Beth weeping and worrying, and tired of watching Gabriela act like the most important thing in the world is what she wears. That's not embracing life; that's hiding from it. I thought it was time they both put things

110

in perspective. Lost their props and crutches, and had the chance to see things differently. They'll be better for it, Otto. It'll bring out the best in them.'

'Or destroy them completely.' He starts striding forward again. 'Do you have any idea what could happen to Beth out there in Gabriela's body? Do you? The girl gets a headache if there's too much traffic on the road or she gets 99 out of 100 in a quiz, and now you've sent her out into this— this—' Although among other gifts he has one for words, at the moment Otto is having trouble finding ones to describe Los Angeles. 'City of Angels' are three that are definitely out. '—this circus with a freeway running through it.'

'Heavenly host! She's a girl, Otto. She'll be fine. You just have to relax.' She follows him outside. Their car is at the kerb. 'That's your problem, you know. You take things too seriously. You never relax. Not ever.'

'A corpse couldn't relax with you around, Remedios.' He slips something into the valet's hand and climbs into the car. 'The only thing to be thankful for is the fact that, despite all appearances, you're on our team.' Though she might do them more good if she went over to the other side.

'What are you going to do?'

'As if there's anything I can do. You're the one who did it. You're the one who has to undo it.'

'So why are you in the car? Where are we going?'

Otto starts the engine. '*We're* not going anywhere. *I'm* going to keep an eye on Beth. For the love of Lazarus, Remedios, she can't even walk in those shoes.'

'And what am I supposed to do while you're cruising all over LA, having a good time?'

'Isn't that obvious? You're going to keep an eye on Gabriela.'

And how atrociously unfair is that? He gets to swan around the most glamorous city ever created in a sports car and she has to sit on a bus? 'But her group's just going on one of those dull tours. Museums, Otto. I don't want to go to museums.'

'Maybe you'll learn something.' Unlikely though that seems. 'Maybe it'll bring out the best in you.'

ONE GIRL'S HEAVEN IS ANOTHER GIRL'S HELL (AND THE SAME IS TRUE FOR ANGELS)

Gabriela's head rests against the window as she stares blankly at the passing streets, Professor Gryck's voice winding itself through her thoughts. Like twine being woven through ribbons of silk. What is the real Beth Beeby doing right now, Gabriela wonders. Is she leaning against a worktable at the studio, giving her opinion on a new design? Is she pinning material onto a body form? Maybe she's having a private moment with Taffeta in her office, discussing Gabriela's future over coffee, Taffeta purring, 'You know, honey, I see great things for you. I'd love for you to work with me . . .' That seems unlikely. Even a girl with Gabriela's creativity finds it hard to picture Beth suggesting adding a pleat or taking a tuck or talking loud enough to impress Taffeta. But she has no trouble imagining Beth and the others slipping through the luscious hills of Hollywood in the back of the limo, on the lookout for celebrities. Maybe they're already on The Strip, having the shopping spree that makes all others look like buying a pair of shorts for gym. The shopping spree Gabriela's been dreaming of.

She sighs. For sure, the real Beth Beeby isn't having as miserable a time as she is. Oh, how Gabriela wishes that she'd made a break for the front door when she saw the car outside the hotel. That's what she should have done. There would have been a big drama with screaming and crying and everything, and nothing would have been solved, but it wouldn't have made things any worse. There's no way things *could* be worse. If she'd made a major scene like that, all they'd probably have done is send her home. And then she remembers that home isn't where her clothes and jewellery and all her other stuff are but where Beth's mother, the talking clock of doom, is. So things *can* get worse. Possibly even much worse. God and all the saints in Heaven help her, if some miracle doesn't get her back into her own body, she's going to be living with Mrs Beeby. She only just manages not to groan out loud. As sure as Prada makes bags, she, Gabriela Menz, is in Hell. *I don't know what I did to deserve this*, thinks Gabriela, *but whatever it is, I promise, if I ever do it again, even totally by mistake or because I'm being blackmailed or something, I won't shop anywhere but Walmart for the rest of my life. Just pleasepleaseplease get me out of here.*

But the being who might get her out of here— the being who got her into this mess—is curled up in a window seat at the back of the bus, thinking about the small, bronze figure from Mesopotamia

113

on display in the last museum, which brought back a host of memories. Remedios is visible, but although her fellow passengers see her, they don't actually notice her, and if they did—if she happened to speak to any of them, for example— as soon as that person turned away she would immediately be forgotten. Professor Gryck, a woman who prides herself on her eye for detail, counts heads every time they return to the bus, and always comes up with the right number. Indeed, the only person who could notice as well as see Remedios (since she is, in theory, under angelic guidance) is Gabriela, but Gabriela is so consumed by self-pity at the moment that she probably wouldn't notice if a scouting party of aliens boarded the bus.

Nor is Gabriela the only one feeling sorry for herself. The small, bronze figure, which once adorned a box in which Remedios kept incense, is not the only thing to bring back memories. There were images of places and people Remedios knew. There were bracelets and necklaces like ones she's worn. Cups like ones she's drunk from. Books she saw written. Canvases she saw being painted. Even part of a wall she once leaned against on a hot July day. The visitors moved around her, listening to their tour tapes or reading from their books and leaflets. Talking. Chewing gum. Checking their phones. Thinking about lunch. They might say, 'Isn't that beautiful . . .?' or 'Isn't that moving . . .?' or 'Wow, what a cool ring . . . !' But whatever it was would be forgotten before they left the room.

The more Remedios had seen, the less delight she'd felt. That knife, that leather shoe, those coins, that painting of sunset over a field that is now blocks of apartment buildings—these weren't even memories, they were remains. Empty shells—to be crushed underfoot or swept away by the tides. And then there's Professor Gryck herself. She may be an expert on the Norse sagas, but her grasp of the rest of the world's history leaves a lot to be desired. How endlessly dull and boring the woman is. How inaccurate. How easily she believes half-truths and lies. Gabriela is not the only one who suspects this may be Hell.

Gabriela sighs again as the small blue bus navigates the traffic, its passengers sitting in orderly rows like guests at a wedding. *No*, thinks Gabriela. *Not a wedding. A funeral.* For this is the day joy died.

While the other tour buses—big and shiny, with some fast talker at the front pointing out the sights and dishing the dirt—go from movie studio to movie studio and famous restaurant to homes of the stars, their bus (no more than a big van) goes from museum to museum with Professor Gryck reading from her notes on the cultural highlights of Los Angeles. Monotonously. If there is anything in these cultural highlights that is more interesting than a pair of white socks, Professor Gryck has managed to overlook it. So far this morning, they've seen paintings of kings, paintings of bowls of fruit, paintings of squares of colour, and paintings of jagged lines. They've seen statues of sun gods, Greek gods, Roman gods, Egyptian gods, demons with human bodies and animal heads, monsters with hooves, tails and pointed beaks, a couple of horses, an Aztec dog, dancers made out of coat hangers and a pickled pig (which, according to Aricely, represents the futility of life). They've seen bowls and pots and cups and tiny clay figures and jewellery from across time and around the world. They've seen an installation of light bulbs and a table made from cereal boxes. Even Delila's beginning to feel like she might have died but doesn't know it yet.

As if reading Gabriela's thoughts, Professor Gryck, in an unexpected display of democracy, suddenly says, 'If there's anything we've left out that you feel should be included, I'm happy to entertain suggestions.'

Gabriela answers automatically. 'I do!' She waves her hand like a flag of truce. 'I have a suggestion.'

But if she hoped the flag would save her from being shot at, she was wrong. Professor Gryck doesn't like her suggestion.

'I'm not saying we have to go in or anything. We can just drive by it,' argues Gabriela.

Professor Gryck heaves a haven't-I-had-enough-from-you-already? sigh. 'I thought we settled this matter, Beth.' Students don't argue with Professor Gryck—especially ones who are still in high school.

Though not everyone seems to understand that.

'No, we settled the other matter.' Unlike many people, Gabriela doesn't flinch from meeting Professor Gryck's gimlet gaze. She can tell that Professor Gryck is an unhappy, frustrated woman. Just look at the outfit she's wearing: the shoulders are too wide, the sleeves are too short, the pattern isn't matched up and it makes her legs look stumpy. It practically screams misery. No wonder she's such a bossy old cow. 'You decided that it isn't important for us, as writers, to experience the living, breathing city of Los Angeles. I get that.

This is something totally different.'

'As I said before, Los Angeles is not all bright lights and glamour.' Professor Gryck is certainly proof of that. 'What we're here to experience is its culture. Not its razzamatazz.'

'Yeah, but that's what I mean, isn't it?' Although patience, resilience and fortitude aren't necessarily the first words that come to mind when thinking of Gabriela Menz, it is a testament to those qualities that she doesn't shriek with exasperation. Professor Gryck may have a string of letters after her name, but none of them seem to spell out l-o-g-i-c. 'If we're doing the super culture tour, then what's a bigger cultural landmark than that?'

'The Max Factor Building, Beth?' Professor Gryck sounds as if she suggested that Superman comics are literary masterpieces. 'You consider that a cultural landmark?'

'Yes. Yes, I do.' Gabriela's policy has always been to let a smile be her parachute out of any possible unpleasantness, and so she smiles now. 'It is where make-up was invented, Professor Gryck.'

The other contestants have been listening to this exchange as though they weren't, but now they all react, giggling in a surprisingly childish way for tomorrow's great writers.

'Don't be ridiculous,' says Professor Gryck when the merriment dies down. 'They've found make-up in Egyptian tombs.'

'But it was Maximilian Faktorowicz who was largely responsible for developing the modern cosmetics industry.' Even without the benefit of Mr Faktorowicz's products, Gabriela's smile is radiant. 'And he did make the term "make-up" popular, Professor Gryck, which is a very

117

significant part of our cultural vocabulary. So I think that counts.'

Professor Gryck might well wonder where Beth suddenly acquired all this poise and confidence—and specialist knowledge—but she doesn't. She's too surprised. Last night she would have bet that the only time Beth Beeby ever used the word 'make-up' was in relation to an exam, yet here she is with an encyclopedic knowledge of the history of the cosmetics industry. 'I really don't think—'

'A very large part of the culture of this country has to do with what American business created in the twentieth century,' continues Gabriela. 'Mass production. The industrialization of everything. Fast food. Where would we be without McDonald's or Henry Ford, Professor Gryck? Ask yourself that.'

Professor Gryck is now annoyed as well as surprised. 'Ms Beeby, if you don't mind, I really don't thin—'

'They changed the whole world, Professor Gryck. And Max Factor is part of that. I mean, we drove past that old church—'

'Nuestra Señora Reina de los Angeles.' Professor Gryck's voice sounds like something being chopped. 'The historic site of the original pueblo.'

Remedios grunts to herself. That's exactly what she means about inaccurate and blind. *There were people here before the Europeans, you know*, thinks Remedios with a certain amount of darkness. Luckless Lucifer but this woman is irritating as well as dull.

Gabriela is shaking her head. Sadly. 'You're not telling me that's more culturally important than

118

creating a billion-dollar indust—'

'Oh, look!' cries the professor with unconcealed relief. 'Here we are! This is one of the greatest museums in the country!' She pops to her feet like a Jack-in-the-box. 'Don't anyone leave his or her seat until the bus comes to a complete stop.'

'Somebody email Dante and tell him we've found a new circle of Hell,' mutters Delila.

Professor Gryck, who considers herself as knowledgeable about the art world as about Norse sagas, leads the way once again. The twenty contestants, one angel and Mr Solman follow. Most of the contestants surreptitiously play on their phones or send each other texts, but as they did at the first two museums they visited, Esmeralda, Jayne and Aricely cluster around Professor Gryck as if she's the mother hen and they're the baby chicks. They talk in clear, serious voices, giving their opinions as though when they're not committing the whole of world literature to memory they're boning up on world art.

The group stops in front of a painting of two men and a dog standing under a tree.

'Look at that brushwork,' says Aricely.

'It's his palette that's so special,' says Esmeralda.

'What an interesting use of shadows,' says Jayne.

'I have data-overload. I need a break,' Delila whispers to Gabriela. 'I'm going to the ladies. Pay attention so you can tell me if I miss anything really interesting.'

Gabriela stands behind the others, feeling as though she may fall asleep on her feet, and thinking about how much she hates museums. She might as well have spent the morning looking at blank walls. She felt nothing for the combs and

119

clips that once styled some long-ago woman's hair. Nothing for the jewellery that was once worn by girls not all that dissimilar to her. She didn't look at the statues or pictures and think, *That person was once alive just like I am—and had hopes and dreams and disappointments and problems just like I do.* (Though probably not the problem she has today.) Now, as she listens to the background gabble of Professor Gryck, the Bad, the Boring and the Real Pain in the Neck, and waits for Delila to come back, it's all she can do not to sob out loud. Surely there is more even to Beth's life than this.

'I couldn't agree more,' says a voice Gabriela has never heard before. 'I mean, museums are like zoos for objects, aren't they? There's no blood. There's no life. There's no *context*.' Remedios snaps her fingers. 'They're worse than zoos; they're more like mausoleums where the bodies have been buried alive.'

Gabriela turns around, about to ask how a stranger can know what she's thinking, but the sight of this stranger shoves the question from her mind. Behind her is a blue-haired girl—possibly her age, possibly a little older, even possibly a lot older, it's kind of hard to tell—wearing rolled-hem tweed shorts, a linen shirt and multi-belted vintage motorcycle boots with a strip of red down the back. She carries a saddlebag instead of a pocketbook. Her only jewellery is a heart-shaped moonstone in a silver setting on a silver chain. Gabriela can tell that the girl mixes her own make-up—not even her eye shadow is a commercial shade. And those have to be contacts; nobody has violet eyes like that. But the clothes and the eyes aren't what really catch Gabriela's interest. There's something about this

120

girl—something indefinable, but so strong you can almost smell it—that surrounds her like an aura. Though that isn't how Gabriela puts it to herself, of course. What Gabriela thinks is, *Wow! This girl is really awesome. If you could bottle her, she'd make the most amazing perfume!*

'I mean, just think about it.' The girl smiles; the air around her seems almost to glow. Those can't be her teeth, either. And God knows what she uses on her skin. 'An artist or a craftsman pours heart and soul and passion into creating something unique and beautiful—'

Thinking of the futility of life as represented by the pickled pig, Gabriela clears her throat.

'I'm not talking about the pig,' says Remedios, who has more than one complaint about this morning. 'I'm talking about something unique and beautiful. Something that speaks through time like the voice of Life itself, saying—shouting—"I am here!" and "We are here!" and "Let the songs of our souls be heard in Heaven!" And then what happens? It gets stuck on a wall or in a cabinet, and all these people trudge past like they're looking at postage stamps, while they think about how their feet hurt or where they're going next.'

'Are you a tour guide?' asks Gabriela. Though it does seem unlikely—she's never heard a tour guide talk about singing souls or the voice of Life.

'Do I look like a tour guide?'

'No. You look like a model. Or a designer.'

'Oh. Really?' Remedios tilts her head to one side, as though a new and sudden thought has just occurred to her. 'Are you interested in clothes?'

Gabriela looks around to make sure Professor Gryck isn't looming behind her, and lowers her

121

voice. 'Well, yeah. As a matter of fact I am.'

Remedios grabs her arm. 'Come on. You have to take a look at this.'

In a separate alcove off the room where Professor Gryck is reeling off dates and lifeless details is the portrait of a young woman. The light, though subtle, makes her look alive, as if her eyes might blink; as if her skin is warm. There's a window behind her, looking out on a churning sea. The young woman's blonde hair is intricately twisted and braided, held up by finely carved pins. She wears a shawl loosely draped over her shoulders and a finely patterned burgundy-coloured dress—whatever hangs from the silver chain round her neck is lost in its bodice. Her hands are folded in front of her and her eyes are looking straight at you, missing nothing; her smile suggests that she knows something you don't. She is almost hypnotically serene. Gabriela steps closer. All morning she's been looking at pictures and sculptures and busts, but it is only now that she actually sees what she's looking at—and suddenly understands what her new friend means about the voice of Life and being heard in Heaven.

And for the first time she thinks: *This girl was real—is real*. Really walked down streets; laughed and cried; saw the same sky and moon and stars that Gabriela sees; watched leaves drift to the ground and spring petals fall like snow; had things she longed for and things she feared. Just like Gabriela. Who also now realizes how alone she often feels. She stares at the face staring back at her. She can imagine her getting up in the morning and deciding what to wear. Imagine her washing. Fixing her hair. Smoothing out her skirt. Choosing a pair of shoes. She wonders what she's thinking. Where she's going next. What she and the painter talk about as she sits there, looking at Gabriela across the centuries. And for an instant, Gabriela has the sensation that if she tried just a little harder she could hear what the young woman has to say.

'Those were awful times,' says Remedios. 'He would've been burnt alive for heresy if it hadn't been for her.'

Gabriela doesn't move her eyes from the picture. 'Who?'

'Ra— the artist.' Remedios sighs. 'He fell in love with her, of course.' She sighs again. 'It was a love that could never be, and he knew it. He was lucky to be alive—to be able to fall in love. You can see that in the intensity of the colours and in the details—the ring . . . the flower . . . the cat asleep at her feet. And the dress. He had the dress made especially for her. Designed it himself.'

'It's beautiful.' Gabriela moves a little nearer. The style is as dated as the pyramids, but the material . . . What an evening gown that material would make. What a showstopper. What a masterpiece. 'Is that brocade?'

'No, it's embroidered.'

'That's impossible.' Gabriela gives a little laugh. 'It can't be.'

'Oh, but it is. Look. That's not a weave. Look at how delicate the work is. And the colour's slightly off. The thread's silk. It was dyed to match but there's the tiniest difference . . . '

It's exquisite. Remarkable. Gabriela's never seen anything like it; never even imagined anything like it. And it looks so real. Not a painting, but warp and weft and delicate, tiny flowers of silk. She is overwhelmed with the sense that if she touches that canvas—touches that fabric, that girl—she'll know what it means to be really alive. She reaches out her hand.

And sets off every alarm in the room.

*   *   *

The assumption Beth made about Gabriela Menz (that she would collapse from the strain if she had to so much as lift her little finger) has undergone a certain amount of revision this morning. Although Gabriela has never been seen to take notes, hand anything in on time or carry anything heavier than a pocketbook if there's some boy around to do it for her, she can't possibly be as lazy as she seems. Not if she's made the finals in the design competition; not if she wants to make this her life's work. Even if fashion were more necessary to life than a gold toothpick; even if it were a useful industry that contributed more to the world than back problems; even if you weren't spending your time making the same things over and over but in different colours and fabrics—even then, Beth *still* wouldn't do it. The girl has to be clinically insane. Being a commando would be a softer option.

Beth is exhausted. She feels as if she's been up for days, doing oral exams in a foreign language that she's never studied while balancing on her toes. The finalists have been frantically rushed and herded from one department to the next—from the pattern makers and cutters to the machinists and embroiderers—and seen dozens of items of clothing in various stages of production, and dozens of workers in various states of stress. If

124

Beth were to close her eyes (and not instantly fall asleep) she would see people waving things at her—pieces of fabric and lengths of trim, belts and bows and handfuls of buttons, skirts and bras and shimmery tops—and hear them screaming: *What do you think? Take a tuck in the shoulder? Put shirring on the bodice? Trim the neckline with lace? Lower the skirt? Shorten the skirt? Sequins? Rhinestones? Ethnic embroidery? Appliqúe? That dress with these shoes? This jacket with that hat? Leggings or footless tights?* Expecting immediate answers. Shouting even more loudly when they don't get them. Acting as if the fate of the world depends on six millimetres of trim.

At the moment, Taffeta Mackenzie is marching into the main room of the Madagascar studio, much like a small tornado in high-heeled boots. The six finalists follow in her wake, not like shadows, but slaves. The staff all look up, greeting them affably but nervously—they know what to expect. Taffeta goes from station to station— introducing people, explaining things, looking at samples—her heels clicking, her smile solid. She stops to examine the dress on a body form.

Beth and Lucinda exchange a look. By now they know what to expect, too. No one shouts louder than Taffeta Mackenzie.

It's been the same everywhere they've gone. Taffeta Mackenzie may be sweet as corn syrup when she's socializing, but when she's in work mode she's more like lemon juice laced with strychnine. *You call that a pattern? I don't call that a pattern. I call that where the cat was sick . . . Are you blind? A gazelle could sew a straighter seam than that . . . When I tell you to get me something, I mean*

125

now, not tomorrow! Not next week . . . You call this finished? *What are you, working for the competition* . . .?

Now Taffeta stands beside the body form, holding the dress between the tips of two fingers as if it's a blanket infected with smallpox. 'Would someone please tell me what this is supposed to be?'

'Uh oh,' whispers Lucinda. 'Here we go.'

Eyes are downcast, heads bent. Everyone's trying not to breathe.

'No one?' Taffeta Mackenzie's melt-that-ice-cap eyes turn to Beth. 'Miss Menz? You've had some very interesting opinions today.' Downcast eyes or not, glances are exchanged. They all know that this isn't a compliment. 'Maybe you could help me out here.'

Beth gazes back at her blankly, but her heart sinks down ever closer to the centre of the earth. *Merciful Minerva! Is this day going to do nothing but get worse?*

It's a trap, of course. Taffeta Mackenzie is a driven, tireless and remorselessly efficient woman with a very low tolerance of anyone she thinks is slow, dull or a fool. Which is unfortunate for Beth, because another opinion that has had some overhauling this morning is Taffeta's opinion of Gabriela Menz. Last night, Gabriela was the brightest star in Taffeta's sky, but in only a few hours Beth has managed to bring that star crashing down to Earth where it ended up at the bottom of the ocean. For Beth, crippled, uncomfortable and caring less about ruching, double darts and kick pleats than most of us care about leaf mould, has found it hard to pay attention or act as if she's

126

really interested in the studio's activities. Which means that every time Taffeta has asked her a question, Beth has looked startled and said, 'I'm sorry?' At first Taffeta just laughed as though Beth were a pet that had done something amusing like get its head stuck in a paper bag. 'Don't be sorry, Gabby. Just tell me what you think.' But soon the small amount of patience that trims her personality began to unravel.

'Oh, really?' she smiled when Beth gave her opinion of the black tunic with the crochet detail. 'Old-fashioned?'

'That's very interesting,' she murmured when Beth answered her question on trouser lengths. 'You certainly do have an original POV. One would almost think you come from a planet where everyone wears skirts.'

'Do tell . . .' she simpered when Beth picked the sample blouse she liked best. 'I would have thought from what you said last night, Gabby, that your taste would be a little less Wisconsin mall.'

'You may be more of an original than I thought,' she commented as she marched them through the machine room. It was difficult to tell from her smile whether this was a good thing or not.

Which is why the question, 'Would someone please tell me what this is supposed to be?' is obviously a trap.

What is Beth supposed to say? That it's a copy? That it's the wrong colour? That the sequins look like a slug trail? Lucinda reaches over and squeezes Beth's hand. 'Don't say anything,' she whispers. 'Just faint.'

If only she could. Beth has fainted on numerous occasions but she is not in her own body today, and

Gabriela's refuses to faint on demand. Beth clears her throat. And for perhaps the very first time in her life, Beth thinks: *What the heck? She's already annoyed with me.* The only person looking at her is Taffeta Mackenzie. 'It's a dress.' She nods. 'Yes, it's definitely a dress.'

Everyone stops breathing, even Taffeta, who for nearly two entire seconds is so enraged by Beth's answer that she can't even speak. But then, just as she opens her mouth to show how good she is at shoot-to-kill sarcasm, the security alarm goes off.

Saved by the high-pitched whine.

*   *   *

High in the hills over Hollywood, Otto sits in the flash red convertible, keeping an eye on the house into which Beth and the others disappeared, and enjoying the stillness and calm of the neighbourhood. This is more like it. It may not have the immaculate beauty of a primordial forest or an untouched mountaintop—of the Earth when it was young and humans younger—but it's close enough for now. No traffic-clogged roads. No clamour and din. No frenzied activity. No Remedios Cienfuegos y Mendoza. This part of the city still remembers what the world was once like. The sky is blue, the grass is green, the sun is warm and the smog settles down in the valley. If he keeps his eyes on the shimmery trees, he can imagine himself somewhere else—some other hills, some other perfect day, some other link in the chain of time.

Nevertheless, the morning moves slowly, every minute taking its own sweet time. It's so quiet up here that even the birds whisper. The only people Otto sees are in cars, glancing over to give him suspicious looks, or the occasional runner in designer shorts and matching sweatbands, worried about her or his heart. But as much as Otto enjoys the calm, he is impatient to get things moving; to return Beth and Gabriela to their own bodies; to get back to Jeremiah where much less can go wrong. His gaze wanders up and down the road, and his thoughts wander with it. It isn't just the Devil who finds things for idle minds to do. Where, Otto wonders, do the people who live in these houses walk their dogs? They will have dogs; he knows that from the magazines he's seen. They'll be small dogs with big names that have their nails manicured and wear diamond collars; the descendents of wolves bred into toys. They must have to do their business like any other animal. Otto frowns. Where are the dogs? In most places he has been—and that, of course, is most places— no matter what century, no matter if there was a war on or a hard winter, you always saw dogs. Otto likes dogs. He peers over the car door. There's no evidence anywhere that a dog has ever walked down this road. Or that anyone else has, really.

For all Otto's complaints about big cities and wanting peace and quiet, just sitting waiting has obviously started to bore even him. He gets out of the car, giving his idle feet something to do. As soundless as the minutes themselves, he walks down the empty road—nonchalantly, as if this isn't a neighbourhood in which the only people who walk are servants going to or from work. He sniffs the air. There's an intricate weave of aromas: jasmine . . . coral trees . . . jacarandas . . . chlorine

129

... grass ... several strands of expensive perfume ... weed killer ... and—

Otto stands at the edge of the property that houses the Madagascar studio. Does he smell a dog? He sniffs again. It could be. Or it could be an old, wet wool jumper left to dry under a hedge. Rather than take the driveway, he goes up the side of the house. Magnolia. Wisteria. Bone meal. Is that barking he hears? Barking or shouting, behind the closed windows and doors. He leaps over the wall.

A cat could walk under the motion-sensor beam of the laser-security system that protects Madagascar, and an insubstantial angel could walk right through it. But not a young man in a white suit and a Panama hat.

NOT EVERYONE LIKES TO SHOP

Otto couldn't believe how quickly the peaceful neighbourhood transformed itself into a war zone. All that shrill, siren-like shrieking. And the screaming and shouting. And the guard suddenly charging across the lawn. At least he found the dog. It was a great brute of a creature, with too many teeth and too much gum and a madness in its eyes. Otto got out of the backyard of the studio a lot faster than he got into it, and collapsed in the car, consoling himself with the thought that the day could only improve.

Unfortunately he was wrong.

When the girls finally emerged and got into the limousine, he assumed they were going to lunch.

He imagined white linen tablecloths and polished floors and a soothing violin concerto playing in the background. Perhaps not an establishment as elegant as the restaurants of old Vienna, but somewhere sophisticated and calm where he could relax and keep an eye on Beth at the same time.

Instead, they went shopping.

Otto has never been involved in any serious, twenty-first century shopping before, and he has no intention of ever being involved in it again. The pushing. The shoving. The grabbing. The frenzied emotions. The arguments. The snarling and snapping. The remorseless determination. Poor Otto hasn't seen such single-mindedness outside of a war.

Angels, however, are very resilient, and now here he sits at a sidewalk café, an iced lemon-sorbet tea with mint and a plate of chocolate macaroons in front of him, recovering from the traumas of the morning. He watches the street—the cars moving along the road like conveyor-belt ducks at a shooting gallery; the people almost dancing. So this is Los Angeles. Laidback. Mellow. City of Angels. City of Dreams. There is an almost liquid quality to the light—possibly to the air itself—that makes everything seem not quite *there*. As if it's only a mirage. An image on a screen. An enchanted place that appears and disappears like a ghost (or an angel).

Otto leans back in his chair. What with driving in traffic that either moves like a stampede or suddenly stops dead for no apparent reason, the hours spent just waiting for Beth to come out of the studio, the burglar alarms and the stress of shopping, it's been a hellish morning—but now he finally feels himself starting to relax.

He sips his tea, suffused with a new sense of peace. Or possibly relief. At least Remedios isn't with him. And nothing bad has happened to Beth. Her face—Gabriela's face—is pinched with strain and she's hobbled by her shoes, but she hasn't been rushed off to a hospital or thrown herself in front of a bus (two of the tragic fates he has imagined for her). Otto has no reason to think that anything more will go wrong. Everything's going to be all right. All he has to do is see Beth safely back to the hotel this evening, meet up with Remedios and Gabriela, and make sure that the girls' paths cross.

But the mellow image of Los Angeles is only an illusion. It has always been a city of violence and greed. And Otto's feeling of well-being is only an illusion, too.

As he reaches for another macaroon, Otto notices heads turning to look at something behind him. Probably a movie star, he thinks. Otto lost interest in the cinema when colour was introduced, but nonetheless, because he always took quite literally the admonition to do as the Romans when in Rome, he, too, turns to see who it is.

The woman coming towards him is tall and willowy with a billowing mane of blonde hair, and she's wearing a hot-pink jumpsuit, high-heeled sandals and aviator sunglasses. It takes him a few seconds to realize that he not only recognizes her; he knows her. It is, of course, Remedios Cienfuegos y Mendoza. What a coincidence. He puts his glass down so hard that he knocks the spoon off the table.

Because the aviator glasses, though stylish, are very dark—and because her mind is on things

132

that don't include Otto Wasserbach—Remedios is more or less on top of him before she sees him scowling at her from the other side of a low railing. *Fire and brimstone!* If only she'd seen him first, she could have made a run for it. But, as Caesar's army crossed the Rubicon, Remedios crosses Santa Monica Boulevard. She comes to a stop beside him. 'Why, Otto! What a surprise! I never expected to see you sitting on the street eating cookies.' She smiles as though she's happy to see him. 'I guess LA is working its magic even on you!'

There is no return smile. Indeed, his thin lips have almost disappeared in disapproval. 'And you are doing what here exactly?' The cacophony of sounds that surrounds them—horns and engines, sirens and beeps, voices and music and ringtones—is so loud that, although she's only a few inches away, Otto almost has to shout.

'I'm talking to you, Otto.' She lowers her shades so he can see her wink. 'What do you think I'm doing?'

'I'll try again. What are you doing here, Remedios?' he repeats, but they both know that what he means is: *Going back on our agreement? Looking to interfere some more?*

'I'm not doing anything. A little shopping . . . A little sightseeing . . .' She gives him a smile that has gladdened the heart of more than one repentant sinner. 'We can't help people if we don't understand them. And we can't understand them if we don't do what they do. Can we?'

He takes a gentlemanly sip of tea. 'But you're not supposed to be "sightseeing" or "shopping". You're supposed to be with Gabriela.'

'And what about you?' Remedios leans against

133

the railing, shaking her head so that the curls move around it like wings. 'What are you doing grooving on the LA scene? I thought you were keeping an eye on Beth.'

'I am keeping an eye on Beth. She's limping a little, but otherwise she's fine.' He slaps her hand away as she reaches for a cookie. 'They've been shopping for what seems like an eternity, but their car will be picking them up in less than an hour. I thought I'd take a break.' Otto finally manages a smile, but it's a wan one. 'Unlike you, I find shopping to be just another name for Hell.' His sigh would disabuse anyone of the notion that angels don't suffer. 'So much effort for so appallingly little.'

'Does that mean you don't like the outfit?' Remedios spins around, causing traffic to slow and horns to honk. 'I found this fantabulous vintage shop down one of those alleys. It's really incredible what you can get in this town.'

'I hardly recognized you at first. That hair!'

She gives her head a shake. 'It's a wig! You can get a wig to look like anybody you want.'

'You look like you've stepped out of a seventies' detective series.'

She makes that face she does when she thinks she has something on him—half sugar, half acid. 'I thought you didn't watch TV, Otto. I thought it was beneath you. How would you know what they wore in seventies' detective series?'

'Somebody had to turn the set off.' He looks up at her, still unsmiling. 'So now that we've dispensed with the chitchat, let's go back to where we started. What are you doing here, Remedios? You're supposed to be watching over Gabriela.'

Remedios slips over the railing and into the chair across from him as though she is made of air. 'Don't get yourself all agitated, Otto. Gabriela's not going anywhere. She's either on the bus or in a museum.'

While he was watching the traffic, Otto absent-mindedly made a small bird from his straw wrapper, but now he absent-mindedly starts to undo it, smiling for the first time since he saw Remedios bearing down on him like a bad omen. 'You're certain of that?'

'Of course I'm certain. You'd love the woman who's running things. She has them on the timetable of a high-security prison. She doesn't even let them out to feed.'

Otto nods towards the other side of the street. 'Who's that then?'

Stoke up the fires of Hell! Why is she so trusting? Remedios knows you can't rely on humans. The minute you turn your back, they're picking apples and sneaking out of museums. She doesn't bother to look round. 'How many guesses do I get?'

'If I had the tiniest smidgen of faith in you, I'd almost be willing to believe that you arranged this so we'd be able to switch them back sooner rather than later.' Otto pushes his cup away. 'But it's far more likely that it's just a coincidence.' He smiles. 'On the other hand, it is a lucky one.' The powers that be, he thinks, are clearly on his side.

She makes another grab for the last cookie on his plate. 'I take it you already have a plan.' She takes a bite.

'As a matter of fact, I do.' Otto pushes back his chair. 'I'll fetch the car. You stay with Gabriela. The limo's meant to be picking Beth and the others

135

up near The Hyatt soon. I'll make certain it never arrives and get her out to the boulevard. All you have to do is make sure your girl is on that same pavement and—'

'Boom, Shiva!' says Remedios through a mouthful of macaroon.

'Amen,' says Otto. He gestures to the empty plate and cup and the crumbs scattered over her jumpsuit. 'I'll leave you to take care of the bill.'

But he hasn't noticed Beth behind him. Remedios sees Beth's eyes fall on Otto just before he vanishes, and the look that comes over her face. *Well, bless my stars*, she thinks. *Beth not only sees Otto and remembers that she sees him, she's also afraid of him. How ironic! Afraid of Otto Wasserbach. It's like being afraid of a feather.* But from Remedios' point of view, of course, it's a very useful thing to know.

And with that, she, too, disappears.

*   *   *

Sunset Plaza, shopping centre to the stars. It has everything a girl who believes in the Three Cs—Cosmetics, Clothes and Celebrity—could possibly want: the upmarket stores, the chic cafes, the luxury cars cruising past, the tourists taking pictures from the windows of buses and rental cars. And today, it not only has all of that, it has the finalists of Taffeta Mackenzie's fashion competition as well. Though some are here more than others.

Beth is present in body only, and it isn't even her body, of course. She trails behind her companions like a wheeled toy on a string. Paulette, Nicki, Hattie, Isla and Lucinda all bubble with

136

excitement, but Beth's face is flat with worry and pain. What does she have to be excited about? She can't see any way out of the nightmare she's in. Not today. Not tomorrow. Not ever. Paulette, Nicki, Hattie, Isla and Lucinda laugh and chat as they try on shoes and dresses, tops and trousers, studying themselves critically in mirror after mirror, one eye always on the lookout for someone famous so they can tell their friends back home. Beth props up walls and thinks about Gabriela, having the time of Beth's life while Beth limps through this torturous day, one eye always out for the man in the Panama hat. As if things aren't bad enough. Oh, how she wants to go home. More than that, oh, how she wants to be back in her own body; back in her own body and home.

Every few minutes, Lucinda glances over her shoulder to make sure she's still with them, but the others don't care. If they're not complaining because she's so slow or so unhelpful, they're ignoring her completely. After the humiliations of the morning, they no longer feel they have to be nice to her or pretend that they like her. She is no longer the person they want to be; she's the person they're glad they aren't. If it were up to them, they would have lost her an hour ago.

Nicki, Hattie, Paulette and Isla all sail through yet another glass door; and Lucinda looks back and beckons. Beth watches Lucinda disappear, and then looks left, right and behind her before she follows them inside. She positions herself near the door, where she can easily see the entire floor and anyone who leaves or enters, and then she sinks back into her reveries of doom, gloom and whether or not an exorcist could help her.

'OK, I give up.'

Beth blinks, aware because something the colour of plums is swinging dangerously close to her face, that someone is talking to her. 'I'm sorry?'

'I've had enough.' Paulette still holds the shoe she was examining, but her eyes, narrowed to slits as if she's judging the finest hand-stitching, are on Beth. 'What exactly is wrong with you, Gab? It's like we're shopping with a malfunctioning robot.'

Where to start? Leaving aside Problem A: there's the pain in her feet; the ache in her back; the ice cubes her toes have become and the feeling that she's being refrigerated; her general fatigue at having spent so many hours in the sweatshop of glamour; and her low morale after a morning of being yelled at. And, finally, there's the fact that *he's* following them. Following her. That's what's wrong.

Beth was facing the wall of glass overlooking the back yard of the studio when the alarm went off. She automatically shifted her eyes from Taffeta Mackenzie to the windows behind her, and there he was—the man from the hotel. He was standing near the west side of the yard, looking up at the house. Then everyone started talking and running to the doors, and the security guard and his dog were charging across the lawn, and even though Beth couldn't have done more than blink, he was gone.

It can't be him, she told herself. *You have him on your mind, that's all. It wasn't anybody.* A natural illusion. It's the kind of thing that happens all the time. People think they see a ghost (or a man in a Panama hat), but really it's only a reflection, the light beams bent into something else. The guard

138

searched all over, but he didn't find any trace of an intruder. It was probably just a glitch in the system, or a very large cat. The guard said it was impossible to get over that wall without a ladder. ('Unless he's a circus performer,' said the guard. 'Or Spiderman.'). And even if someone did manage to get into the yard, there was no way he could get back out without being seen. And if he didn't go over the wall, how did he leave? Fly?

But then, as they were getting into the limo to come shopping—Beth hobbling behind the others with Taffeta shouting after her, 'For God's sake, Gabby, buy yourself a pair of shoes that fit!'—a glint of red caught her eye and she glanced over to see a red sports car parked further up the road, out of sight of the studio. You'd think he'd have the sense to ditch that stupid hat.

'Well?' demands Paulette. 'I asked you a question, Gabriela. What is up with you?'

'Me?' Beth's smile is as delicate—and as temporary—as the flowers glued to the shoe in Paulette's hand.

'No, your cousin in Michigan.' Paulette points the shoe at her. 'Yes, *you*. What's going on? I asked you three times if you thought this would be better in another colour, and when you finally bothered to answer you said, "Yeah, it's nice".'

'Well, that's what I meant.' Beth may not be able to walk in Gabriela's shoes, but she has no trouble lying in them. 'That they'd be nice in another colour.'

Paulette eyes her as if her mascara has run. 'No, you didn't. You've been on automatic since we got here.'

'I may be a little distracted . . . '

139

She didn't see him following the limo. Which she thought must mean that he really was a figment of her imagination or that he'd given up. No to both. She's seen him since. Strolling past a window. Going into the store next to the one they're in. Standing in a doorway on the other side of the street. Disappearing up a flight of stairs. Vanishing around a display of scarves. It's always just a glimpse, an image at the corner of her eye; and when she looks again he isn't there. But she knows he is.

'A little?' Isla comes up beside Paulette. With her long red hair and liking for lace, Isla may look like the heroine of a romantic novel, but she snorts like a truffle hog. 'I bet you don't even know what stores we've been in.'

Beth wouldn't know these stores on a normal day—a day when the face looking back at her from the mirror behind Paulette is hers and no one would think of asking her opinion about a pair of shoes. She doesn't have a clue.

'Of course I know.'

'No looking at our bags,' warns Nicki, shifting hers out of sight. 'Go on, name them.'

'Don't be ridiculous,' says Beth. 'We don't have time for games. We still have a lot of shopping to do.'

'And that's another thing.' Hattie, who only a minute ago was at the other end of the room trying on her sixth pair of boots, has somehow materialized beside Isla. 'You haven't bought anything. Not one single thing.'

Beth smiles sweetly. 'I haven't seen anything I like.'

'We've been here over three hours,' says Hattie.

'That's like going to a supermarket and not seeing any food.'

'And what about the guy in Transcendental? What was up with that?'

Beth doesn't recognize the name, but she knows exactly which store Isla means. She was going through the motions of looking at tops in the boutique where some actor whose name she can't remember apparently shops all the time, when she *knew* for certain that the man from the lobby was right behind her. She could feel his eyes on her. 'Just what is it you think you're doing?' she shrieked as she swung round. 'Why don't you leave me alone?' Only it wasn't the young man in the white suit; it was an older man in jeans, a cowboy shirt and a cowboy hat (in her defence, his hat was white) looking for a present for his granddaughter. Beth apologized eight times.

'I told you, it was a mistake. I thought he was someone else.'

'Who?' asks Nicki. 'I didn't think you knew anybody in LA.'

'Or maybe you do,' says Paulette. 'You keep looking over your shoulder.'

'Hey, that's right!' Hattie snaps her fingers. 'Even in the car you kept looking back all the time.'

'Maybe she's pretending she's in one of those old movies she likes so much where everybody's a spy,' says Isla.

Beth fidgets. She should have known that, with whatever grudging respect they'd had for Gabriela now gone, it was only a matter of time before they jumped on her like a pack of hyenas on the carcass of an antelope. 'You're all making a big deal out of nothing.'

'What's going on?' Lucinda strolls up to them, a new shopping bag swinging from her arm, looking wary. 'You guys look really serious.'

'We're trying to figure out why Gab's acting so weird,' says Nicki. 'And don't say you haven't noticed.'

Oh, Lucinda's noticed. From the minute she woke up to the sound of sobbing, Lucinda's noticed. The clothes, the make-up, the apologizing, the clinical amnesia when it comes to anything to do with fashion, the fact that Gabriela, who last night was as graceful as a gazelle, can barely walk. It's like she's a different person to the one Lucinda met yesterday. But she was hoping the others hadn't noticed. 'Well . . .' She smiles without any conviction. 'Define weird.'

'Weird like she's not really here,' says Isla.

'Weird like she didn't know what Madagascar was,' says Nicki.

'Weird like she's wearing pyjamas and no make-up,' says Hattie.

'I'll go for weird like paranoid,' says Paulette.

'I don't think that's being weird,' lies Lucinda. 'It's just nerves and stress and excitement and everything.'

'Sure,' says Paulette. 'I can't walk right when I'm feeling nervous either.'

'I can hardly leave the house,' says Isla.

'OK,' Beth sighs. 'OK, I'll tell you. I guess I should have told you straight away, but I didn't want to worry you or scare you or anything . . .'

'That's very kind of you,' says Paulette, 'but we don't scare that easily.'

'This had better be good.' Hattie looks as if she's trying to swallow her mouth.

'Well, you see, there's this guy. I noticed him first in the hotel.' Beth explains about the young man in the lobby in the white suit and the Panama hat. How he was watching them while they were waiting for the car. How she saw him in the garden at the studio. How she saw him parked up the road when they were getting back in the limo. How she's seen him while they've been shopping. Someone, not Lillian Beeby, has said that a trouble shared is a trouble halved, and as she talks Beth really feels that that is true. After all her anxiety, this is a trouble that can be understood. She should have told them from the start, instead of keeping it to herself. United we stand, divided we fall. Strength in numbers. You don't have to walk alone.

When Beth finishes her story, there is silence for a few seconds. But only a few—and it definitely isn't the silence of fear.

'Some guy's been following us,' repeats Paulette, with as much conviction as if Beth had said that the bustle is coming back into fashion. 'You mean, like a stalker? Is that what you mean?'

'Well, yeah, I guess you could call him that.' Beth makes a scrunched-up face. 'There's something really strange about him.'

Nicki, peering at herself in a compact mirror, says, 'I didn't see anybody strange in the hotel this morning.'

'Me, neither,' says Isla. 'I mean, everybody who stays at The Xanadu has money, don't they?'

'So what if he has money?' Beth snaps. 'That doesn't make it OK to follow us around.'

'I'm just saying that it's not like he's some kind of LA lowlife, is it? He has to be respectable,' argues Isla. 'Guys with money don't do stuff like

143

that.'

'Why not?' asks Beth.

No one hears her.

'Well, personally, I don't understand how you noticed anyone.' Hattie's lips form a narrow, unbending line. 'You were pretty much out of it even then. You hardly said five words while we were waiting, and, if you ask me, they were the only thing that was strange.'

Paulette turns on, rather than to, Lucinda. 'What about you? Did you see this mysterious stalker?'

'Well . . . I—' Lucinda's eyes ping-pong from Paulette to Gabriela and back again. 'I don't— I'm not really sure. There were a lot of people in the lobby this morning.' Her shopping shrugs. 'I can't remember everybody I saw.'

'Well, I know I didn't see him,' proclaims Nicki, 'and I always notice hats because they're, like, my specialty. There's no way I'd've missed a Panama.'

'I still don't see why you're all wound up because some guy was looking at us in the hotel.' Hattie continues to study her as if she's not sure of the decoration or the colour. 'Let's face it, guys always look at us. You'd think you'd be used to it by now.'

'Besides,' says Isla, 'if there really was some guy watching us, then he was probably a director or a producer. They're always looking for new faces.'

If he is a director or producer, then he's one who spends his time riding around town and climbing into people's gardens.

Paulette's smile is full of ill will. 'Nobody but you saw him in the garden, did they?'

'I can't explain that, but he was definitely there!' Beth's voice is, for her, unusually loud and firm. There's nothing like chronic frustration to make a person forget her shyness. 'I saw him as clearly as I see you. He was right there in the back yard. If he wasn't there, why did the alarm go off like that?'

'The guard said it was a malfunction,' says Paulette.

'It happens at our house all the time,' adds Isla.

'And we were all right there,' says Hattie. 'Right next to you. So if you saw him so clearly why didn't we see him, too?'

Nicki laughs without a stitch of humour. 'Maybe he really did fly away.'

Blessed are the peacemakers, a group that can now count Lucinda among their number. 'Look, it's been a long morning. Why don't we get some lunch or at least a drink,' she says. 'There's a café a couple of doors down.'

Beth, who, met with so much resistance, is starting to doubt herself, jumps at the suggestion. 'That's a great idea!' Lunch, that's what she needs. She hasn't had anything to eat all day. Maybe that's all that's wrong with her—hunger. That and being in someone else's body. She's hungry. Hunger makes you hallucinate. Everybody knows that.

They come out of the shoe store and turn towards the café. Beth freezes.

Sitting at one of the tables, talking to a man with his back to Beth, is one of those LA types that Beth's mother warned her about. Several times. There are undoubtedly quite a few things that she might be discussing with the man at the table, most of them illegal, but the improbable blonde isn't the reason Beth has stopped like a phone whose battery has suddenly died. It's the man. He may be facing the opposite way, but she knows him instantly.

'Luce, look!' Beth turns and grabs Lucinda's arm. 'That's him! That's him! Right over there.'

Not just Lucinda, but Hattie, Isla, Nicki and Paulette all look at her.

'Now what?'

'That's him! Over there with the blonde with all the hair!'

Paulette groans. 'Oh, for God's sake. How long are you going to keep this up?'

'No, really. Right over there! At the café! I swear, it's him.'

Hattie is the first to look round. 'Where?'

Beth turns back to the couple at the table.

There's no one there.

*   *   *

Nothing like this has ever happened to Professor Gryck before (nor to anyone else involved, come to that). The entire Tomorrow's Writers Today group was frogmarched out of the exhibition area by the armed guards of this most prestigious of museums. The head of security (an ex-policeman who thought he'd seen everything, but obviously hadn't) wanted to know what the heck Professor Gryck thought she was doing.

'I thought I was educating these upstanding and talented young students,' said Professor Gryck in the voice of an expert. 'That's what I thought I was doing.'

The head of security said it was more like she was training a gang of art thieves. 'They were all over the place. Ignoring the signs. Touching everything. Going over markers. How do you explain that, Professor?'

Professor Gryck couldn't. It never happened; none of her students touched anything; nor did they wander around like straying cattle. 'These are responsible, highly intelligent and gifted young adults, not riff raff,' she informed him. 'They would never do anything like you're suggesting.'

The head of security pointed to the bank of monitors. 'Well, it's all on there. In black and white.' Apparently, they were trying to steal the special exhibit, loaned from the Louvre for the first time, *Unnamed Lady at Window*. The others were causing distractions while that plain, innocuous-looking girl made the lift.

'We weren't trying to steal anything.' Professor Gryck's voice was brittle with exasperation. 'It was an accident, you dolt.'

Calling him a dolt was probably a mistake. They were supposed to have lunch in the beautiful courtyard restaurant of the museum. She'd been planning it for weeks: tables were reserved on the elevated terrace overlooking the fountain and Professor Gryck had gone over the menu, making sure that there was nothing that would cause any of her charges to break out, throw up or go into toxic shock. (Beth isn't the only one who suffers from allergies.) Professor Gryck was looking forward to this lunch. Civilized. Sophisticated. Elegant. The perfect ending to what was meant to have been a perfect morning. You certainly wouldn't want to have a day of art and culture and then eat in some fast-food joint with plastic forks and styrofoam plates.

But even if their reservation hadn't long expired by the time they were released, 'the incident' (as Professor Gryck has come to think of it) ended any

147

chance of them dining at round, marble-topped tables overlooked by priceless sculptures and modern fountains. Though it was ultimately established that she and her group were who they said they were, and that something had gone horribly wrong with the surveillance system, there was no question of them being allowed to remain. Or wanting to. In a civilized, sophisticated and elegant manner—but in no uncertain terms— she and her group were told to leave. And with a dignity amplified by righteous indignation, they left.

And so, in an unprecedented move that broke all of her own rules, Professor Gryck gave the contestants free time for a quick lunch.

'You're to stay on this block.' She waved her arm back and forth so they'd know which block she meant. 'We'll meet back here in exactly one hour.' She looked directly into Beth Beeby's glasses. She knows whom she blames. There was only one person in that alcove; one person myopically close to that precious portrait. 'Don't any of you be late. Do you understand?' Professor Gryck needed a drink. 'Promise me that.'

Everyone promised. Or almost everyone.

'But we're not supposed to leave the block,' Aricely is saying now.

They've finished their quick lunch and have half an hour to spare. Esmeralda, Jayne and Aricely want dessert. Gabriela wants to do some shopping.

'It depends how you define block.' In so many ways it has been a demoralizing, not to say deadening, morning. The only bright spot was that painting—that painting whose life and passion was just within her reach. Until the alarms went

148

off and she was rudely hauled away. If she really were Beth Beeby, Gabriela would still be crying and apologizing. Since she isn't, what she wants is to give herself a treat. Some foundation and a little blusher, for example. And maybe a scarf—filmy, flimsy and glinting with colour. Something to cheer her up. Surely she deserves that little crumb of happiness? Gabriela thinks so. 'We're not leaving the area; we're just going to a different section.' The Sunset Plaza section. 'It's, like, two minutes away.'

'I don't see why you have to go shopping,' says Esmeralda. 'As I say in my essay, unbridled consumerism is destroying our nation's—'

'Yeah, I know,' interrupts Gabriela. This has been mentioned before. 'It's destroying our nation's soul. Only I'm not emptying the nearest mall, Esmeralda. I'm just getting a couple of things I forgot. I must've left my make-up bag at home. I don't have anything with me.'

'Maybe if you call Professor Gryck—' begins Aricely, but Gabriela cuts her off, too.

'What's wrong with you guys? So far we've been in a bus and a museum, and a museum and a bus. Don't you want to just walk around a little? See the city without a piece of glass in front of your face?'

Jayne frowns. 'But Professor Gryck—'

'Isn't going to know we went anywhere, because we're going to be right where she left us when the bus comes back.' If they ever get out of here, that is.

'But what if something happens to us?'

'What could possibly happen to us in half an hour? We're not rafting across the Pacific. We're just going into a couple of stores.'

149

'I still say Professor Gryck's not going to like it,' says Esmeralda.

'Geez, Louise . . .' groans Gabriela. No wonder Beth chews her nails, if this is what her friends back home are like. 'Trust me. She's not going to know.'

Delila has been silent throughout this exchange, looking as if she's watching a play and is trying to follow the plot, but now she says, 'Well, you can count me in.' She missed a lot of the excitement in the museum because she was in the toilet; she isn't about to miss any more.

'What about the rest of you?' Gabriela smiles encouragingly. As much as she'd like to leave them behind, if Professor Gryck does catch them disobeying her orders, she wants the others to be with her. Safety in numbers. Divided we fall.

Aricely looks at Jayne. Jayne looks at Esmeralda. Esmeralda looks at Gabriela.

'What are we going to tell Professor Gryck if she finds out we disobeyed her?'

'We'll tell her we had to help Beth get a special non-allergic, organic kind of sanitary pad,' says Delila. 'She's met the girl. She'll believe that.'

Gabriela's spirits are almost immediately restored by being out on the street. This is more like it. The energy of so many people going somewhere, and going there in a hurry, hums through bone and steel; cellulose and concrete. Even on so short an acquaintance (and most of it from behind glass) she knows that Los Angeles is so much more than any other place she's ever been. There is nothing ordinary or dull here. Nothing humdrum. Everything sounds louder; looks brighter; smells stronger; moves with a shimmer or a bounce. She feels as if her blood is foaming

150

with excitement. Why would anyone want to live anywhere else? She loves LA! And LA, of course, should love Gabriela. She should fit right in; she should look like she belongs. Wearing her faux snakeskin zip-back heels and the ivory-coloured shift with the beadwork. Heads should be swivelling, elbows nudging. *Look at her! Who's that? She is, like, sooo cool!* But LA doesn't love her; it doesn't even know she's here. She's not a goddess; she's a geek—a lot more invisible than the air. The only advantage this gives her is that she's wearing shoes that allow her to walk easily and quickly. Half an hour is a long time when you can stride.

'Wow, will you look at those two over there?' whispers Aricely; as if there is any chance that she can be heard on the other side of all that traffic. 'They look like they're out of a movie.'

Gabriela glances over. Not a movie she'd watch. 'Good God, retro seventies.' She shudders with distaste. 'Bell-bottom jumpsuits weren't a good idea then, and they're really not a good idea now. And look at her hair! She looks like she's got a dog on her head.'

Jayne and Esmeralda aren't interested enough to look, but Delila is trying to remember if she saw the man in the white suit at breakfast. He seems kind of familiar. And he's good-looking, in an old-fashioned, European way. And it's not just the hat he's holding in his hand, or the James Joyce sunglasses. He looks as if he speaks several languages; as if he's spent a lot of time sitting in cafés, but not here—where there's a man at the bus stop holding an iguana and a woman who looks like Marilyn Monroe skating through the traffic— in much older cities of narrow streets and buildings

151

that were built long before any white man put his foot down here. But though it's only been a second or two, when Delila turns back for another look, there's no one there.

CROSSED PATHS

They're running late, of course.

'Where do you think you're going?' says Esmeralda as Gabriela heads towards another display of beauty products. 'We have to leave. *Now*.'

'But it'll only take a minute.'

'We don't have a minute,' says Aricely.

Jayne holds out her arm. 'Do you know what time it is?'

Gabriela groans inwardly. She made a mistake; she should have left them in the restaurant with their faces in plates of cake. Two mistakes: they're not the Bad, the Boring and the Real Pain in the Neck; they're the Grump, the Nag and the Talking Clock. 'I just have to get one more thing and I'm done. I swear it.'

'That's what you said ten minutes ago.' Jayne is still holding out her arm. 'What is it now?'

'Eye-shadow foundation.'

'Eye-shadow foundation?' repeats Jayne. She wears the expression a medieval serf might wear if she were told that, one day, men would fly through the air and walk on the moon. 'Are you serious?'

'I completely forgot. You've been rushing me so much . . .'

'You know, this sounds like something you can

live without,' says Aricely. 'I've never even heard of such a thing before.'

'Just because you've never heard of it, doesn't mean it doesn't exist,' says Gabriela.

'And who, disguised as a plain-Jane, serious fiction writer is really Super Shopper, able to leap whole counters at a single bound . . .' intones Delila, but she intones with a smile. Unlike some people, Delila is having a good time. If she'd wanted to spend the weekend in a museum, she could have stayed in Brooklyn.

The 'some people' who aren't enjoying themselves are, of course, Jayne, Aricely and Esmeralda. They'd much rather be reading a thousand-page novel. Gabriela's 'a couple of things I forgot' encompassed much more than those few words suggested. They thought she meant a lipstick and maybe an eyeliner. The basics most girls can't leave the house without. They wear make-up; they understand that much. But they all put on make-up the way they put on gloves and a scarf in winter— because they feel they have to. There's no art to it. No method. No plan. Which means that it isn't a subject Jayne, Aricely and Esmeralda know much about—and they are girls who like to be the experts in any situation. But in this instance, it's Gabriela who's the authority. She doesn't put a barrette in her hair without considering the effect. She has to test each pot, tube, brush, compact, palette and pencil; each skin, lip and eye colour, and balance them out against each other. Everything has to match.

'Well, if you want to be late for Professor Gryck, that's fine with me,' says Esmeralda. She pushes on the door. 'But we don't. We're going.'

Delila gives Gabriela a nudge. 'They're right,' she whispers. 'We're running on empty here when it comes to time. We better get moving.'

Gabriela sighs. With resignation. She hasn't put up with all their moaning and griping to be the only one to get into trouble; she has no choice but to go with them. She hugs Beth's backpack and, despite the fact that she doesn't like to sweat, gamely trots up the street after them. Delila, built for endurance rather than speed, brings up the rear.

It seems to be a longer way back than it was coming, but at last they see the rest of the group, hovering on a not-too-distant corner.

'Well, I'll be danged,' grunts Delila. 'We really do have guardian angels. I think we're actually going to make it.'

'Oh, my God!' Gabriela stops dead, her eyes wide and her mouth open in shock, staring through the river of traffic at something across the road. From her expression, it might be a UFO or a Hollywood star.

'What's wrong?' Delila only just manages not to plough into her. 'What is it?'

You couldn't say that Gabriela's forgotten about Beth. How could she when every time she looks at her hands she sees Beth's savaged nails, when every time she glances in a window she sees her plain, pinched face? But, having other things to occupy her mind, she has managed to put Beth out of her conscious thoughts for most of the morning. Until now. For what she sees across the street is not, of course, a UFO or a Hollywood star. It is herself, Lucinda, Hattie, Nicki, Isla and Paulette, standing near a bus stop with bags of shopping in their arms.

'Oh, my God!' Gabriela repeats as a bus pulls

154

up to the kerb, obscuring her view. They must be waiting for the car to pick them up. Delila's right—they do have guardian angels. This is her chance to talk to Beth, just put down in front of her like a present. She can take her aside, have a quick word. Suddenly, for some inexplicable and illogical reason, she thinks that everything will be OK if she can just get to Beth before the car arrives and takes her away.

'What is it?' Delila asks yet again. 'Is it somebody you know?'

As a general rule of life, it isn't advisable to cross Sunset Boulevard in between lights. A chicken could cross the Autobahn as safely. Anyone will tell you that. Unless, of course, traffic is bumper-to-bumper and not moving. But it isn't bumper-to-bumper now, and it's moving very quickly.

Gabriela, however, isn't thinking. All she knows is that she has to get to the other side. She hurls herself into the traffic, and, rather miraculously, for only a few seconds that no one will remember, every car, bus, bike, skateboarder and skater on the boulevard freezes and she runs through them unscathed. Esmeralda, Aricely and Jayne, who are almost where they want to be, don't know there's no one behind them any more. Delila runs after her.

But when Gabriela reaches the sidewalk, Beth and Lucinda are no longer waiting at the kerb; they're walking up a side street towards the hills.

And after them goes Gabriela, like a bloodhound that's caught the scent.

*   *   *

155

It's a well established fact that things can always get worse. We tell ourselves that it's always darkest before the dawn, but sometimes it's darkest before it gets really, really dark. This is something Beth has always known. Yet, today—a day that got off to such a phenomenally bad start—as they wait to be picked up by the limo, it seems it's something she's chosen to forget. She's been put into somebody else's body. She's been harangued and hassled by the Lady Macbeth of the fashion world. She's been frightened out of her mind by a Hollywood sleazeball who seems to be able to disappear at will. She can't even think about her mother or she'll start to hyperventilate. But now, she's convinced herself, everything's going to be all right. Tea at The City of Angels College of Fashion and Design to meet the rest of the staff. The big party tonight to meet everybody who's anybody in the LA scene. Nothing else can go wrong. It can't. How could it?

The six of them are waiting near the hotel as instructed—as, indeed, they've been waiting for the last fifteen minutes—when, from Gabriela's bag, an instrumental version of the song 'Hotel California' suddenly starts playing. Beth's been surreptitiously texting the same message to Gabriela and checking for messages and missed calls all morning—every time she's alone for a minute or goes to the bathroom. Her heartbeat stumbles. It must be Gabriela. She fishes the pink cell phone from the bag and holds it in front of her. It's not her number, but that doesn't mean it isn't Gabriela. Beth was way too tired to charge her phone last night, Gabriela could be using Delila's phone. Beth can feel the others looking at her. But she can't talk to Gabriela with Lucinda, Nicki, Hattie, Paulette

156

and Isla surrounding her, listening to every word. She glances over at them.

'Well, who is it?' demands Paulette.

Beth looks back at the phone. 'I don't know. It doesn't recognize the number.'

'For God's sake, answer it!' orders Hattie. 'Find out who it is.'

'Maybe it's the driver,' suggests Lucinda. 'You know, explaining why he's late.'

And maybe if she stalls long enough, Gabriela will give up for now.

'It's probably one of my friends. They must've gotten a new phone.'

'But they wouldn't be calling you now,' says Isla. 'They know you're busy.'

The song continues playing.

Paulette takes a step towards her. 'Are you going to answer that, or what?'

Beth takes a step back. 'But why would the driver be calling me?'

'It doesn't matter.' Hattie pokes her. 'For God's sake, Gabby. Just answer the phone! It could be important.'

Beth turns so that the others are looking at her back. To her relief, it isn't Gabriela. It also isn't the driver. The driver has a deep, rich voice that makes you feel as if you're sitting by a fire on a snowy afternoon. The driver is always calm, even when someone cuts him off. This voice is high and thin, and belongs to someone who is almost never calm.

'Thank God I finally got through to someone!' screeches Taffeta MacKenzie. 'What the hell is wrong with everyone today? Did they all throw their phones into the ocean?'

'I'm sorry,' says Beth. 'Who is this?'

157

'Who do you think it is?' snaps Taffeta. 'Your fairy godmother?'

'Ms MacKenzie?' ventures Beth.

'Where are the others? Why don't they answer their phones?'

The others move closer, their whispers like the buzzing of bees. *What is it? What's the matter? What does she want?*

'But their phones didn't ri—'

'There's been a change of plan. This is not supposed to happen, of course. For what that damn limo costs, it should be as infallible as the Pope.'

'Something's happened to the car?' guesses Beth.

'Yes, something's happened to the car. It's broken down. On the freeway! He can't break down in town. Or near a garage. Oh, no. He has to break down on the freaking freeway. What was he even doing there?'

'I'm sorry. I—'

'You'll have to take a cab. Go out on Sunset and grab the first cab you see.'

'Bu—'

'I'll pay for it when it gets here.'

The line goes dead.

Traffic is heavy, but moving fast. In the few minutes it took them to reach the main road, more than half a dozen cabs have gone by, but now there isn't one. They wait. And wait.

'How can there not be one single cab?' moans Isla.

'There's some kind of curse on us.' Hattie is looking at Beth.

'You can say that again.' Paulette is alternately shaking her phone and holding it to her ear. 'This

158

is, like, totally dead.'

'I knew I'd have time to go back and look at those shoes again,' grumbles Hattie.

'Why couldn't she have called us a cab?' complains Nicki. 'It's not like we know our way around.'

Beth, still nervous that the man in the Panama hat is going to show up again, isn't listening. She looks up the road. There are several buses coming, but still no sign of a cab. Beth sighs. She doesn't notice Aricely, Jayne, Esmeralda, Delila and herself hurrying along on the other side of the street because, just as a bus starts to move towards the stop a few feet away from them, a car parked further up the road suddenly shoots into traffic—so that she can now see the small red sports car parked behind it.

The bus moves up to the kerb. The doors open. It will come as no surprise to learn that—along with drugs, sex, germs, vitamin deficiencies, sink holes, falling airline debris, cell phone radiation and killer bees—riding on public transport in Los Angeles is among the thousands of things that Beth's mother has warned her about. According to Lillian, the only people who use it are people who have no choice—the poor, the criminal and the insane. There have been horror stories: robberies, knifings, infections, violent outbursts—even hijackings. Didn't Aunt Joyce have her wallet taken right out of her bag? But for once Beth doesn't heed her mother's advice. Panic overrides Lillian's dark prophecies. She doesn't know what the man in the sports car wants, but she doesn't really want to find out . . . 'Come on!' she orders.

Hattie, Isla, Nicki and Paulette all look at her as

if she's mad, which is an understandable reaction.
   Lucinda follows her on.

*   *   *

Remedios sits at a café near the bus stop. Her wig sits on top of several burger boxes in a garbage can on the corner. The only thing on her head now is a baseball cap with the inscription: *Have a Nice Day!* She watches Beth and Lucinda disappear inside the bus, the door shutting behind them so quickly you'd think they were tiny fish being swallowed by a whale. And she watches Gabriela sprint through the stilled vehicles, Delila behind her, and—thinking that she sees Beth—straight past Remedios and up a side street.
   Remedios is feeling pretty pleased with herself. Otto knows that she paused time and traffic and got Gabriela across the boulevard as she was supposed to, but he doesn't know that, because of her, Gabriela thought she saw Beth going up into the hills and followed. Nor does he know that Beth saw him, and got so scared she jumped onto the bus that just happened to come along before the swap back could be made. He'll know that his plan has been thwarted, but he won't know whom to blame. She really is one very accomplished angel. Remedios turns her head enough to be able to see the red sports car, its driver still trying to figure out what just happened. Resisting the temptation to wave at him, she slips from her seat and is gone.

*   *   *

Sodom and Gomorrah, what in the name of God's

blue sky is Beth doing? She's getting on a bus! Why in Heaven is she getting on a bus? You might think that Otto, having experienced it for quite a long time now, is beyond being surprised by human behaviour, but it seems that he isn't. She was supposed to wait for the taxi—which, of course, wouldn't appear until Gabriela was right beside her, but instead she's getting on a bus! And not just any bus—she's getting on the *wrong* bus! He feels like shouting at her. 'Are you crazy? Where do you think you're going? You're headed for the ocean!' She's supposed to be going to The City of Angels College of Fashion and Design, not the *verdammte* sea. Why would she do something so stupid?

Otto watches Beth vanish into the moving billboard that is the westbound Metro, its body covered with a teaser for a popular TV show and bored-looking faces at the windows; and then he glimpses Gabriela striding into the hills. *Fire, flood, famine and plagues of locust, rodents and disease!* He bangs his head against the steering wheel, just as if he's a real Californian. How could Remedios have blown such a simple task? Beth was standing there, waiting for a cab that wasn't going to come. Gabriela was charging through the traffic as if it were no more than a mirage. They should have stood within inches of each other. They might even have touched! For the love of Lot, how much easier could it be? And, instead, what happened? Beth got on the bus before Gabriela reached the sidewalk, and Gabriela, guided no doubt by the illogic peculiar to teenage girls, kept right on going.

It is, of course, unseemly for an angel to groan out loud, but Otto is definitely tempted. He should, perhaps, be above such petty emotions as

161

anger and the childish desire to push Remedios Cienfuegos y Mendoza into the Pacific Ocean, but Divine Beings have never been short of a temper—and he isn't above anything at the moment; he's right down in the thick of it: traffic, crowds, pollution and enough noise to make it a major miracle that the dead manage to sleep at all. And it hasn't even occurred to him yet that Remedios' failure to swap the girls back was deliberate.

Otto stares at the smiling, toothy faces painted on the back of the bus as it lumbers up the road. This is all his worst fears of what might happen to Beth parading around Los Angeles in the body of Gabriela Menz come true. Does she even know where she's going? Will she know when she gets there? And what if she doesn't get there? What if she gets off at the wrong stop? Is waylaid by some tanned lothario and never seen again? Drowns in the Pacific? When it comes to imagining worst-case scenarios, Lillian Beeby could take lessons from Otto.

'Don't worry, Beth!' he calls after her. 'I'm on my way!' Then bangs his head on the steering wheel again as another car hits him from behind.

CITY OF MORE THAN ANGELS

'It's called pay and ride, sister.' The driver, well aware of the dangers of making eye contact with strangers in Los Angeles, isn't looking at Beth. 'No pay, no ride. I don't give change.'

Lucinda tugs on her arm. 'Maybe we should just get off,' she whispers.

162

In Beth's normal life, she would already be gone. All the driver would have had to do is clear his throat and Beth would have turned as red as sunset over the Gulf of Mexico, stammered an apology and backed down the steps (probably into someone trying to get on). But Beth is not in her normal life, and so she doesn't feel guilty about not having the exact fare; nor does she feel that she has no option but to obey the rules. What she does feel is an overwhelming desire to get somewhere she considers safe as quickly as possible, and right now that somewhere is The City of Angels College of Fashion and Design, where Taffeta Mackenzie awaits them in a diabolically bad mood. There's nothing like being hounded by some crazy creep to make Taffeta MacKenzie look like the soft option.

In her normal life, Beth never tries to argue or make excuses because it never really works for her. There is something about her face—the serious line of her thin lips and the fairly permanent look of worry in her eyes—that makes her look insincere and uncomfortable when what she wants to look is vulnerable and sweet. But today Beth's face belongs to Gabriela Menz, a girl who's been getting her way with a smile and a flutter of eyelashes since the day she was born, which gives Beth all the confidence she needs to try.

'Please,' says Beth, wheedling but not begging. 'I know it's a lot to ask, but we do have money. We just don't have the exact fare.' She holds up a crumpled bill. 'If you let us on, maybe somebody can give us change.'

Perhaps because this is such an extraordinary request, the driver finally looks over at her. This is a man whose job keeps him in an almost constant bad mood, but for some reason that bad mood is momentarily replaced by a feeling of warmth and kindness, as if an angel is whispering in his ear, *Oh, come on. Give the poor kid a break.*

'Forget it.' He winks. 'I won't tell, if you don't tell.' He waves them on and closes the door.

The bus lurches back into the traffic, which is now moving like a river in flood.

Beth stops abruptly only a few steps down the aisle. She has never been on a city bus before, and, like a desert nomad seeing snow for the first time, she is both intrigued and a little alarmed. She stares down the aisle. Narrow seats filled with weary-looking people, dingy windows and a floor that's been trodden on by hundreds of filthy feet. There are probably enough germs on this bus to bring down the entire west coast. Music leaks from iPods and MP3 players; someone shouts—to whom exactly isn't clear—'Yeah, well I care more about what my parrot thinks than your opinion!' The air conditioning isn't working, and the heat combines with the smells of sweat, pollution, chemical fragrances and things that probably shouldn't be named to create an aroma that is fairly unique to the public transport system of LA. Many of the passengers have their heads bent over newspapers, books or phones, but, with the exception of the blind man with the dog, the ones who aren't absorbed in some activity stare back at her. Unblinking. Many of them give the impression of being fairly unstable. The guy with the beaded necklace and the tattoos. The old lady with a bag of light bulbs on her lap. The man in the tuxedo. The woman in the shower cap who's talking to herself. The woman all in black saying the rosary. The

164

youngish man rocking back and forth in his seat at the back.

And yet Beth realizes that for once in her life she isn't afraid. Now that she's over her initial surprise, she feels almost excited. She, Beth Beeby, is on an LA bus, without her mother, and the world hasn't come to a horrible end. The spectre of Lillian Beeby in rubber gloves with a bottle of disinfectant under her arm, muttering about epidemics, may not be far away, but the actual flesh-and-blood person is. It's as if she's been released from a cage.

Lucinda, however, is nervous. 'Gab?' she hisses in Beth's ear. 'Gab? What the hell are we doing here?' Lucinda followed Beth onto the bus without thinking, indeed without actually being aware of what she was doing, pulled along by some strange compulsion. And now she finds herself on a crowded city bus without being able to say how she got here or why. She's never been on a city bus before, either. Indeed, the only city she's ever visited is Portland, Maine, and Portland, Maine is not LA. Up until this point, that fact has been in Los Angeles' favour; but now she's not so sure. LA's supposed to be all about glamour and glitz—beautiful people wearing fabulous clothes—but all that stopped dead at the door of the Metro. In here it's just regular people with the glamour and glitz of dollar-store flip-flops. It is safe to say that had Lucinda heard Lillian Beeby's warnings about public transport, she wouldn't have ignored them the way some people have.

Beth turns around. Lucinda looks the way Beth has always felt until now. Insecure. Anxious. 'We're just taking a bus, Lucinda. Like millions of people do every day all over the world. It's no big deal.'

'Yeah, but why?' The way Lucinda remembers it, one minute they were standing on a street frequented by celebrities, and the next here they are in a place where no celebrity would be caught dead—unless they were making a movie.

There's no point Beth mentioning the stalker again; even Lucinda thinks she's making him up—making him up or losing her mind. She'll have to lie. 'Because I got tired of waiting for a cab, Luce, that's all. We don't want to be late for the reception, do we?'

'But what about the others?' Though Hattie, Paulette, Nicki and Isla are now far behind them, Lucinda looks towards the rear window as though they might still be in sight. 'I mean, they're getting a cab. If we'd waited—'

'They could've come with us. Nobody stopped them.'

'Well, yeah, but—'

'Trust me, we're better off on a bus. Look at the traffic. Even if Moses is their cab driver, it's going to take them ages to get through this. It's more like a parking lot than a road. I guarantee you we'll get there before they do.'

'You mean, *if* we're on the right bus,' says Lucinda.

If they're on the right bus? Beth blinks. Until this moment, it hadn't occurred to her that there was a right bus and a wrong bus; she just wanted to be off the street. But perhaps it should have occurred to her. Perhaps then she might have realized before the driver shut the door behind them that a bus going west is unlikely to take you to a college on the east side of the city. The miracle is that Lucinda hasn't figured this out for herself.

166

And yet, this realization doesn't upset Beth any more than the bus itself. Yesterday it would have been so traumatic that by now she'd be nauseous, weeping and probably breaking out in a rash. Today it doesn't really seem like much of a problem. They'll just stay on here till she's certain they've lost the guy in the red sports car—and then they'll take a cab.

'Come on,' says Beth, in her new role as the voice of reason and calm. 'Let's sit down. If it is the wrong bus we can get off.'

They find two seats near the middle, behind the woman in the white kimono and the old lady carrying every light bulb from her apartment in a 7-Eleven bag.

'I think you should call Taffeta and tell her what happened,' says Lucinda. Sitting down has not made her feel any less nervous.

But Gabriela's phone is no longer working. 'There's something wrong,' says Beth, giving it a shake. It's lit up like a Christmas tree, but less use in transmitting sound than a tin can. 'I can't get a signal. We'll have to use yours.'

The frown Lucinda has been wearing since they got on the Metro deepens. 'But I thought Taffeta said mine wasn't working.'

'Well, maybe it is now. It's worth a try.'

Lucinda can't remember where she put her phone, and while she searches through all her bags, Beth leans back against the seat—and is so relieved to be sitting down at last that she slips off her shoes and closes her eyes.

Several people get on at the next stop. Two women with small children. An elderly Rasta. A young white guy wearing jeans, a plain T-shirt, a Dodgers' baseball cap and cheap sunglasses, like thousands of other ordinary Californians. But he is not an ordinary Californian; he is the Divine Emissary Otto Wasserbach, who has had to abandon his car to follow Beth. This is against all of his own rules, of course; his being here is proof (if proof were needed) of how seriously he takes his job (and of how much he wants to do well so he can go back to working on his own again). He would rather be just about anywhere else. Being on this bus is a little closer to suffering humanity than Otto cares to get. *Give me your tired, your poor, your huddled masses . . .* may be the motto of the Statue of Liberty, but it is not his. He'd much rather keep the huddled masses at a safe distance. He can feel the tiredness; sense the anxieties; smell not only the perfumes and aftershaves, but the disappointments and disasters; hear, below the rumble of the engine and the leaking music and the cell-phone conversations, the sad stories of bad luck and betrayal. What if they all start crying at once? What if they all start praying?

Otto moves cautiously up the aisle, his gaze darting from person to person, trying to find a place to sit where he can keep an eye on Beth and get her safely to where she's meant to be, without finding himself embroiled in someone else's problems.

He finally takes a seat across the aisle from where Beth thinks sleepily about foot binding and Lucinda discovers her phone in a shoebox, next to the man with the tattoos and the beaded necklace, who seems to be sleeping peacefully. Otto blocks out every sound around him, focusing on the job he's here to do. He closes his eyes, concentrating, and can see LA before him as if it's a toy city; see every building and road; see where the bus is and the route it's meant to take—and see where he wants it to go instead. *Turn left*, thinks Otto, and left the Metro turns, arcing gracefully in the direction it's not supposed to go and down a road it was never meant to be on. Otto, it seems, can meddle just as well as Remedios when pushed.

The driver doesn't seem to notice that he's heading south by a circuitous route that will eventually take the bus to the eastern end of Pico Boulevard. The passengers—who know that the way to travel on public transport is to act as if you're somewhere else—are so lost in their thoughts, or their music, or their cell phones that they don't notice either. The bus rolls on, hurtling past stops where people stand open-mouthed and waving, down streets that have never actually seen a bus before.

And then someone rings the bell.

It is, in fact, the woman wearing the shower cap who rings the bell. She has suddenly looked up from her book and realized that she has no idea where they are. She thinks that she must have passed her stop. This has happened to her before.

The bus doesn't so much as slow down, sailing past another group of disgruntled would-be passengers.

This time the bell rings a little more urgently.

Others look up from their books, papers, phones or iPads and realize that they have no idea where they are, either.

Someone shouts out, 'Oy! Where are we going?'

Someone yells, 'Hey! This isn't the right way!'

Someone screams, 'What's wrong with you? Stop

the bus! We wanna get off!'

It's this shouting, yelling and screaming that wake up both Beth and the tattooed man. Beth blinks. The tattooed man also blinks, but then he clasps his neck and bellows, 'My snake! What the hell's happened to my snake? George? Where'd you go?'

Snake? Otto's eyes snap open, and in that instant he realizes his mistake. The man beside him wasn't wearing beads, as Otto supposed; he was wearing a small snake—apparently named George. Snakes and angels have a history, and it's not a particularly good one—certainly not from the snake's point of view (which is mainly flames in your face and feet coming down on your head). Unlike everyone else on the bus, George knows an angel when he smells one, and silently and speedily unwound himself from round his owner's neck almost as soon as Otto sat down.

Now more people are screaming. Some are screaming to stop the bus. Some are just screaming because the thought of a snake loose on a bus has that effect on them. The ringing of the bell has become constant. Lucinda lets out a concrete-cracking screech and jumps onto her seat.

'What's going on?' frets the blind man, tapping his cane. 'What's going on?'

Otto remains calm. He has no more love for serpents than they have for angels, but he has to stay in control. If he doesn't, there's no telling what will happen. And then not only will he really be in trouble, but it will be trouble for which he can't blame Remedios.

The bus steams on as though no one is shouting or ringing the bell. As a certain atmosphere of panic takes over, attempts are made to phone for help, but no one can get a connection now. Oblivious to the ringing bells and the shrieks and screams and shouts for him to stop, the driver keeps going, humming a song he heard on the radio this morning.

'George! George!' calls the tattooed man. And, though George has never been known to speak, pleads, 'George! Where are you? Come to Daddy! Please!'

Interestingly enough, Beth, though terrified of microbes and the possibility of being struck by a piano, is not afraid of snakes. In fact, she was very fond of the garter snake her sixth-grade class kept as a pet. So when she sees a flash of colour under the seat across the aisle, heedless of the dirty floor and danger of being kicked in the head by someone more squeamish, she drops to her knees and scoops it up.

'It's OK!' Beth yells. She cradles the snake gently, cooing, 'There, there, George, it's all right. It's all right now.' But the general panic doesn't abate. 'It's OK! I have him!' she yells again, and this time holds the snake aloft.

The flailing snake makes the woman in the kimono jump, and the small dog that was up her sleeve leap to the ground, barking hysterically.

The guide dog—a calm and responsible animal who has been trained not to get agitated, even when people are shouting and snakes are swinging in the air—forgets all his training when he sees the other dog scampering around like an electronic toy with a short circuit, and charges down the aisle.

Things are now seriously chaotic in a way that not even the biggest critic of Los Angeles' Public

Transport System could have predicted.

Beth, as we know, is not a girl to assert authority. Not only would she not normally say 'boo' to a goose, she wouldn't say 'boo' to the picture of a goose. This, however, has been a difficult and trying day, and she is standing in the middle of a Metro bus, barefoot, wearing pyjama bottoms and holding a snake named George that looks like a beaded necklace when it isn't flicking its tail and darting its tongue in and out of its mouth in terror.

'Everybody calm down! Do you hear me?'

Heads turn. Everybody hears her. Indeed, many people who know Beth, including Mr Sturgess, would be surprised at how loudly she can speak if she really needs to.

'Get a grip on yourselves! There's no reason to panic!' Her eyes go from one end of the bus to the other, glancing over the young man in the Dodgers' cap and almost catching for a wing beat but moving right on. 'Just calm down!'

It's as if Jehovah has leaned over a cloud and given a command. The bus stops suddenly, and everybody on it stops, too. An almost preternatural stillness descends. Though this, as it happens, has less to do with Beth's exertion of authority than it does with the police cars—sirens whooping and lights flashing—that are blocking the road.

As the police officers get out of their cars and approach the bus, Beth suddenly realizes why the young man in the Dodgers' cap seemed vaguely familiar, and turns back for another look.

There's no one there.

*　　　*　　　*

172

Gabriela doesn't see Beth and Lucinda get on the bus, of course. Remedios has seen to that. Indeed, as she reaches the other side of the Strip, Gabriela is sure that she sees Beth—sees herself—striding up into the hills of Hollywood with Lucinda, bright boutique bags bouncing against their hips and sunlight shining off their hair. California girls; smiling and happy, without a care in the world. Gabriela doesn't wonder by what miracle she managed to cross through traffic that a gnat would have had trouble navigating, or why the other girls aren't with her and Lucinda, or even why they're walking when they have a chauffeured limousine to take them everywhere. She thinks she knows what's going on. They must have changed the venue for the tea, moved it from the college to Madagascar's studio. Given what the traffic's like in Los Angeles, it's probably quicker to walk.

Gabriela is not an overly cautious girl, and now she doesn't hesitate long enough to flick a piece of lint from her sleeve. Beth finally seems to be within reach—within reach and virtually alone. Talking to her may not solve their problem, but it has to be a step in the right direction. It's definitely a lot better than spending the rest of the afternoon in another museum. Marvelling at how quickly she can walk in sensible, if unattractive, shoes, she follows the bright and carefree girls as they effortlessly climb into the hills, going further and further away from Sunset Boulevard. But no matter how fast she walks, Beth and Lucinda are always ahead of her, turning a corner or darting down an unexpected path, almost shimmering and just out of reach.

Above the frantic activity of the valley, the thickly wooded streets twist and wind up these famous hills where holly has never been known to grow, crossed by dozens of narrow lanes that end suddenly, as if they've forgotten where they were going.

They aren't the only ones.

Coming to a stop at last, Gabriela looks around the cul-de-sac at the opulent houses half-hidden behind small jungles or high walls, puzzled. There is no one around. No one sitting on a porch. No children playing; no dogs barking; no cat sitting statue-like in a patch of sunlight. It might be a movie set and not a real neighbourhood at all if it weren't that they can hear the low, electronic hum that hovers in the air, the swish-swishes of a sprinkler somewhere near, the muffled sound of a mower, the thwack-thwack of a tennis ball being hit back and forth on someone's private court. Where are Beth and Lucinda? It's as if they vanished into the air.

Delila comes up beside her. Staggers. She's out of breath and breaking a sweat; it's been a longer walk than Gabriela thinks.

'You don't mind if I ask you a personal question, do you?' Delila huffs. Just as Lucinda followed Beth onto the bus like a lemming pitching straight over a cliff, Delila unquestioningly trotted after Gabriela, somehow assuming that they both knew what Gabriela was doing. Only now, finding herself high in the hills with a view worth millions, and, somewhere in that view, Professor Gryck and the other contestants annoyed and wondering what happened to them, Delila finally realizes that she has no idea what that was. 'Would you mind telling me what the hell we're doing up here in Never-Never Land?'

Unfortunately, it doesn't seem that Gabriela knows either.

'I . . . I saw somebody I know.' Her sigh is no less heartfelt for being silent. 'At least, I thought I did.'

Her arms folded across her chest, Delila eyes her room-mate in what can only be described as a suspicious manner. 'You saw somebody you know? *Here?*' She glances at the nearest house, the top of it rising grandly from behind a screen of trees. This is not a neighbourhood of low-income housing. '*You* know somebody who lives in a house with eight bathrooms and a swimming pool?' She tilts her head to one side as if trying to get a better view. 'Who's that? Somebody you met the last time you bought make-up on Sunset Boulevard?'

Gabriela gives her a don't-be-silly smile. 'No, of course not. I never—'

'Well, who then? I didn't think you knew anybody in LA.'

Gabriela doesn't know anyone in LA. But Beth Beeby does. And suddenly Gabriela hears Lillian on the phone this morning saying in her hand-wringing voice: *You know Aunt Joyce would be happy to run over with anything you need, honey . . .*

'Well, you're wrong. It just so happens that I have an aunt who lives here.' She's pretty pleased with herself for remembering this. 'Aunt Joyce.'

'Your auntie?' Delila's entire face seems to narrow. 'Your auntie lives in LA?'

'That's right.'

Delila's eyebrows come together, as if holding her thoughts in place. 'Up *here*? Your aunt lives in one of these mansions?'

Gabriela shakes her head. 'No. No, she lives

175

in—' Gabriela searches her memory for a name in the area that isn't Hollywood. 'In Santa Monica. In a bungalow. But I thought it was her.' Her smile is as thin as organza. 'I figured she was taking a walk.'

'From Santa Monica? You thought she walked here from *there*?'

Gabriela laughs. 'Well, obviously it wasn't her, was it?'

'Hold on. Obviously *who* wasn't her?' Delila's expression of scepticism takes on an edge of concern as she remembers a small but significant fact. 'Since you decided to take me mountain climbing, the only person I've seen who wasn't in a car was that dude with the umbrella selling maps. Way back when.'

Gabriela opens her mouth and shuts it again. She was going to say that Delila *must* have seen them—they were as clear as the stitching on a pair of jeans—but, of course, this is not a day that plays by any of the usual rules. 'You didn't see those girls— those two women up ahead of us?'

Delila looks as if she's planning to suck the truth out of Gabriela's words through a straw. 'Do I look like I did?'

No. No, she definitely doesn't look like that. She looks as though the only person she's seen was the lonely map seller under his beach umbrella.

Delila stares into Gabriela's eyes. 'Leaving aside the tiny fact that I never saw these women of yours up ahead of us, where would you say they are now? You know, just a rough guess.'

'Well . . .' Unless Beth and Lucinda went—very silently and very quickly—into a house or managed to get into someone's yard, they couldn't have got back to the through road without passing Gabriela

176

and Delila. 'I don't know. I guess they must've gone into one of these houses.'

'How? By osmosis? Because I, for one, didn't see anybody walking up a driveway or hear any doors opening or shutting, either.'

Gabriela laughs the way she used to when she knew what she was doing. Yesterday. 'Maybe they were beamed up.'

Hahaha.

Delila's look of concern deepens. 'Why is it that I get the feeling you're not being exactly a hundred percent honest with me? Why would that be?'

Gabriela makes an I-give-up face. 'Because you're right, Del. I haven't been completely honest.' Gabriela is in a very interesting position. Since Delila won't believe the truth, she has no recourse but to come up with a lie that she will believe. 'I should have levelled with you, but you know . . .' She shrugs. 'I guess I just feel kind of dumb. I mean, I don't want you to think I'm not as serious and into culture and everything as the rest of you . . .' Her voice trails off.

'I'm still listening,' says Delila.

Gabriela rocks back and forth. 'Well, it's just that . . . it's just that I really couldn't face looking at any more old pictures. I mean, my God, we can do that any time. You don't even have to leave home to look at old pictures. You can do it online. But we're in Los Angeles! We're here! Really here! Even people living on ice floes dream about coming here. So, I don't know, when I saw the hills up there like a magical kingdom, I thought, *Hey, let's be spontaneous—*'

Delila's mouth looks the way vinegar tastes. '*You* thought we should be spontaneous?'

'Uh-huh.' Gabriela's smile couldn't be more enthusiastic if it were waving pompoms. 'I figured we could have an adventure.'

'An adventure?' repeats Delila. '*You* wanted to have an adventure? I thought having an adventure for you was drinking water that doesn't come out of a bottle.'

Gabriela laughs. 'I guess LA must be working its spell on me.'

'Or maybe you're over-medicating.'

Gabriela laughs again. 'No, really. I feel like a new woman.' She could even tell her which one.

'Yeah? Well, you're going to have to excuse me, but I come from Brooklyn, the Capital City of Doubt.'

'What does that mean? That you don't believe me?'

'You could put it that way,' says Delila. 'Don't get me wrong, Beth. I'm not saying museums aren't like wheatgrass juice—a little goes a real long way if you ask me. And the Good Lord knows I was starting to lose the will to live cooped up with the smarter-than-thou brigade all morning. Personally, I'd just as soon be up here seeing how the rich folk live than dragging around with the culture coven all showing off to each other how smart they are. Only I still have this niggling feeling that there's something else going on with you today.'

Meet Delila Greaves: poet and psychic.

Gabriela doesn't blink. 'With me?'

'No, with your dog.' And Delila proceeds to tick off the major events of the day on her fingers. 'First we had the food fight. Then the great art theft. And now charging up into the Hollywood hills like you were in some kind of marathon . . . '

178

'OK, I did start the food fight. I admit that. They were just being so incredibly irritating, it was like having pins stuck under your nails. I had to do something. But what happened in the museum was not my fault.'

'You were the one who tripped the alarms.'

Geesh, the girl's like a prosecuting attorney. 'Yeah, I did . . . but that was an accident. And I explained why I decided to come up here.'

'Because you were being spontaneous.' Delila is shaking her head. 'Only you are not a spontaneous kind of girl. And you are also not the kind of girl to throw fruit or touch priceless oil paintings. Or argue with a professor. There's something else you're leaving out—'

'But there isn't,' protests Gabriela. 'Really, Del. I mean, you act like you know me and everything about me, but you don't. You've just met me.' She opens her arms in a let-me-embrace-the-world gesture. 'I'm full of surprises.'

'Well, I hope that one of your surprises is a talent for dealing with really angry academics, because if you think the Gryck is going to be in a good mood next time we see her, you're the one who's in for a mighty big surprise.'

'Don't worry,' says Gabriela with a confidence that doesn't belong to Beth, and probably shouldn't belong to her, either, right now. 'I can handle her.'

'Oh, yeah, I noticed that. Especially when we were being marched out of her favourite museum. She seemed really charmed by you then.'

'She just needed somebody to blame. And anyway, I don't think it was me she was really mad at. I think it was the security guards. They were the ones who caused all the trouble.'

179

'Are you delusional? You've been working every everlasting nerve in that woman all morning.'

Gabriela dismisses this information with a wave of her hand. 'I don't think it's me, Del. The Gryck's a very uptight type of person. You can tell by her shoes and the way she does her hair.'

'Really?'

'Totally. I think she has a very deep-seated neurosis. So I don't—'

'Beth Beeby? Earth to Beth!' Delila cups her hands around her mouth. 'Beth, this is ground control trying to make contact. No matter what shoes she wears, Professor Gryck is going to be madder than you've ever seen anybody. We have got to get back to the group pretty pronto.'

'OK. You don't have to get all warped. We'll go back right now.' There's certainly nothing to keep them here since Beth and Lucinda have vanished as if they'd never been there at all.

'Well, I'm glad to hear that. And you know the way?' This is definitely a question and not a statement.

'We'll go back the way we came,' says Gabriela. What could be easier?

'And you remember what that is?' persists Delila. 'Because I can tell you right now that sure as there's snow in Alaska, I do not have a clue. I might as well've been blindfolded for all I saw. I just followed you.'

'Yeah, of course I know.' Gabriela has no idea. The network of lanes and cul-de-sacs that snake through the lush hills are more like a maze than a recognizable trail. Which side of the hills are they on? Is she looking towards Sunset Boulevard or the valley? Did they come from the left or the right?

180

Have they been going in circles or been walking miles?

'Good,' says Delila. 'And that would be . . .?'

'Well . . .' Gabriela points to a large white house to the left, its terracotta roof vivid against the shimmering green of the trees and the delicate blue of the sky. 'Didn't we come past that?'

'Beats me. Maybe.' Delila points to a similar sprawl of terracotta below them. 'Or maybe it was that one we passed.'

'Well, what about that map you took from the hotel? You still have it?' Since she doesn't have to worry about dirt or showing her underwear or wrinkling her clothes or any of the other things that spell sartorial disgrace, Gabriela plonks herself down on the kerb 'Let's take a look.'

Delila drops beside her. 'You look at it. I'm going to see if I can save us from total annihilation.' She thrusts the map into Gabriela's hands. 'I'm calling the Gryck.'

This, however, turns out to be a wish more than a statement of fact.

'Damn.' Delila shakes her phone. 'All I'm getting is noise.' She shakes it again. 'It sounds like I've contacted a planet that's being pelted with asteroids.'

Gabriela looks over at her. Delila hardly wears any make-up. She thinks sandals are dress shoes. She's never had a makeover or been to a spa. Her eyelashes are her own. She does her hair herself. She wouldn't recognize a fashion statement if it sat on her lap. What are the chances she can actually work a cell phone?

Gabriela holds out her hand. 'Give it to me.' For a few seconds, she studies the small, black rectangle in her hand the way one might study a nineteenth-century candle-making machine—*you do* what *with* that? Like Beth's phone, it's not exactly the last word in mobile telecommunications; more like the first. 'This thing still works?'

'Yes, it still works. It was dandy as candy this morning. Remember? When I texted my grandma?'

'Well, maybe it's because we're way up here.' Gabriela, too, gives the phone a shake. 'You know, maybe we're too far from a signal.'

Delila, it seems, has quite a repertoire of sarcastic, you-have-to-be-kidding-me faces. 'Because we're up *here*? We're in Beverly Hills, Beth, not the Andes. These people would have a signal if we were in the middle of the apocalypse.'

She's right, of course. Movie stars and directors live in these houses: people who probably take their phones into the bath with them. People whose phones wouldn't dare not work.

'Yeah, but their phones aren't going to be relics from the past, are they?' says Gabriela. 'That's probably why they work up here.'

Delila is also developing quite a repertoire of world-weary sighs. 'So let's try your phone.'

But Beth's phone is in their room at The Xanadu, inside her suitcase at the back of the closet so that the voice of Lillian Beeby can't dog Gabriela through the day.

Delila laughs. 'I should've known it was too quiet. Your mother'd be calling you every five minutes if she was on a space shuttle halfway to the moon.' Delila slips her own phone in her backpack. 'We'd better find Sunset quicker than a flea jumps, then.' She stands up. 'What does the map say? How far away are we?'

In the closet that is Gabriela's mind, there isn't really a lot of room for the finer points of navigation. Most places she goes, she's taken. Which means that the only way Delila's map would tell her anything worth knowing is if it could actually talk.

'This thing isn't really any good,' she says, folding it away. 'You know, it tells you where Rodeo Drive and Grauman's and Universal Studios are. Stuff like that.' She waves vaguely down the road. 'I still think we should just go back the way we came.'

'And you're absolutely sure that's it?' Delila isn't so sure; she isn't very sure of anything any more.

Hope pushes up the corners of Gabriela's mouth. 'Positive. What goes up has to come down, right?'

This will turn out to be less a statement of fact than a prophecy.

You might think that anyone living in a neighbourhood such as this—a neighbourhood with such valuable properties and such priceless views—would be in a perpetual state of bliss. Living the dream. But Remedios Cienfuegos y Mendoza has been looking around while Delila followed Gabriela, and Gabriela followed a mirage, and as she would be quick to tell you, you'd be mistaken. This is not the home of happiness. Put another way, it's a lot easier to build an infinity pool than achieve bliss.

As Gabriela and Delila march off in the wrong direction, a jogger rounds a bend two blocks away. He is not one of those look-at-me urban joggers in Lycra shorts and aerodynamic trainers. He is a tall, heavy-set, tired-looking, perennially grumpy, grey-haired man in busted old high-tops, baggy work pants and a faded T-shirt who trots more than jogs. He performs this ritual every day only because he spends a lot of time sitting down and his doctor says he needs the exercise—or else. He is listening to Pokey LaFarge and the South City Three play a song that makes him want to drift down a river on a raft with one hand in the water and the sun in his eyes.

The man in the work pants (who lives in a very expensive house with a really terrific view) is an example of what Remedios means when she says it's easier to build a swimming pool than capture bliss. Drifting down a river on a raft is something this man always dreamed of doing when he was young. Just throwing some things in a bag and going wherever the current took him. Being free in the moment, with no ambitions and no plans; no things he felt he had to be or do. Indeed, it's something he often dreams of doing now. But now, of course, his life is full of ambition, plans and things he has to do. Responsibilities. Expectations. He sits in his beautiful living room or on his shaded deck, gazing out on the terrific view, but it doesn't make him happy. He wants to hear crickets and woodpeckers calling; the splash of fish jumping; the crackle and rustle of deer along the shore. He wants to be that boy again, to get back his dreams. And, as he comes around the next bend, he is imagining dragonflies grazing the water; leaves rattling; the sighing of trees. Which is why he doesn't see Gabriela and Delila as he passes.

And they don't see him because they are arguing about whether or not they're going the right way. Except that they both know it should be in the sky, they can't agree where the sun should be. Over there? Over here? Over there? They remember different landmarks, when they remember any landmarks at all. Gabriela would bet her favourite boots that they passed that lime-green house with Roman blinds on the way up; Delila would wager her favourite books that they didn't.

'I hope you speak some Spanish,' grunts Delila as they round another twist in the road. 'Then you'll be able to get a job as a cleaner or something when we never find our way out of this place.'

'It's not like we're lost in the Amazon jungle,' Gabriela snaps back. 'I mean, God, Del . . . The rate you're going, you could probably make the Olympics worrying team.'

'Only since I met—' A sudden agonized scream from behind them cuts Delila short. 'What the hell was that?' She looks around. 'Do they have wild boar up here?'

But although there are wolves and coyotes in the Hollywood hills, there are no wild boars as yet. The agonized scream came from the jogger they don't remember passing, whom they find lying on the ground, breathing heavily and groaning.

'Are you all right?' they call as they hurry over to him. And, because he has his eyes closed and doesn't respond, shout again, 'Sir! Sir! Are you all right?'

He should have known something like this would happen. Die if you don't exercise; die if you do. He's afraid to move. Everybody knows that the people in this neighbourhood don't walk anywhere unless you count to and from the car. And most of them run first thing in the morning or on machines. So if he can't walk, then he may be here for hours

185

before someone finds him. Finds him, or runs over him. But then, feeling them more than hearing them, he realizes that he's already been found, and opens his eyes expecting to see someone's gardener or housekeeper.

Two teenage girls stand over him, looking vaguely concerned. He doesn't really like teenagers. He doesn't really like most people, but teenagers he finds especially depressing. At an age when they should be wild and irreverent and kicking up dust, they worry instead about what they're wearing and what people think of them. *Ooh, you have the wrong kind of shoes . . . the wrong jeans . . . the wrong nose . . .* They're always plugged into something, like lamps. Though these girls, amazingly enough, don't seem to be attached to anything: no phones, no iPods, no iPads. They can't come from around here, where the girls are all wannabe stars or spoiled princesses. Indeed, from the look of them—sweaty, slightly dishevelled, strangers to beauty parlours and hairdressers; the one dressed for strolling through an Eastern market, the other for an English boarding school in the fifties—they might come from another world entirely. Not that this makes him feel any more kindly towards them.

'I'm all right.' He pulls off the headset. 'I just slipped.'

'We'll help you up.' Hands reach towards him.

He bats them away. 'I'm all right, I tell you. Just got a little winded.' He doesn't like being ignored, but he doesn't like people fussing over him, either.

The large, flamboyant girl says, 'You always have that green tinge to your skin?'

The skinny, flat-looking girl says, 'You sure

186

you're OK?'

'Yes, I always have a green tinge to my skin. And of course I'm OK. I didn't land on my head.' But when he tries to stand the pain knocks the breath right out of him. 'My ankle—' he gasps. 'I must have sprained it . . .'

Gabriela kneels down beside him. 'It's swelling fast.'

He winces as the accidental movement of his foot causes another jolt of pain. 'I'm not blind. I can see that.'

'You're not exactly Prince Charming, either,' says Delila, as she kneels on his other side. 'We're only trying to help you, you know.'

He does know that; he just wishes he didn't need any help. 'I'm sorry. I'm just—' He's never in a very good mood lately. He holds out a hand. 'I'm Joe.'

'Ga— Beth.'

'Delila.' She starts untying his laces. 'It doesn't look broken.' Delila has three male cousins who live next door to her grandparents and is, therefore, something of an expert on limb injuries. 'It probably is just a sprain. But we should get this sneaker off.'

'It could be a fracture.' Gabriela and her friends have sustained any number of clothing-induced injuries, so she is something of an expert, too. She forages through her bag and pulls out the scarf Beth carries in the event of sudden drafts or dust storms. 'We can bandage it with this. But you'd better not try to walk on it.'

'No fear of that.' His smile comes out more as a grimace. 'I couldn't walk on it if I wanted to.' He looks from one to the other. 'I left my phone at home, but maybe if one of you could call my housekeeper—'

'My phone's kaput,' explains Delila. 'And Beth left hers at the hotel.'

Gabriela smiles as if she's used to life without a cell phone. 'How far away do you live? We can help you get there.'

'Just a couple of blocks, but I don't think two young—'

Gabriela waves this away, too. 'It's not a big deal. I've done this dozens of times. Really. It's all about balance.'

'Besides,' says Delila, 'you're not that much taller than I am. And my granddad, Johnson? He sells old bottles. I'm used to lugging heavy things around.'

'We had to do this one time when my friend Hedda sprained her ankle because she got her heel caught in a crack in the sidewalk,' Gabriela informs him as she and Delila position themselves on either side of Joe. 'It was really thin? The heel, I mean. It just wedged itself in. She went down like a bowling pin. You should've seen it. It was worse than yours. It looked like she was morphing into an elephant.'

'One . . . two . . . three . . .' counts Delila, and they heave him to his feet.

'You see?' says Gabriela. 'And you're not crying the way Hedda was. It makes it a lot easier.'

'Give me a few minutes,' he grunts. 'I may be crying by the time we get to my house.'

He lives close by compared to, say, Las Vegas, but it's still a good distance to be hauling a grown man, especially quite a large one, under the afternoon sun. Free to talk about things other than books, paintings and foreign films, Gabriela and Delila tell him what they're doing in LA and keep up a constant stream of chatter to try to distract him from the pain. Delila talks about Brooklyn and her grandparents and recites a poem she wrote about the New York subway called *World Soup with Music*. Gabriela talks about her unfair and largely undeserved problems with Professor Gryck and the gruesomeness of the morning and how they were nearly arrested.

By the time they get to Joe's house, they're all laughing.

His housekeeper is out. He forgot she was going to the market.

'Damn woman,' says Joe. 'When you don't need her, she's always underfoot; when you do, she's miles away.'

They drop him on the couch, and Delila props up the bad leg with pillows while Gabriela goes to the kitchen for ice. She comes back with a bag of frozen peas.

'This is what we used on Hedda,' she tells him, not mentioning that what the hospital used on Hedda was traction. 'And it really works. Plus you don't have ice melting all over and you can just stick it back in the freezer and have it for supper.'

He leans against the cushions with a sigh of relief. 'Today, this really is the City of Angels. I can't thank you two enough.' He manages to smile without wincing. 'My saviours.'

Gabriela adjusts the bag of peas. 'The only thanks we want is directions back to Sunset. You know, before the Gryck calls out the National Guard.'

'The short cut would be good,' adds Delila.

'I'd take you myself if I could drive. Explain to your professor that you're so late because you were

189

being good Samaritans.'

'I don't know why,' says Delila, 'but I don't think the Gryck's really going to care.'

'You should see the shoes she wears,' says Gabriela. 'They're the shoes of a person with very little flexibility.'

'And what about my shoes?' Joe waggles his good foot. 'What do they say about me?'

Gabriela gazes at his feet for a few seconds, considering. 'They say you're younger than you look.'

The shortcut, as it turns out, is to leave by the back door and go straight down through the jogger's property, where they'll be able to slip out through the bordering shrubs.

On the hill that overlooks Joe's home is a mansion that was built to look like an old Spanish mission, complete with a bell tower—which, in fact, has never housed a bell but is a bedroom. The hacienda, as it is known in the neighbourhood, belongs to a very famous director who at the moment is in France. It's from the window of the bell tower that Remedios has been watching Gabriela and Delila. She saw them stride up the road in the wrong direction. She saw them pass the jogger. She most certainly saw him stumble and fall. She saw them go to his aid. And now she sees Gabriela and Delila making their way past the swimming pool and the gardens and the koi pond. But she turns away before they emerge onto the road, straight into the arms of the waiting police—though she does allow herself a very small smile.

BETH, GABRIELA AND THE LAPD

Interestingly enough, Gabriela and Delila aren't the only ones having an unexpected meeting with members of the Los Angeles Police Department this afternoon.

'So let me get this straight.' Officer Wynlot looks from his notebook to Beth. 'You and your friend got on the bus because you saw some guy in a red sports car.'

'The stalker,' says Beth. 'He's been following us all morning. He even got onto the property of the Madagascar studio and set off the alarms.'

'In his car?' Officer Medina is Officer Wynlot's partner.

Beth shakes her head. 'No, he wasn't in the car then. He was on foot. He was in the car when we were waiting for a cab. That's why I got on the bus.'

Officer Wynlot nods, almost as though this is making more sense to him than anything else he's heard in the last half hour since they stopped the runaway bus. 'Right. Because you thought he was following you.'

'I didn't *think* he was following us.' Not only is Beth not blushing, she seems to have forgotten how to stammer and whisper as well. 'He *was* following us. He was everywhere we went at Sunset Plaza.'

'In his car?' asks Officer Medina.

'Of course not,' snaps Beth. Among the many fears Beth seems to be overcoming this weekend is her fear of figures of authority. 'On foot.'

'Wait a minute.' Officer Wynlot is looking at his notes again. 'You said this guy was on the bus?

191

When did he get on the bus?'

'I don't know. I didn't see him until the snake got loose. He must've changed his clothes.'

'He changed his clothes?' Many people think that Officer Medina has a lovely, melt-your-heart smile, but Beth is not one of those people. 'First you see him in his car, so you get on the bus. And then he somehow ditches the car, changes his clothes and gets on a couple of stops after you?'

'I don't know how he did it,' says Beth, 'but he was definitely on the bus.'

Officer Medina moves his mouth as though he's impersonating a fish. 'Well, he wasn't on it when we searched it.' This is an accusation, not a statement. 'And we talked to every passenger that came off your bus and there was no one like the guy you described.'

Officer Wynlot sighs. 'What about you?' He turns to Lucinda. 'Did you see this "weird" guy on the bus?'

'Well . . .' Slowly and reluctantly, Lucinda shakes her head. 'No, I didn't see him on the bus. But—'

'Now that's kind of interesting.' Officer Wynlot looks thoughtful as well as interested. 'Because Miss Menz here says that he was sitting next to the tattooed man, but the tattooed man didn't see this guy either. He says nobody was sitting next to him. How do you figure that?'

'I didn't see him because I was busy trying to get my phone to work.'

'Of course. So that explains why the guy sitting next to him didn't see him either.' He taps his pencil against his notebook. 'But you saw him when you were shopping?'

'Well . . .' Lucinda's eyes dart towards Beth. 'Not

192

exactly.'

Officer Medina takes his turn to sigh. 'Not exactly "yes" or not exactly "no"?'

'Well . . . '

'And when he broke into the back yard of the studio?' persists Officer Wynlot. 'You must've seen him then.'

'Well . . .' Lucinda shrugs. 'I was looking at something else then.'

'I thought he set off the alarms.'

She shifts from one foot to the other. 'Well . . . they did go off . . . '

'So what you're saying,' recaps Officer Wynlot, 'is that you never saw this man who your friend says was following you around all day.'

Lucinda does some more foot shifting. 'Well . . . '

'What the heck is going on here?' Shaking his head, Officer Medina directs this question to his partner. 'Are we in the Twilight Zone or something? The bus driver went in the wrong direction on a route that doesn't exist, but he never noticed. And nobody on the bus noticed either. They just rolled along like they were on their way home.' He turns his attention to Beth. 'And now you're reporting a stalker that seemingly can be in two places at once, change clothes in a matter of minutes, and who's invisible to everyone but you.'

'You know what they say,' says Beth. 'Truth is stranger than fiction.'

'It is today,' says Officer Medina.

Either out of kindness, or because they think Beth is delusional and poses a threat to both herself and public order, the policemen take her and Lucinda the few blocks to The City of Angels College of Fashion and Design. Up until now, there was never any possibility that Beth would ever be brought home in the back of a cop car, but if she had Lillian Beeby would have fainted on the spot. Taffeta Mackenzie, however, is not the sort of woman to get upset just because someone in her care turns up with a police escort.

'How very kind of you to return our lost sheep,' purrs Taffeta, smiling at Officers Wynlot and Medina as if they were fantastically wealthy fashion gurus and not poorly paid public servants. 'Are you sure you wouldn't like a cup of coffee or tea?'

But showing up in a police car and showing up with bare, filthy feet and your clothes dishevelled because you were wrangling snakes and dogs on a bus filled with hysterical people are two different things. The smile vanishes the minute the officers leave.

'Good grief, girl!' Taffeta points one dagger-like nail, midnight blue and flecked with gold, at Beth's heart. 'Your hair! Your clothes!' Her delicate nose twitches. 'God help us, you smell like drugstore aftershave and cheap perfume. What in the name of Christian Dior is that on your blouse?' She peers closer. 'Is that excrement?' It's a good guess. In fact, the tiny smudge on Beth's blouse is snake poo. 'And your feet! What the hell happened to your shoes?' She puts a hand where her heart can be presumed to be. 'You look like you've been herding cows. Barefoot.' Taffeta puts a hand to her cheek, but although she is careful not to disturb her make-up, this is a sign that she couldn't be more upset if someone had dumped a case of red wine on the entire Spring collection. 'I think, Lucinda, that you should go to the tea. I want to speak to Gabriela alone.' She sits down at her desk as

194

Lucinda, with a last, worried look at her roommate, closes the door behind her. 'All right, I want the whole story,' says Taffeta. 'And let me tell you, it had better be really, really good.'

It is, as we know, a really, really good story. But, good as it is, Beth can tell that Taffeta Mackenzie doesn't believe her any more than Officers Wynlot and Medina did.

As Beth's tale of menace and mayhem comes to an end, Taffeta purses her mouth, risking smudging her lipstick, and sits back in her chair. 'It's not that I'm not sympathetic,' she says after a few seconds' pause. 'I've been there myself, honey. When I was a top model and had my face on every magazine in the solar system, there was this madman who became obsessed with me. And let me tell you, it scared the bejabers out of me. It got so bad I wouldn't go anywhere by myself. Even to buy a pair of shoes.' She taps her fingertips on the edge of her desk. 'But there is one big difference between my guy and your guy . . .' *Taptaptap.* 'The guy who was stalking me wasn't invisible, Gabriela. His name was Sam and he installed air conditioners.'

'But my guy's not invisible. I saw him. I—'

'You didn't even take a picture of him. Why didn't you take a picture of him if he's real?'

'I didn't think . . .'

'And nobody else saw him, did they? You admit that none of the other girls saw him, even though you say he followed you all the time you were shopping. I was right there when the alarm went at Madagascar, and I didn't see him.' Taffeta smiles. 'How do you explain that, Gabriela?'

'Well I guess I can't, but—'

'Even Lucinda never saw him, and she's been

with you all day.'

'But that doesn't mean he wasn't there,' argues Beth. 'It just means nobody else saw him.'

'Or maybe she didn't see him because there was nothing to see. Just some guy being a little admiring.'

'A little admiring?' Following her around like he was a balloon on a string that was tied to her finger?

'Honey, Lucinda knows and you know, too— men are going to follow you around. That's why you look like you do. Well, not like you look now—' Taffeta gives a delicate shudder. 'But like you usually look. That's the point of all the make-up and clothes and the diets and everything. That's the price of beauty.'

'Being stalked by some psycho is the price of beauty?' What kind of a world is this?

Taffeta leans forward, eyeing Beth as if she were a piece of flawed fabric. 'Look, honey, you haven't been yourself all day. Don't think I didn't notice. As soon as I saw you this morning I said to myself, *Taffeta, we have a little situation starting here. This is not the young goddess you met last night. This is not the girl who sent that awesome portfolio. Not the girl who designed the angel dress. Something's gone horribly wrong . . .* '

Beth stares back at her, wavering between horror and hope. Is it possible that there is some explanation for what's happened to her, and that Taffeta Mackenzie knows what it is? Has this kind of thing happened before? Is it part of the magic of Hollywood? The part no one ever talks about? 'I haven't been myself?'

'No. Definitely not. You are not the real

196

Gabriela Menz. And that is not a good thing.' Taffeta shakes her head. Mournfully. 'Your outfit didn't come together at all today; it was like you dressed on a boat in a storm in the dark . . . You're not wearing any make-up and you've been hobbling around like you have beans in your shoes and never wore heels before . . . But when you wanted to put that tailored shirt with those cropped beachcomber trousers—' Though it happens rarely, for almost a full half-second Taffeta Mackenzie is at a loss for words. 'Well, I just couldn't believe it. I would've been less shocked if my favourite model had put on a hundred pounds and started shopping in charity shops.' She smiles as if the fabric she's been considering is worse than she'd feared. 'It was only then I figured out what was happening.'

She knows? She really knows? Maybe it's some kind of rare natural phenomenon like the Bermuda Triangle or a shower of frogs. But peculiar to Los Angeles. The Los Angeles Syndrome. It's all Beth can do not to fling herself on Taffeta's desk begging, *Well, tell me! Tell me what it is!*

'You did?'

'Uh, huh. It's obvious.'

'Really?'

'Sure,' says Taffeta. 'It's nerves. Nerves are a killer. This is a big deal for you. Maybe you're a little overexcited. Wound up. I've been there, too, honey. When I first started out, I was a bundle—an enormous, jiggy bundle of nerves—and they were all being jabbed with needles. I shook. I puked. I even *sweat*.' Her expression darkens with the horror of it all. 'But you'll get over it. Trust me. It's like actors get stage fright.' She stands up. 'So I'll tell you what we're going to do.' She comes round to where Beth is sitting and eases her out of the chair. 'You're going to go back to the hotel and get ready for tonight. You'll miss the tour of the school, but that can't be helped. We can't have the staff seeing you like this. I'll tell them you have a migraine. Tonight's when you girls meet the major players. I want you to look like you were beamed down from Heaven. You're going to take your place at the party and show them all what you've got. Because that's what this town and this business is about. The show must go on!'

I'm not even in real life any more, thinks Beth. *I'm in a movie. Any minute now this woman's going to start singing and dancing.*

'Well, I—'

'Let's get something straight, OK? You've been messing up all day, Gabriela. And I can't put my patronage behind someone who messes up like that. Think jungle. You either eat or you're eaten.' She gives Beth a look that says she's on the verge of being someone's dinner. 'So this is your chance to prove I wasn't wrong about you. That you have what it takes.'

Suddenly Beth feels cold, as though someone has opened a window behind her that looks out on winter in Iceland. What she's messing up are Gabriela's hopes and dreams—and in a rather spectacular way. And if she's doing that, then there's a very good chance that Gabriela is doing the same for her. Every god there ever was can't help her now. Even if she somehow manages to get back in her own body, her life has been ruined forever.

'Do you understand what I'm saying?' Taffeta's smile holds as much amusement as a hanging.

'Don't blow this, Gabriela.'

Beth barely has the strength to nod. 'I won't.'

'That's the spirit.' With one hand Taffeta guides Beth out of the office and down the hall, and with the other she calls for a cab. 'And then we're going to forget this day ever happened,' she says when they reach the entrance of the school.

'That's fine by me,' says Beth.

*   *   *

The police officers who apprehend Gabriela and Delila as they squeeze through the hedges at the bottom of Joe's property are Cecilia Rueda and Ivan Zokowski. Officers Rueda and Zokowski have been patrolling the area since earlier this afternoon, when several people reported a prowler in the neighbourhood. That the prowler wasn't described by anyone as two teenage girls is immaterial as far as the officers are concerned. They've known thieves use small children, dogs, monkeys and even—once—a bird to help them. Why not teenagers who look as if they might be selling candy to raise money for their school?

'So, you young ladies taking a short cut?' asks Officer Zokowski.

He isn't smiling in the friendly way of the policeman in Jeremiah who helped Gabriela when her bike had a flat, but she smiles back at him anyway. 'Yes, we were. We're in a hurry.'

'I'll bet you are.' Officer Rueda isn't smiling either.

'It's just that our group is waiting for us.' And Gabriela explains that they're in LA for the weekend with the other finalists in a writing competition and that they're touring the cultural highlights of the city today. 'We got separated from them and we're trying to get back to Sunset Boulevard.'

It's unclear whether or not the officers have heard a word she said; if they heard, it certainly didn't make any impression on them.

Officer Zokowski snorts. 'Through Beverly Hills?'

'Are you aware that this is all private property around here?' asks Officer Rueda. 'Why would you be coming out of somebody's yard?'

'We told you.' Gabriela continues to smile. 'Because we were taking a short cut.'

Delila doesn't smile. 'We weren't hurting anything,' she says. 'It's not against the law to walk on the grass in California, is it?'

'And anyway,' Gabriela interrupts before either cop can answer Delila, 'we had permission.'

'Did you?' Officer Zokowski pulls out his notebook. 'And who gave you that?'

Delila points through the shrubs. 'The man who lives in that house up there. Joe.'

'Joe.' Sunlight glints off Cecilia Rueda's badge. 'And his last name is . . .?'

Gabriela looks at Delila, who is looking at her. 'Well, he didn't tell us his last name, but—'

'Get in the car,' orders Officer Zokowski.

No one answers the door of Joe's house.

'We told you,' says Gabriela. 'His housekeeper's out and he can't walk.'

'Because he sprained his ankle jogging.' On the lips of Ivan Zokowski the word 'jogging' somehow sounds like 'picking daisies'.

'That's funny.' Cecilia Rueda looks musingly up

at the house. 'I would have thought someone living in a place like this would have their own gym.'

'I don't know if he does or not.' Gabriela is still smiling. 'I only went to the freezer for the peas.'

'I'd like to take a look in your bags,' says Officer Zokowski.

'Oh, for Pete's sake,' groans Gabriela. 'Do we look like terrorists or something?'

Delila, the granddaughter of a man who has lost count of how many times he's been arrested for civil disobedience, says, 'I don't think so. I know my rights. You have to have a reason to search our bags.'

'You were acting suspiciously.'

Delila sighs. 'We were walking across the lawn.'

Gabriela was hoping that the officers would realize how ridiculous they're being and give them a ride back down the hills, but she can tell that, between Delila's belief in sticking up for herself and the kind of day this is, that probably isn't going to happen. Instead, she has an image of them being bundled back into the police car and thrown into a holding cell with people whose dress sense is even worse than Beth's. 'Why don't you call Professor Gryck,' she suggests. 'Professor Cybelline Gryck? She's our chaperone for the weekend. She'll vouch for us.'

Officer Rueda looks as if she's been invited to telephone Santa Claus. 'You have a number for this professor?'

Professor Gryck is standing outside the bus when they arrive, her hands clasped and her sharp features softened by concern. 'I can't tell you how worried we've been,' she says several times to the officers. 'They've never been to LA before. I was

201

afraid something terrible had happened.' This isn't actually true. Beth Beeby may present herself as mild-mannered and unassuming, but Professor Gryck knows that this is only an act. In reality, Beth Beeby is a troublemaker, a subversive force who has no respect for the rule of law. Che Guevara in grey trousers, generic trainers and a cheap barrette. Even the fact that Professor Gryck couldn't get through to her or Delila on their phones didn't make her worry for their safety. They were AWOL not MIA. Nonetheless, she does worry about her own reputation, and couldn't stop the lurid headlines that raced through her brain like a runaway train: *Visiting Teens Missing from Tour . . . Girls Found at Bottom of Pool . . . Tomorrow's Writers Dead Today . . .* And it would be all her fault for leaving them on their own while she restored her shattered nerves with a glass of white wine. How would her career ever recover from that? Instead of Dr Cybelline Gryck, leading authority on the Norse sagas, she'd be Cybelline Gryck, the woman who lost those poor, innocent girls. 'I can't tell you how grateful I am,' she says several more times. 'You're a credit to the force.'

Piled with praise, the officers are modest. They're glad they could help. It's not every day they have a happy ending.

'I can't apologize enough for any trouble you've been caused,' says Professor Gryck, who apparently can't. 'I really am very sorry.'

'No trouble,' says Ivan Zokowski. 'We were just doing our job.'

But as soon as the patrol car moves back into traffic, all traces of empathy and concern vanish faster than an ice cube tossed into a volcano.

'Why did you wander off like that?' demands Professor Gryck. 'What in the name of God were you thinking?' Now her expression is as dark as the inside of the barrel of a gun. This is yet another thing that has never happened to Professor Gryck before.

'We're really sorry, Professor Gryck,' says Gabriela. 'But we did have a good reason.'

'That's right,' Delila chimes in. 'There were seriously extenuating circumstances.'

Sadly, Professor Gryck doesn't believe their story any more than Taffeta Mackenzie believes Beth's.

'Your aunt?' Professor Gryck's voice is sour with doubt. '*Your* aunt was hiking through Beverly Hills?'

'No, it wasn't my aunt,' repeats Gabriela. 'I just *thought* it was my aunt.'

'Like you thought you helped a jogger who sprained his ankle?'

'How could he answer the door when he couldn't walk?' argues Gabriela.

'And anyway he probably fell asleep right away,' adds Delila. 'From the shock.'

'I'm surprised *I* haven't fallen asleep from the shock,' mutters Professor Gryck. So far, the weekend hasn't gone according to plan. Not according to *her* plan. The competition and all its fanfare and publicity were supposed to add a contemporary, media-wise coda to the distinguished book that is her academic career, but it's turning into a Three Stooges movie. Or it would if she allowed it to. Which she won't. From now on, Cybelline Gryck, PhD, isn't taking any more chances. 'Nothing can go wrong tomorrow.

203

And by "nothing", I specifically mean nothing that has to do with *you*, Beth Beeby. You won't start a food fight. You won't set off alarms. You won't go wandering around private property.'

Tomorrow is the awards ceremony. The distinguished academics and writers who judged the competition will, of course, be attending, but the very large and rare feather in Professor Gryck's literary cap is the fact that she has persuaded one of the greatest and most reclusive figures in American literature to present the prizes. No one knows about this except the organizers; if news leaked out, there would be a tent city of reporters and photographers and slightly rumpled-looking, intense young men outside the hotel in a matter of minutes. Professor Gryck has not worked so hard for this coup, and to keep her secret, to have the day ruined by a high school student. 'I'm going to be watching you as if I'm a broker on the verge of bankruptcy and you're the stock market, is that clear? The only time I won't have my eyes on you is when you're sleeping.'

With some effort, Gabriela manages not to bang her head against the side of the bus. This day just gets better and better.

*   *   *

Outside a small taqueria on the busy boardwalk, a couple sit at a table with a view of the ocean, paper plates of food in front of them.

'Look at you, eating Mexican!' crows Remedios, as though this is a personal victory for her. 'I thought you said Mexican food's the revenge of an oppressed and conquered people.' She scrunches up her face in horror and distaste. 'All those nasty chillies.'

'I'm hungry.' Otto's run around so much today you'd think he was a racehorse, not an angel. And then, of course, there was all the palaver on the bus—dogs . . . snakes . . . hysterical women . . . police officers . . . 'And in any case, I didn't call you here to discuss my diet, Remedios. We have more pressing concerns.'

Remedios watches him, amused. 'You know, I've never seen anybody eat a burrito with cutlery before . . .'

'Don't try to change the subject.' Otto points his plastic fork at her. 'I want to know what happened. I did my part. All you had to do was get Gabriela on the same piece of sidewalk as Beth at the same time and swap them back. What was so hard about that? That was our understanding.'

It was his understanding, not hers. Remedios bites into her lunch in a non-committal way.

'However,' Otto continues, 'for some twisted reason of your own, you didn't do that, did you?' Otto cuts his food into remarkably even slices. He may be upset, but he's still neat. 'You just sat there and watched them charge off in opposite directions as if they were being chased by rampaging Cossacks.'

'I don't know why you're blaming me. I am not responsible for the unpredictability of humans, Otto. Beth just bolted for that bus like a frightened horse.'

'You could have stopped her.' He pops a slice of burrito into his mouth.

'I'm so sorry, Otto.' Remedios is the voice of sweet reason. 'But if you recall, you told me very

205

specifically to look after Gabriela. Not Beth.'

He flaps his fork at her. 'You didn't stop her either!'

This, of course, is true. And because it is true, Remedios takes another bite and chews slowly. 'You know, humans may have invented guns and nuclear weapons and drone bombers, but they also came up with the black bean burrito—and the black bean burrito's really good.'

'You could have stopped Beth,' repeats Otto, 'but you didn't. You sat there and watched her go off on that bus like a lamb to the slaughter.'

'She didn't go off to the slaughter, Otto. She went downtown. It's not the same thing at all.'

'That's what you think. That bus was almost literally Hell on wheels. What is it with this city? It's usually only religious wars that bring out so much insanity.'

'She wasn't hurt, Otto. Everything turned out just dandy.' Remedios reaches for the salsa verde. 'And just for the record, since you seem to think everything's my fault, I'm not the one who caused a major international incident.' She smiles at him as she scoops up a spoonful of sauce. 'That would be *you.*'

And that would be why he's changed his clothes again. Just in case the police are looking for him.

'I wouldn't call it major, Remedios.' He forks another piece of burrito. 'It was just one bus.'

'It's all over the news already.' An angel would never gloat, of course, but she can't resist a slightly smug smile. 'By tomorrow it'll be in every paper on the continent.'

'I think that's very unlikely.' He certainly hopes that it is. Even though Otto holds her completely

206

responsible for everything that's happened, he can see that it might not appear that way to everyone. 'Things like that must happen here all the time. And, in any event, it's a national—not an international—incident.'

'That woman from Tokyo had to be sedated.'

'That wasn't because of me.' He wipes hot sauce from his mouth with a yellow napkin that says *The Whole Enchilada* in red lettering. 'That was because of the snake. And the dogs.'

'It wasn't the snake or the dogs that made the bus go the wrong way. For *miles*.' She points the salsa spoon at him. Accusingly. 'I heard that the driver may never recover. He keeps repeating, over and over, "How did it happen? How did it happen?"'

'Oh, he'll be fine.' Because human emotions are so undependable (they cry at weddings, but bomb whole cities without blinking back a single tear), they are also irksome and exhausting. You never know what insignificant incident is going to set them off. 'There was a lot of screaming towards the end. It probably jangled his nerves.'

'The screaming, of course. How silly of me. Driving like a zombie and finally being stopped by the cops had nothing to do with it.'

Otto slips another slice of burrito into his mouth. 'I only did what I had to do.'

'And that's what I did.' She picks up her burrito and takes a bite, a noticeable amount of the stuffing falling back onto the table and her paper plate. 'What I had to do.'

'Putting Beth on that bus? That was what you had to do?'

It's not easy to sound indignant with a mouth

full of rice and beans, but Remedios manages heroically. 'Excuse me, Mr Wasserbach, but I thought we'd been through that. I didn't put her on that bus.' Though she did, of course, make the bus available. 'She got on all by herself.'

He picks up a pepper. 'And you expect me to believe that?'

'It happens to be true.' If only technically.

Otto watches her closely for the slightest shimmer, but much to his chagrin, there is none. And yet he'd be willing to wager that she isn't telling the truth. Not Remedios Cienfuegos y Mendoza, the DIY angel.

'And in any case, you're the one who's looking after Beth,' says Remedios. 'Not I.'

'But that doesn't change the fact that you were meant to switch them on Sunset. Beth was standing right there at the kerb. Gabriela crossed the road. Everything was perfect. I was all set to pick you up, check out of the hotel and go home. But, no. Next thing I know, Beth's going west and Gabriela's disappeared. How could you have botched that? What went wrong?'

'Beth got on the bus; that's what went wrong.'

'And Gabriela? What happened to Gabriela?'

'Gabriela's on the tour bus with old Dragon Breath.' Still not even the shadow of a shimmer. 'Where do you think she is?'

'Well, how would I know?' One minute he's as good as shaking the sand of Los Angeles out of his shoes and the next there's a snake hissing at him and a dog bouncing off his knees. 'I just hope you don't lose track of her again.'

Remedios licks sauce from her fingertips. 'Otto, what difference would it make? We can switch them back in Jeremiah.'

'What? After you've ruined their lives?' He pushes his empty plate away. 'Because that's what you're doing, you know. I, for one, certainly don't imagine that Gabriela's doing a better job of being Beth than Beth is of being Gabriela. Or are you going to tell me that she is? That she's going to emerge from this weekend triumphant and covered in laurels?'

Remedios, too, pushes her empty plate away. 'She's doing a great job.'

Unfortunately, because of the sunlight reflecting off the ocean and the hazy quality of the air, he still isn't sure whether or not he caught a shimmer.

DESPITE APPEARANCES, THINGS CONTINUE TO GO DOWNHILL FASTER THAN A CAR WITHOUT BRAKES

Crying usually helps. At least in Beth's experience it does. It helps you get through the worst day or the bluest mood or the longest, darkest night. Indeed, Beth spends a lot of time by herself; and a lot of the time that she spends by herself is taken up with tears. How many days has she sat in the corner stall of one of the school's girls' rooms, weeping because of a poor grade or a spotlight of laughter following her down a hall? How many nights has she lain awake with her cat, Charley, curled against her humming like a small motor, worrying about all the things that might go wrong tomorrow, or the next day, or ten years from now? How many weekends has she sat in her room, poor-me drops splashing onto her homework because everybody else is at a party or out on a date? Almost too many to count. But a good cry is like a spring cleaning of the soul; afterwards she feels, if not better exactly, at least refreshed.

And that's how she plans to spend the rest of the afternoon once she gets back to the hotel and is finally alone: sobbing her heart out. God knows she has enough cause; she could cry a river the size of the Rio Grande and no one would blame her. Besides, what else does she have to do? She can't even call her old room—call herself—because there won't be anyone there. They won't be returning to the hotel till after the play. Just the thought of what she's missing nearly gets her started; she'd been looking forward to seeing a play that wasn't performed on the stage of the high school auditorium by kids she's gone to school with most of her life.

The cab driver, however, has other plans. He is a gangling, beaming man with an unpronounceable name and the personality of a Labrador pup. As soon as she shuts the door he starts talking.

'Are you a model?' He grins at her over his shoulder. 'I get a lot of models. There's almost as many models in this city as actors. I get a lot of them, too. Always in a hurry. Rushrushrushrushrush. But you can't go faster than you can go, you know? That's just a fact. And I say to them, God didn't make all the beautiful things in the world so you could keep looking at your watch, you know?' He more or less throws the cab into traffic. 'So are you?' he goes on. 'Are you doing a show at the college?'

Able to tell the truth for the first time all day,

Beth says no. 'No, I was just— I was just visiting the school with a friend. Actually, I'm a writer.' And she explains that she's in LA for the weekend because she's a finalist in a national competition.

'A writer? Now that is something.' He glances into the mirror, a colourful collection of talismans and chotskies swaying gently below it. 'I'd never guess that. You don't look like a writer.' He laughs. 'But a book doesn't look like its cover, you know? What do you write?'

'Short stories. But some day I want to write a novel.' Barefoot and no longer bashful. 'That's what I really want to do.'

'A novel! Now that is a thing to want!' For some reason his laugh makes her think of cinnamon. 'You know what you should do? I'll tell you. You should write about me!' With one hand he cuts into the next lane and with the other he thumps himself on the chest. 'You wouldn't believe the life I've had. It would be a best-seller.' And while he weaves rather recklessly through the traffic, rarely looking at the road, but frequently shouting good-naturedly at drivers who are even worse than he, he tells her the story of his life. Which, at a rough estimate, contains enough material for a dozen novels, each of them marked by hardship and struggle, and quite a lot of *joie de vivre*. He laughs again. 'Everything but the kitchen sink, you know? And every word is true.' He sounds his horn as a man in a Humvee comes close to ending the story once and for all. 'And then I came to this country,' he finishes up. 'Where anything can happen, you know?'

'Yes,' says Beth, 'I know.'

The cabbie comes from a place where you might also say that anything can happen, but most of it

211

is unpleasant. 'Here, I have a chance. I can make the best of things, you know? Nothing's perfect, but you can make the best of things.'

Does she? *Make the best of things . . . the best of things . . .* The three shells and the plastic Snoopy hanging on a red ribbon from the mirror clack against the wooden cross and the glass beads on the piece of string. *Make the best of things.* Instead of the worst.

Horns honking and brakes squealing, the cab lands in the drive of The Hotel Xanadu.

Beth stands on the pavement, waving good-bye until he disappears. And then she marches into the hotel. But instead of going upstairs, she goes straight for the beauty parlour on the first floor. If she is going to make the best of things, she might as well have someone who knows how to style hair and put on make-up take charge.

*   *   *

The party is being held in the Grace Kelly Room of The Hotel Xanadu. The walls have been decorated with blow-ups of *Vogue* covers through the decades and tiny star-shaped lights have been strung from one side of the room to the other. Waiters weave through the throng like bees through a meadow, carrying trays of canapés that are more a suggestion of food than a meal. As Taffeta promised, everybody who is anybody on the LA fashion scene is here—models, designers, journalists, buyers, and all their PAs. Many of us are nervous of meeting new people, and Beth has always been more nervous than most, often making herself ill with worry. But tonight she is as

212

fearless as a blade of grass. Tonight she is Gabriela Menz. She spent nearly an hour just staring at her made-over reflection in the bathroom mirror, saying silently to herself, *Think Gabriela, think Gabriela* . . . And it seems to have worked. She greets each new person with the confidence and efficiency of an assembly-line worker installing her part of an engine. Smile, shake hands, murmur something about Los Angeles or fashion or how excited you are to be here; smile, shake hands, murmur something about Los Angeles or fashion or how excited you are to be here; smile, shake hands, murmur something about Los Angeles or fashion or how excited you are to be here . . .

Beth stands near the door, propped against the wall for both moral and physical support. Tonight she is wearing shoes that make the ones she had on earlier look like loafers and a dress that fits her like a bandage. The skirt is so short it feels as if there's a fan blowing on her thighs. Her eyelashes feel as if they've been glued together (which they have) and her face feels as if it's been varnished (which it might as well have been). But she knows she looks like a million dollars. Indeed, she doesn't look like *just* a million; she looks like a million packed in a Louis Vuitton bag and locked in the trunk of a Bugatti Veyron. Lucinda practically swooned when she saw her. The other girls looked like their smiles hurt them. Taffeta, who tends to dole out compliments like a miser doling out alms, adjusted the shoulder of Beth's dress and said, 'Well, that's more like it, Gabriela.'

Think Gabriela Menz, Beth tells herself. *Be her* . . . She does a pretty good job. Most of the talk is about clothes. Who's wearing what. *Isn't*

213

that a McCartney . . .? Do you think that's really a Morgana . . .? What are going to be the big names next season and the season after that. *Sambucco . . .? Wu . . .? Austin Finch . . .?* The major trends. *Mid-calf . . .? Maxi . . .? Mini . . .? Feathers . . .? Bows . . .?* Beth listens, laughs and nods, giving the impression that whether or not something is cut on the bias or double-stitched are questions that keep her awake at night. *What do you think about linen?* someone asks, but all Beth can think of is bandages—the mummy look—all the rage this spring. She smiles and nods. *And what about crops? Corn? Wheat? Beans?* She smiles and nods some more. Giving up on ever having a real meal again, she nibbles and sips. She knows Taffeta is watching her—measuring her, judging her—so she makes certain that Taffeta likes what she sees. *That's more like it . . .*

Thinking that—at least in this part of the nightmare that her life has become—the worst must now be over, Beth allows herself a sigh of relief, as slim as the hips on a size 0 model. But it could be a sigh too soon.

Suddenly, a hand grips her arm—lightly and firmly as plastic cuffs.

'Gabriela, honey,' purrs Taffeta. 'I have some people here you absolutely *have* to meet.'

The people Gabriela honey has to meet are Mo and Inda Linger, two of the hottest young designers in the country, and Estella Starr, a model whose face could only be seen by more people if it were put on a postage stamp. Beth turns to find them all lined up behind her, and smiling. It's like staring at a wall made of Chiclets.

'This,' says Taffeta, her cool fingers still on Beth,

'is the girl who designed *that* dress.'

This announcement is greeted with a chitter of approval.

Ohmigod, really . . .? Awesome . . . Fantabulous . . .

'I can't believe you're still in high school,' says Mo. 'This is kind of embarrassing, but when I was your age I was still following the flock, baa baa baa . . .'

Inda laughs, a sound reminiscent of a bottle of soda being shaken. 'I don't want to be the one to make the bad pun, but, really, your angel dress is so divine . . .'

'I'm starting my own label,' says Estella, 'and that dress is just the kind of thing I'm looking for. Only maybe I'd change the bodice detail and drop the hemline? What do you think about that?'

Beth has got through the evening with nods and smiles, and so she nods and smiles now, in an enthusiastic if ambiguous way.

'Though I do wonder about the palette . . .' murmurs Estella. 'It could be that stronger, less innocent colours would really set off the purity of the design and give it an even sexier edge.'

Beth nods; Beth smiles. 'Um . . .'

'You know what I really wanted to ask you?' cuts in Inda, the glitter in her false lashes seeming to make her sparkle. 'I know that you're incredibly talented, but what and who are your inspirations?'

'My inspirations?' echoes Beth. How on earth should she know? Not only does she have no idea what dress they're talking about, the clothes she buys don't have names. They might as well be asking her which architects or scientists have influenced her the most. *I owe everything to Christopher Wren and Isaac Newton.*

215

'Gabriela?' prompts Taffeta.

'Well . . . my inspirations . . .' Beth mumbles. 'That's a very good question.'

Taffeta's smile glints like sharpened steel. 'I believe it is. And we'd all like to hear your answer.'

'Well . . .' It may be true that the only thing Beth knows about 'fashion' is how to spell it, but there is something that she does know quite a lot about and that, of course, is literature. She takes a deep breath, and plunges in—substituting the words 'fashion' and 'designers' for 'writing' and 'writers' where appropriate. 'I don't think I can pick just one or two influences. I just sort of immerse myself in all the styles and trends from today and yesterday and decades and centuries ago . . . I mean, fashion is organic, isn't it?'

'Oh, but organic materials are so expensive,' murmurs Inda.

Mo nods. 'We do a lot of stuff for the big outlets. You can get certificates to say things aren't made in sweatshops, but organic material really jacks up the price.'

'No, I didn't mean that. I meant that it's kind of a living thing. You see something here that you like, and then something else there. And then you start putting things together or taking out the best parts, and it all starts to grow, doesn't it?'

Because no one responds, Beth keeps going, chattering on as if she's a sound system that's been programmed for continuous play. If she had half a second right now to think about it, she might wonder why she's always been less articulate than a talking doll; stuttering and stumbling, certain her opinions will be as welcome as a contagious disease. She starts to warm to her subject, gesturing

216

emotively and making expressive faces, only vaguely aware of the women in front of her, the voices around her, the waiters sidling past.

No one ever looks at the waiters at this kind of thing, but Beth doesn't know that and while she talks her eyes move from Taffeta and Mo Linger to the young man standing behind them, who is proffering a silver tray, but looking at her.

Beth stops mid-word, staring back at him as if he's holding not a platter of miniature Thai spring rolls, but a very large and fiery sword.

Taffeta clears her throat. 'Gabriela? Gabriela? You were saying?'

'That's him!' cries Beth, pointing over Taffeta's shoulder. 'Ms Mackenzie, that's him!'

The polite smile vanishes from Taffeta's face. 'Excuse me?'

The others look to where Beth is pointing, but now there is no one there, just a white-coated back gliding effortlessly through the clusters of guests.

'It's him!' Beth points towards the retreating waiter. 'It's the man who's been following me!'

'Gabriela.' Taffeta's voice is low but urgent. It sounds as if her teeth have been cemented together. 'Gabriela, not now.'

'But it is! It's him! I'll prove it!'

It is Beth's intention to charge after the waiter; to stop and confront him; to make him face her once and for all. The only thing wrong with this plan is that she's forgotten that one of the reasons she's been propped against a wall all evening is because she is balanced on her shoes like a book on a bottle.

*　　　*　　　*

There have been times in Professor Gryck's life, as there are in the lives of all of us, when she has said things she didn't mean and made threats she never intended to keep, just because she was angry or wanted to seem as if she was in control. But this is not one of those times. This afternoon, Professor Gryck is as good as her word and sticks as close to Gabriela as a pair of tights.

'No, no, Ms Beeby!' she calls as Gabriela prepares to take the empty seat next to Delila on the bus. 'You'll be sitting up front with me.'

Oh, goody.

And so, as the shadows slowly lengthen over the City of Angels, the Tomorrow's Writers Today group makes its way to yet another repository of human culture. The others can all surreptitiously send texts or emails or play games while Professor Gryck reads from her guidebook, but Gabriela— wedged in between the shatterproof glass of the window and the sturdy, unyielding form of Cybelline Gryck—has no choice but to keep her eyes open and focused on the good professor and not on the more interesting sight of the city outside the bus. But though she looks as if she's paying attention, her mind wanders off on its own.

As the bus creeps through the traffic-choked streets, Gabriela finds herself thinking not about herself, for a change, but about Beth. Now that she has some small idea of what it's like to be Beth, Gabriela has stopped thinking of her as some alien life form and started thinking of her as a real person. Like the girl in the painting. Like whoever wore the jewellery or ate from the clay bowls that they saw. Like Gabriela herself. Someone with longings and fears. Someone with dreams. That Beth's longings, fears and dreams are very different to Gabriela's doesn't seem to matter any more. And if Gabriela often feels lonely, then how lonely must Beth feel? Competing with girls like Aricely, Esmeralda and Jayne; bossed around by people like Professor Gryck; fussed over and controlled by her mother; terrorized by even the air she breathes. Beth is no match for any of them. And at that thought, Gabriela sits up a little straighter, and the determined look she had when she successfully put in her first zipper comes into her eyes. So far today she's done no more than complain, sulk, systematically destroy everything Beth's worked so hard for and come close to getting arrested. What she needs now is to repair some of the damage she's done. And not cause any more. Which can't be as difficult as it sounds. All she has to do is not do anything and say even less. The day is half over. How can she fail?

Because they lost so much time what with 'one thing and another', as Professor Gryck put it (clearly meaning Beth), they have to adjust their itinerary and spend the afternoon in the contemporary art museum, which is much nearer the restaurant and the theatre than the museum Professor Gryck originally chose. Gabriela would have preferred an afternoon of Etruscan relics—anything so long as you can tell what it is—but she walks demurely beside Professor Gryck, keeping her face expressionless and her mouth shut tight, without so much as a sigh. Even when Jayne becomes almost lyrical over a model house made entirely from garbage, Gabriela merely smiles vaguely and says nothing. When Aricely decides she likes the hillock of dolls' heads even more than the pickled pig they'd seen in the morning, Gabriela simply nods as though carefully weighing the merits of each. And when Esmeralda talks for five minutes and forty-five seconds about how the black canvas with the purple stripe down one side is a moving meditation on the relationship between hope and fear, Gabriela refuses to catch Delila's eye.

None of this brings an actual smile to Professor Gryck's face, but at least she isn't shouting. So far, so good.

But not that far, and not for long, as things turn out.

For, as both Otto and Remedios would be quick to point out, good intentions pave the road to Hell, and despite Gabriela's efforts to have as low a profile as a hem stitch so that all her mistakes can be forgotten and forgiven, things take a turn for the worse at dinner. The entire group sits at a long line of tables in the middle of the restaurant, Gabriela and Delila on either side of Professor Gryck. The conversation is all about writing and who the greatest American writers of the last hundred-and-fifty years are. Gabriela keeps her eyes on her plate and her expression blank. If she could, she wouldn't listen, but because this is less a discussion than a duel of strongly held opinions, it is impossible to turn it into background noise. Munchmunchmunchmunch . . . *turgid . . . overwritten . . . brilliant word play . . . deconstructionism . . . historiographic . . . dialectic between authority and community . . . postmodern violence against the conventions of narrative and form . . . parodic punning . . . structural complexities*

220

. . . *slurpslurpslurpslurpslurp*. There is nothing in any of their comments that makes reading the novels they mention sound like a particularly good idea.

And then, just when the dinner plates have been cleared and the ordeal is almost over, Professor Gryck turns to her and says, in the tone of someone daring you to throw a stone at that very large window, 'I must say, Beth, that I'm surprised you have nothing to contribute to this discussion. After all, you hope to write a novel yourself some day, don't you?'

Gabriela looks up from the dessert menu. 'Excuse me?'

Everyone nearby is looking at her; especially Professor Gryck with her know-it-all smile. The woman really is the human equivalent of a hangnail.

'I said I'm surprised you haven't contributed anything to our discussion.' If Professor Gryck's smile were a dress it would be a severely cut sheath, something futuristic and angular, and possibly made out of sheet metal. A dress to disguise not flatter. 'I was under the impression that you know as much about literary criticism as you do about novels.' This definitely sounds like a challenge.

One to which Gabriela rises with a smile of her own. 'I do.' And that much, of course, is true. She knows little about novels, and equally little about literary criticism. But Professor Gryck's expression is so insincere that it makes Gabriela wonder why she's baiting Beth this way—like a matador waving his cape at the unsuspecting bull. Especially after the arguments the two of them have had today; you'd think she'd be grateful Beth finally shut up. And it is because of that that she forgets she's

221

meant to do nothing and say less. 'I do have one question.' Gabriela pushes the dessert menu aside. It seems that in some small corner of the closet that is her brain (possibly on a high shelf, right at the back), part of Gabriela has actually been paying attention, and this is the part that speaks now. 'I was just kind of wondering why all the writers you've been talking about are men. Every one of them.'

Professor Gryck's smile hovers on her lips as if looking for a safe place to land.

'Excuse me, Ms Beeby?'

'I mean, women write literature too, right? It's not like it's a college fraternity or anything like that. They're allowed to join.'

Everyone else stops talking, drinking, chewing and even swallowing. It's possible that one or two of the contestants are holding their breath. Someone clears his throat.

That someone is Mr Solman, who looks as if he is either about to laugh or cough. 'Well, of course they are,' he says, with the positive joviality you'd expect from a representative of a powerful corporation. 'There's nothing excluding women from the great community of the written word. Not nowadays. And they do.' Because Gabriela is staring at him with a face less blank than stony, Mr Solman's words are slowing down and his eyes keep darting to Professor Gryck. 'Write. Literature. Very good literature.'

'Then how come all the writers who've been mentioned are men?' Gabriela asks again.

Professor Gryck comes to Mr Solman's rescue. 'There are many major writers who are women, as you well know, Ms Beeby,' she says, her voice as

222

stiff as starched cotton. 'Jane Austen . . . Virginia Woolf . . . George Eli—'

'Then why aren't any of them up for Great American Novelist?' insists Gabriela.

Professor Gryck glances at the others, allowing herself a small but humourless laugh. 'Well, for openers, they're all British.'

Gabriela rolls her eyes in an exasperated, annoyed-by-a-snag way. 'You know what I mean. I haven't heard anyone mention one woman. Not even quickly. Not even because some famous male writer liked her stuff.'

Professor Gryck folds her hands, leaning forward slightly. 'Perhaps you'd like to mention some then, Ms Beeby.'

Behind the writers' group, a young woman sits by herself at a table for two, finishing her meal and flicking through the book on Babylonia that Professor Gryck bought in one of the museums they visited (and which she thinks she left on the bus). Remedios has been as unsuccessful as Gabriela at completely ignoring the conversation at the contestants' table, and so has found herself almost sedated by it. But now she looks up with amused curiosity. Is it possible that things are finally going to get interesting?

Much to Gabriela's surprise, there seems to be even more information on that high shelf at the back of her closet, put there unbeknownst to her by Mr Sturgess and suddenly, if inexplicably, discovered by Gabriela, for into the silence that has engulfed them like a giant plastic bag she suddenly hears herself say, 'Maya Angelou . . . Edith Wharton . . . Alice Walker . . . Harper Lee . . . Kate Chopin . . . Toni Morrison . . . Anne Ty—'

'No one would argue that those novelists haven't produced some very fine work,' Professor Gryck interrupts her, 'but I don't know that any of it can be considered truly great.'

'Why not?' asks someone nearby—but not so near that Professor Gryck can tell who it is. 'What criteria are you using to measure greatness?'

Professor Gryck sits up a little straighter as her smile becomes noticeably thinner. 'I'm afraid the simple fact is that, on the whole, women tend to write more domestically and personally—about relationships and that kind of thing—while men deal with the larger, more profound issues.'

'Like what?' This time there is no doubt who spoke.

'Like everything, Ms Beeby. War . . . philosophical and existential questions of existence . . . power . . . meaning . . . government . . .'

'And those things don't involve relationships?'

The only ones smiling are Delila and Remedios.

'Well, yes, of course they do. What I meant was that women are more concerned with the emotions . . . with love stor—'

Gabriela nods. 'You mean like "Romeo and Juliet"? "*Anna Kare*—"'

'Good Lord, will you look at the time?' Professor Gryck waves a hand at the waiter. 'I'm afraid we can't have dessert after all. We'd better get going or we'll be late for the play.'

*   *   *

As far as Gabriela is concerned, the good thing about the theatre is that it's dark and no one is going to ask her to say anything. She can just sit there, invisible and mute, and in a couple of hours they'll be on their way back to the hotel and she can go to bed and forget this day ever happened— at least until the morning. As soon as the lights dim, she starts to relax. Gabriela has only been to a real theatre once before, and that was to see the musical so mocked by Jayne at breakfast. This play is not a musical. It is also long and convoluted, making it difficult for Gabriela to tell who is who and what is what. The actors are dressed in modern clothes, but they don't speak like real people speak—or even like the unreal people in movies speak. Nor do they have microphones, so that you have to listen really closely to hear what's being said. But even when Gabriela hears what's being said she isn't always sure what's going on. There are at least two characters who, as far as she can tell, never actually make an appearance.

Gabriela falls asleep.

As soon as they emerge from the theatre, Professor Gryck makes it clear that her limited supply of patience and forgiveness has officially run out. 'You've been trying to make me look a fool all day. Are you purposely trying to undermine me? Is that what you're doing?' she demands. 'I'm an academic so I'm used to backstabbing and treachery, but not from my students!' She might possibly understand that someone who has spent the day trying to get arrested might be so tired from her efforts that she falls asleep in one of the greatest plays ever written, but did Gabriela have to *snore* in the middle of one of the most beautiful and moving speeches in the English language, as well? 'You could have heard a pin drop!' Professor Gryck keeps saying. 'A pin drop! But what did

225

we hear? We heard you snuffling like a pig after truffles!'

The other phrase she keeps repeating is 'insult to injury'.

And indeed, even as they finally enter the hotel, Professor Gryck is saying, 'As if that wasn't enough, you had to add insult to injury!'

'I said I was sorry,' says Gabriela, who has—and who very much *is* sorry. 'It's not like—'

Gabriela was about to say (also not for the first time) that it wasn't as if she'd deliberately snored during a tense moment on stage. The reason she doesn't finish this sentence is because it is right then that she notices a tall, skinny scarecrow of a woman in pink pedal pushers, pink baseball cap and a shirt that identifies her as a member of a bowling team in Long Beach, running towards them, shrieking, 'There you are! At last! Oh, praise the Lord you're alive! I was beside my wits!'

There is no doubt in Gabriela's mind that this badly dressed woman is shouting at her. She's looking right at her and waving her arms. Who else could she possibly be shouting at? *Oh God! Now what? Who on earth can this creature be?*

Professor Gryck, also reduced to silence by the sight of a hysterical woman—who clearly wouldn't recognize a Norse saga if it appeared in her bowling bag—charging across the lobby of The Xanadu like a runaway ball, would also like to know who it is.

Interestingly, there are two people in close proximity who can answer that question. The first is Beth. Shoeless again, she is limping towards the elevator with Lucinda when she hears an all-too-familiar voice screeching loud enough to be heard

226

on the other side of the valley. Is there *nothing* that isn't going to go wrong with this day? The second is Remedios Cienfuegos y Mendoza, who is directly behind Delila and Gabriela.

The shock of seeing her mother's sister where she very much shouldn't be makes Beth scream as loudly as if she'd walked into the kitchen and seen a rat scampering over the counter. As we all know, when faced with a dangerous situation, the natural response is either to fight or to flee. Beth chooses flight, but turns around so quickly that she smacks into Lucinda and knocks them both down.

Remedios has been looking forward to going to her suite and watching a movie. Before something else goes wrong. But the galumphing figure hurtling towards them pulls her up sharply. Clearly, something else already has gone wrong. But she is used to thinking quickly and acting even more quickly. So she leans over the shoulders of Gabriela and Delila and says very clearly, 'Ladies, that's Aunt Joyce.'

Although it wasn't Gabriela who spoke, Delila looks over at her. 'Well damn me, you do have an aunt.'

Of course she has an aunt. It's amazing that she doesn't have several uncles and a dozen cousins as well, all of them dressed like they're on permanent vacation and loitering in the lobby of The Xanadu. What the heck is this woman doing here? Now. Hasn't this day been bad enough? The moment is slightly reminiscent of the time she wore that wrap-around skirt to Bessie Malarch's party and it unwrapped itself as she walked into the room. She does exactly what she did then. She takes a deep breath, and—metaphorically this time—picks

227

up the skirt. 'Aunt Joyce!' cries Gabriela. 'What a great surprise! What are you doing here?'

'What am I doing? Your poor mother's worried sick. She's been calling all day and—'

Another scream, this one sharp as a glover's needle, cuts her off.

This scream, too, was made by Beth. Otto, on his way to the elevator to retreat to the calm and safety of the El Dorado Suite, automatically stopped to help Beth and Lucinda up from the floor. So much for giving aid; she nearly blew his ear off. When Gabriela and everyone else in the lobby looks over, several glamorous young women are gathered round two other glamorous young women in a heap on the carpet. (There is no sign of Otto, of course.)

'Would you look at that?' Aunt Joyce gives a snort of disapproval. 'One of those starlets drunk like you read about in the papers.' She shakes her head. 'I thought this was supposed to be a high-class hotel.'

'So did I,' says Professor Gryck.

By the time either Gabriela or Delila thinks to wonder who told them that the woman in pink was Aunt Joyce, Remedios, too, is gone.

THERE ARE THINGS THAT ARE EASY TO BELIEVE ... AND THERE ARE THINGS THAT ARE HARD TO BELIEVE ... AND THEN THERE ARE THINGS THAT ARE REALLY HARD TO BELIEVE

Once Aunt Joyce is assured that Beth is fine, just very busy, and that there is no need for concern, and Gabriela has been put on Aunt Joyce's phone with Lillian Beeby to apologize for leaving her own phone behind today and to assure her that she is just very busy and there is no need for concern, Professor Gryck takes the league-champion bowler for a soothing cup of tea in the hotel's café. 'The girls have an extremely big day tomorrow,' she tells Aunt Joyce. 'They have to get a good night's sleep.'

Gabriela and Delila stand side by side, waving goodbye as the elevator doors close, and then ride to their floor in ruminative silence—Gabriela thinking about tomorrow and Delila thinking about today.

But as soon as the door of their hotel room shuts behind Delila with a click like a Colt revolver being cocked, she says, 'OK, Beth, I'm tired of dancing around in the dark with a blindfold on. I want to know what's going on. And this time I want the whole unabridged story.'

Gabriela doesn't even have enough strength left to groan out loud. 'There's nothing going on.' She throws herself on her bed. 'I don't know what you mean.'

'Oh, yes you do.' Delila stands over her, arms akimbo. 'You know exactly what I mean. I'm not stupid. You've been as weird as a beard on a goldfish all day. And I want to know why.'

'Your poetic imagination must be on overdrive,' says Gabriela, 'because I'm not being weird and there's nothing going on.'

'Am I a mushroom that you think you have to keep me in the dark and feed me crap?'

'Delila, it's late. You heard what Professor Gryck said. We have a big day tomorrow.'

'We had a big day today.' Delila starts ticking

229

off the day's major events on her fingers. 'One: you, Beth Beeby, the girl who's allergic to the word "cow", drank two cappuccinos at breakfast.'

'I'm not allergic if the milk's in coffee.'

'Yeah, sure.' If Delila's expression were a fruit, it would be a lemon. 'Two: you, the girl who wouldn't stand up to a daffodil, started a food fight.'

'I said I was sorry.'

'No, you didn't. And that can be number three. Because last night you apologized for something every five minutes, but today the first time I heard you say you were sorry for anything was after you fell asleep in the play. Which was about three dozen times too late.'

'There's more than one way of saying "sorry".'

'Not for the Beth Beeby I met yesterday. She said *sorry, sorry, sorry* like it was a mantra.'

Gabriela's expression is distinctly on the lemon-side itself now. 'You know, you're wasting your talents being a poet. You should be an interrogator for the CIA.'

'Forget it, I'm not taking the distraction detour.' Delila holds up both hands. 'I'm going to skip over all the minor things like spontaneously running up into the hills and how much you don't know about books and paintings and stuff like that, and how you bought make-up, and how you'd argue with the President. I'm going to go straight to the big fat cherry on today's seven-layer cake.' She leans forward, speaking slowly, as if expecting Gabriela to read her lips. 'You didn't even know who your own aunt was, Beth. You just stood there gawping at her like you were a deer and she was an oncoming car with really bright headlights until that woman said it was Aunt Joyce.'

'That's right! I completely blanked that.' Gabriela sits up, trying to bring back that moment in the lobby. 'There was somebody behind us. Somebody who said "Ladies, that's Aunt Joyce".' Why didn't she pay any attention? She didn't even think to look round. Now it's her who's gawping at Delila. 'Who *was* that? How did she know that was Aunt Joyce?'

'Don't change the subject,' says Delila. 'I don't care who that was or how she knew your Aunt Joyce. What I want to know is who *you* are and why you didn't know her.'

'I'm Beth Beeby.'

'Yeah, right. And I'm Emily Dickinson.'

'Look at me! Who else could I be?' Gabriela gestures at herself. 'You think there are two people in the world who look like this?' Skinny; pinched, sharp features; seriously myopic; anaemic complexion; dull, lifeless hair; toenails like claws and fingernails that look like a chewed cob of corn. 'You know it's me. I look exactly the way I looked yesterday.'

'Even plain looks are only skin deep,' says Delila.

Gabriela sighs. It has, indeed, been a long day. The last reserve of stubbornness and fight she had left was used up on Aunt Joyce. 'You're not going to believe me.'

Delila plops herself down on the opposite bed. 'Try me.'

And so Gabriela tries. She tells her story simply, adding no trimming or embellishments—and offering no explanations.

Delila sits in total silence, listening to Gabriela's story the way families once gathered around the radio in the evening to listen to the latest

231

instalment of their favourite shows.

'Well?' Gabriela asks when she's finished. 'Don't just sit there like you're having your portrait painted. What do you think?'

'What do I think?' Delila, of course, had no idea what story she was going to hear, but she definitely wasn't prepared for the one she heard. 'I think you should be writing science fiction, that's what I think. Girl, I've heard some wild stories. I mean, there are people who say they've seen the Virgin Mary in Bayside, which, you know . . . Bayside? That's pretty out there. But this one beats them all.'

'Only it happens to be the truth.' Gabriela's mouth pinches with resignation. 'Didn't I tell you, you wouldn't believe me?'

'It's not that I don't believe you, exactly.' Delila, after all, does have a grandmother who believes in angels. 'I know there's more in Heaven and Earth and all that stuff. But it is a little hard to get my head around the idea that through some mysterious process you got switched with somebody else. I mean, I haven't checked lately, but last time I looked we were in The Hotel Xanadu, not The X Files.'

'But you said yourself I'm different to how I was yesterday. If I didn't get dumped into Beth Beeby's body, what do you think's going on?'

Delila shakes her head. 'Danged if I know. We don't have this kind of problem in Brooklyn.'

'Well, it happens all the time in Jeremiah. We drop into each other's bodies the way the rest of you drop into coffee bars.' Gabriela is beginning to show a flair for creative writing that she never knew she had. 'We don't even bother going to movies or concerts or anything. If we want something to do

232

we just say, "Hey, let's be so-and-so for a couple of hours tonight".'

'You don't have to get all sarcastic.'

'And you don't have to act like I'm making this up. Just because something's really unlikely doesn't mean that it can't happen, you know.' Gabriela flaps her arms in exasperation. 'I mean, do you think it's easy for *me* to believe it?'

'No, I don't. But it's different for you. You're the person it's happened to. So, even if it seems impossible and improbable, you know it's true. Whereas the innocent bystander doesn't have that advantage. The innocent bystander—which, in this case, is me—has a serious belief challenge going on.'

'Oh, my God! How could I be so dumb?' Gabriela jumps to her feet, smiling for the first time in quite a few hours. 'I can prove it. I can prove what I'm saying's true, can't I?'

'Really? And how are you going to do that?'

'Simple.' Gabriela reaches for the phone. 'We'll talk to the real Beth Beeby!'

*   *   *

Beth and Lucinda also ride up to their floor in a preoccupied silence. Around them, the other girls talk about the party—the amazing clothes, the super-cool people, and how the night couldn't have been more perfect if they'd dreamed it—while the more memorable moments of the evening (memorable because of how horrible and humiliating they were) play in Beth's mind like a slide show and Lucinda checks her arms for bruising.

233

And, almost like an echo of what is happening two floors away, as soon as they reach the privacy of their room, Lucinda says, 'What's got into you, Gabriela? You could've knocked my teeth out whamming into me like that! My father would have killed me after what they cost him.'

Beth drops onto the bed as if she has no bones. 'I'm sorry. I just— I had a fright.'

'You had a fright? Oh, really?' Lucinda kicks off her shoes as if she's angry at them. 'Was that why you screamed when that guy tried to help us up? I thought you'd ruptured my eardrum. I mean, really, Gab. He was trying to help us, not attack us.'

'I'm sorry. He—'

Lucinda holds up one hand. 'No, don't say it. Don't tell me he was your stalker.'

Beth doesn't say anything; she doesn't have to.

Lucinda sighs. 'I thought you said your stalker was one of the waiters. You said that was why you threw yourself across the room like that. But he couldn't be a guest too, could he? There are physical laws, you know. You can't wear two dresses at the same time, and you can't be in two different places at the same time.'

That's what you think, thinks Beth, but what she says is, 'Look, Lucinda, let's just forget it, OK? I said how sorry I am.' Indeed, she's beaten her own record of apologizing once every five minutes by at least two-hundred-and-forty seconds. 'It's been a very stressful day. Let's go to bed and pretend tonight never happened.'

As if.

'Stressful? Stressful means you break a nail or get a pimple five minutes before your date comes to pick you up. It doesn't mean that you forget how

234

to walk in heels. Or that you think every guy you see is a vampire.' Lucinda's lips come together to form a very small 'o', as if she's planning to suck the truth out of the air. 'Anyway, it's more than just tonight. You've been acting really freaky all day.' Her foot taps as though keeping time to music only she can hear. 'And since I'm the one who's been dragged on runaway buses and nearly knocked unconscious, I think I deserve to know why.'

There are quite a few things that it's easier to do if you feel you have nothing to lose. Taking risks, for example. Exposing yourself to humiliation. Telling the truth. And Beth, at last, realizes that she has nothing to lose.

'It's really hard to explain,' she says slowly. 'I mean, *really* hard. I can't even explain it to myself.'

Lucinda sits down, folding her hands on her lap as if she's waiting for the show to begin. 'Don't explain. Just tell me.'

Beth takes a deep, let's-go-up-this-mountain breath. 'I don't really know where to start.'

'Start at the beginning,' advises Lucinda.

By the time Beth gets to the end of her tale, she is in tears and Lucinda is sitting next to her with a box of tissues on her lap.

'Here.' Lucinda passes Beth a handful of tissues. 'Your face looks like it's melting.'

'Humphhumph,' snuffles Beth, dabbing at her eyes.

Lucinda pats Beth's shoulder. 'It'll be OK,' she says, but her tone is more hopeful than convinced. 'Really.' She doesn't dare ask herself how.

'The worst thing is that I'm ruining everything for Gabriela, and she's ruining everything for me,' sobs Beth.

'I'm not so sure that's the *worst* thing.' Lucinda hands her more tissues. 'The worst part for me would be being stuck in somebody else's body.' She shudders involuntarily. 'I mean, even if it's better than the one you had, it's pretty creepy, isn't it?'

Beth looks over at her, blinking. 'You mean you believe me?'

Lucinda shrugs. 'I'm not saying that it sounds really realistic or anything, but, let's face it, yesterday you knew more about fashion than I do, and today I wouldn't let you pick out a pair of socks for me.'

'I could be crazy, though. I could just be making it all up.'

'Yeah, you could be.' Lucinda shrugs again. 'But I figure that if you're not telling the truth, then you're so insane that they wouldn't have let you out of the clinic to come on this weekend in the first place.'

'So that leaves me with just one small problem,' says Beth.

Lucinda raises an eyebrow. 'You mean, what do you do now?'

Which is when the hotel phone rings.

*   *   *

Otto is already stretched out on the sofa when Remedios gets to their suite. He has a cold compress across his forehead, and is eating a plate of canapés and watching TV.

'What's with the washcloth?' Remedios shuts the door behind her.

Otto snuffles. 'I have a headache. A migraine, really. I feel as if my head is being crushed in a vice

236

and tiny microbes in steel stilettos are dancing on the backs of my eyes.'

Undoubtedly, he will blame her for this. 'Poor you,' mumbles Remedios, as sympathetic as a Grand Inquisitor. 'In case you're interested, my feet are killing me.' She flops into the armchair nearest the couch and kicks off the high heels she's been wearing all evening. 'I don't know who invented these things, but I hope he's enjoying Hell.'

'And I think I'm deaf in one ear,' complains Otto. There may be advantages to being human, but he can't see that flesh and blood are two of them. 'Sainted Solomon, but that girl can scream.'

Remedios, wiggling her toes to get the circulation back, stops and looks at him. 'Beth? You're the reason she screamed like that? I thought it was Aunt Joyce.'

'Aunt Joyce was the first scream.' Otto grimaces at the screen. 'The second scream was when I tried to help her get up from the floor.'

'Maybe she twisted her ankle when she fell,' says Remedios.

Otto shakes his head. 'No. She screamed at *me*. She looked me right in the eye and woke the dead of the next five counties.' He shakes his head again. 'And you know what else? She actually came after me at the party! I don't know how she recognized me, but one minute I was serving spring rolls and the next thing I knew she was baying like a banshee and trying to tackle me. Brought down two other waiters and the fashion editor of *The Los Angeles Times*. I was lucky to escape.' He chews thoughtfully on a canapé. 'Of course, she is very highly strung. You might recall that I warned

237

you about that. I said the swap would permanently damage her. But would you listen? No, you wouldn't. They'll be serving frozen yoghurt in Hell before you'd listen to me.'

'Oh, turn off the engine and give it a rest, Otto. Beth's not going to be damaged by the swap. I couldn't make her life worse if I tried, and I'm not. I'm trying to make it better.' For all the thanks she's likely to get. 'Besides, she's not highly strung, she's just neurotic. If she doesn't have something to worry about, she worries about that.' Remedios goes back to wiggling her toes. 'And that wasn't a war cry. That was a scream of fear.' She gives him a sideways look. 'Maybe she's more tuned into you than you think. It does happen. Maybe she's seen you even when you don't think she could have.'

He picks a canapé. 'What are you getting at?'

'Has it occurred to you that she might be afraid of you?'

'Of me?' Otto laughs. 'Why in the cosmos would she be afraid of me?'

IN THE INCUBATOR OF DESPERATION, PLOTS START HATCHING LIKE SPRING CHICKS

Things happen in hotels. The staff is used to that. How many arguments have they witnessed? How many fist fights? How many sleepwalkers padding through the lobby in their pyjamas? How many people trying to smuggle towels and linens out in their luggage? But these things pass, and in just that way tonight's disruptions have passed.

The Xanadu has returned to normal. Humming. Swishing. Bleeping softly. On the seventh floor, most of the guests are still out or already asleep—except in Room 803. In Room 803 nothing has returned to normal, and there is a strong suspicion among its occupants that it never will.

Gabriela and Delila are on one bed; Beth and Lucinda are across from them. There are several minutes of an eerie, so-this-is-what-trench-warfare-is-really-like silence when they first sit down, while the four of them just stare at each other. Delila and Lucinda look awkward and slightly embarrassed, but Beth and Gabriela look merely stupefied.

Gabriela is the first to speak. 'Wow, this is so weird.' She points at Beth. 'I mean, OMG! You are me! You really are!'

And vice versa, of course.

'It's spooky,' says Beth. 'Talk about putting yourself in somebody else's shoes. I'm sitting over there next to Delila, but I'm not. I'm sitting over here next to Lucinda.'

'Can't we talk about something else?' asks Lucinda. 'You two are creeping me out.'

'Oh, I'm so sorry,' says Gabriela, with exaggerated sweetness. 'We certainly don't want to upset *you*.'

'OK, OK, I know it's worse for you,' says Lucinda. 'I just meant—'

'The thing is, what else is there to talk about?' asks Delila. 'The weather? What we had for supper? I mean, it's kind of like what my granddad calls the tank-in-the-room syndrome, isn't it? You can pretend there isn't a tank in the room, but it's there. And, man, it is really big and it's heavily armed.'

239

'But it's not going to do any good talking about it,' Lucinda argues. 'I mean, it happened. But you don't know how. So you just have to hope that it unhappens. You know, eventually. You guys just have to wait till it does. There's nothing you can do, is there?'

'Oh no, you're wrong. There are dozens of things we can do,' says Beth. 'We can snap our fingers. Or chant a magic spell. Or pray to our guardian angels . . .' Her sigh sounds like something breaking. 'We just thought it'd be more fun to see how much we could mess up each others' lives.'

Gabriela groans. 'Oh, God . . . How did you know?'

'How did I know what?'

Gabriela looks over at Delila, but Delila is gazing at her feet as though she's never seen them before. 'Well . . .' Gabriela, too, is suddenly fascinated by Delila's feet. 'I haven't exactly been doing a great job of being you.' She gives Beth a wan smile. 'It's a hell of a lot harder than it looks.'

'It can't be as hard as being you,' says Beth. No dangerous clothes, no tricky make-up, no physical exertion. All she really has to do is just *be*: go to meals; go to museums; watch a play. She may not be gaining her any points, but, realistically, just how many could Gabriela be losing her? 'What does not exactly a great job mean?'

'It means Professor Gryck's really mad at you.' Gabriela's whole face squints, as if a very strong sun is in her eyes. 'She thinks you're deliberately trying to ruin her big weekend.'

'*Me?*' How is that possible? The girl across from her—herself—looks exactly as Beth is: meek and obedient; afraid to talk back to a recorded

240

announcement. 'What have I done?'

'You mean what *haven't* you done,' mutters Delila.

'It's not like I meant to do any of this stuff.' Gabriela's foot swings back and forth. 'It just kind of happened. It's, like, mainly I'm a victim.'

And so the whole tragic chain of events that is today is unwound. The miscalculations. The sudden impulses. The mistakes. The things that were *so* not her fault. 'Plus, your mother thought you were kidnapped,' Gabriela finishes. 'But I think I got that all straightened out.' She finally looks Beth— looks herself—in the eye. 'I'm really sorry.'

'Oh, it doesn't matter,' says the girl who only twenty-four hours ago thought everything mattered—that every single thing in the universe was out to get her. 'Besides, I haven't been doing too well as you, either.' Now Beth's smile takes on a certain wanness. 'I seriously doubt that Professor Gryck is more angry than Taffeta.'

'Taffeta Mackenzie?' Gabriela's image of Taffeta from the night before is of a charming, smiling, laughing woman wearing an awesome cocktail dress and Cartier jewellery. 'Taffeta's mad at me?'

'That's one way of putting it,' says Beth.

Lucinda rolls her eyes.

'It wasn't so bad to start with,' Beth explains. 'At first she just thought I was a klutz and kind of a clown. And she wasn't even that upset about us losing the others and getting on the bus and everything.'

'Or about the police,' says Lucinda helpfully. 'My mom would've gone ballistic if I came home in a cop car, but Taffeta was pretty cool. I figure that

241

kind of thing happens a lot in LA.'

'More often than you think,' says Gabriela. And, although she hadn't planned to mention this part of her story, she explains about Joe and taking the short cut through his property, and being picked up by the police. 'That kind of did it for me and Professor Gryck,' she finishes.

'It was the party tonight that did it for me and Taffeta,' Beth admits. 'It started out great. She thought I looked fantastic and everything was OK again but then it all fell apart in a pretty spectacular way. I think I really—' She searches for the right words to describe how things now stand between Taffeta and her. 'I really nuked the last remaining shred of goodwill.'

'Oh, God . . .' groans Gabriela. 'It's really that bad?'

Beth nods. 'She lost it in a major way.'

'You can say that again,' agrees Lucinda. 'You could've boiled a pot of water on her head she was so mad.'

To explain what happened at the party, Beth first has to explain about the man who's been following her from the moment they left the hotel this morning.

'I don't know how he did it, but I swear that everywhere we went, there he was. It's as if he planted some kind of homing device on me.'

'Only the rest of us never saw him,' puts in Lucinda. And then, catching the look Beth gives her, adds, 'I'm not saying I don't believe Ga— Beth. I'm just saying we never saw him.'

'Because he can vanish into the air,' says Beth. 'And then tonight, there he was at the party. Pretending to be a waiter. Handing out the spring rolls. What was I supposed to do? I couldn't help it. I panicked.' And brought down two waiters, one tray of smoked salmon, one tray of empty glasses and the fashion editor of *The Los Angeles Times*. 'If I mess up tomorrow, it won't matter if we ever get back to our own bodies. You'll never work in fashion unless you change your name and move to Milan.'

Gabriela smiles glumly. 'I think you might have to do something similar. Or write anonymously.'

'Maybe you should both get ill,' suggests Delila. 'Migraines all round.'

'That's a good idea,' says Lucinda. 'I mean, it's not like anybody's going to be devastated if either of you doesn't show up. They'll probably dance for joy.'

'Not Professor Gryck,' says Delila. 'She doesn't really strike me as much of a dancer. But she might click her heels together with a big smile on her face.'

Gabriela moans. 'This was going to be my major moment! I worked so hard. I was going to see *my* design modelled at a real fashion show. And I was so sure I was going to win the scholarship and maybe even get an internship in the summer . . .'

'Well, so was I. But if Professor Gryck thinks I'm trying to ruin her big weekend—'

Beth leans back on her elbows.

Gabriela rests her chin on her hands. 'And Taffeta thinks I'm nuts.'

'Let's not forget the part about something being bound to go wrong,' says Delila.

'That's right.' Lucinda nods. 'I mean, what if *he* shows up at the fashion show? What if you panic and bring down everybody on the runway or something like that?'

Beth groans, but Gabriela raises her head with a thoughtful, what-would-really-set-off-this-blouse look in her eyes. 'But *I* wouldn't.' She looks from one to the other. 'I don't know this guy. I couldn't tell the difference between him and a shoe salesman in Omaha. He hasn't been following *me*.'

'But he *has* been following you—' Beth breaks off. 'Oh. You mean . . . '

'Exactly. I dress as me. And you dress as you. We switch back! Manually. We'll still be in the wrong bodies, but we'll make them look as much like we really look as we can. So you can go to your writers' thing and I can go to the fashion show.' She beams. 'It solves all our problems.'

'But what about next week?' asks Beth.

Gabriela screws up her mouth for a second. 'At least as far as this weekend goes, it solves all our problems. We can worry about next week after this is over.' She hugs herself. 'Oh, Cinderella, you shall go to the ball . . .'

*   *   *

Shortly after midnight, it suddenly starts to rain. This is a surprise rain, unpredicted by any of the sophisticated weather forecasts for the area, and it falls so fiercely and thickly that the lights of the city seem to dim and instead of waking people it drives them deeper into sleep as if they're crawling into a cave for safety.

Otto and his migraine have gone to bed, but Remedios stands at the sliding glass doors of the terrace, staring into the night. Thunder rolls down from the mountains—an avalanche of sound.

Spears of light rip open the preternatural darkness. If you saw her there, you'd see a young woman in a striped cotton nightshirt and fluffy slippers watching a storm, but, of course, that is not who or what Remedios really is. She is formless and timeless; a traveller of centuries and galaxies; as real as light, as luminous as hope.

She is holding something in her hand and as another volley of thunder moves towards the valley, she takes her eyes from the glass to look at it. Sitting on her palm is the small clay figure of a dancer. A thousand years ago, when it was made, it was brightly painted and wore feathers and a tiny necklace made of shells. Then, if you looked at it long enough, it seemed to move; if you held it up against the sky, it seemed to shimmer with the stars. The shells and feathers and paint are all long gone, but as a wave of lightning bleaches the sky, the tiny figure shifts with the drumming of the rain. 'The universe always seeks balance . . .' Remedios murmurs to the dancer. 'That's why it's always changing.'

Another wash of purple light illuminates the skyline.

'Right now it looks like it's seeking revenge,' says Otto from behind her.

She doesn't turn round.

'Everything's going really wrong, Remedios.'

'Maybe.'

'Maybe?' He stands beside her, but what Otto sees as he looks out at the watery night is not what Remedios sees. 'I don't see that there's any maybe about it.'

Remedios folds her hand around the dancer. If something is off-balance, it can only be righted by

245

movement.

'You started this, Remedios,' says Otto. 'And you have to end it. You can't let them go into those award ceremonies tomorrow as someone they're not. You have to straighten it all out.'

A breaker of rain smashes against the terrace doors.

'I will,' says Remedios. 'But I'll need your help.'

ANOTHER EXAMPLE OF HOW THINGS RARELY GO AS PLANNED

'Oh my God!' yelps Lucinda. 'Will you look at the time? We have to get going. We don't want to be late.'

She and Gabriela have been up for hours. Several miracles had to be performed: on Beth Beeby's short, badly cut hair the colour of cardboard; on Beth Beeby's plain face, as exciting as a boiled egg. And then they had to pick the perfect outfit for the first part of the morning's programme—the awards' ceremony.

'That's it,' says Lucinda, fastening the last of a jangle of gold necklaces around Gabriela's neck. 'Let's see how you look.'

Gabriela takes a gulp of air. She hasn't felt this nervous since her first day at middle school, when she changed her outfit three times, brought an extra pair of shoes with her in case she'd picked the wrong ones, and decided to buy her lunch rather than risk showing up with a loser lunch box. 'Well?' she asks. 'What do you think?'

Lucinda steps back and gives Gabriela a

critical appraisal. There was nothing they could do about the length of Beth's hair, but they dyed it blonde and gelled it so that it circles her head like a halo. Gabriela, an artist not only with a needle and thread but with a make-up brush as well, has changed Beth's plain features and sallow complexion into a face that might look at you from the cover of a magazine. The open-toed platforms and filmy dress in a patchwork of different patterns complete the transformation.

'It's incredible,' Lucinda says at last. 'I mean, I knew we could make you look better, but you look better than better. You look—' She hesitates for the bat of an eyelash, as if she's afraid to say the secret words. 'You totally look like one of us!'

Gabriela allows herself a few seconds of being pretty pleased with herself, then she puts Beth's glasses on again so she can actually see and turns back to the mirror for a final check. 'But I still don't look like me.' She frowns at her reflection (in which, if you looked very hard, you might see the unremarkable face of Beth Beeby peering through). 'Everybody's going to know it's someone else.'

'You look more like you without the glasses, so if they don't get too close they probably won't notice,' judges Lucinda. 'Anyway, it's only Taffeta who really matters. If you can keep out of her sight till the show starts, it'll be OK.'

Gabriela raises one carefully brushed eyebrow. 'You think?'

'I *know*. Everybody's going to be all wrapped up in themselves. Besides,' says Lucinda, 'even if somebody does say something, you *are* you, right? You're not Beth pretending to be you. You made

247

that dress. You did your face. You did your hair. You know what to say and how to act. Guaranteed, you'll be able to talk them round.'

Gabriela makes an exaggerated gesture of relief. 'Phew! At least I don't have to pretend to know anything about books any more.'

*   *   *

'What are you doing in there?' Delila rattles the doorknob. 'It's almost show time. Professor Gryck's going to go into meltdown if we get there late.'

'I'm coming! I'm coming!' Beth gives herself one last look in the mirror, puts her spare pair of glasses on, and opens the bathroom door.

Delila whistles. 'Well, kiss my grits,' she says, laughing. 'Will you look at you!' Slowly shaking her head, her eyes move up and down the girl in the sober grey dress and sensible shoes. 'You look almost like you!'

Beth steps in front of the full-length mirror on the closet door. 'What about the hair?' She squints at her reflection through the thick lenses. 'You think the hair's all right?'

Beth and Delila have also been up and busy for hours performing miracles while the rest of their group dreamed and snored, turning the silk purse that is Gabriela Menz into the sow's ear that is Lillian Beeby's only child. They cut off Gabriela's blonde curls, darkened them with a box of henna from the hotel's drugstore and flattened them with Gabriela's electric hair straightener. Topped off with the understatement that is Beth's wardrobe, it's possible that Mrs Menz herself would walk by her without wondering, even for a nanosecond, if

248

that girl reminded her of Gabriela.

'The hair looks dynamic. A little longer than it was, but no one's going to notice that.'

'You mean because nobody looked at me that closely to begin with?'

'That's right.' Delila puts on a deep, portentous voice. 'It's grey and brown and it's wearing glasses—it must be Beth Beeby!'

Beth laughs. 'I knew there had to be some advantage to being geeky and invisible. I just could never figure out what it was.'

Delila picks up her bag. 'So I guess it's time to strut our stuff.'

'At least I can walk without falling over,' says Beth.

*   *   *

At one side of the lobby of The Hotel Xanadu, stands a calendar of the day's events. *Welcome Tomorrow's Writers Today: Cary Grant Conference Hall,* it says in plastic letters. Underneath that, also in plastic letters, it says, *Welcome The City of Angels College of Fashion and Design: Grace Kelly Room.*

On one of the sofas in front of the desk, with a view of both the elevators and the calendar of events, sits Otto Wasserbach in a pinstriped suit and horn-rimmed glasses. Otto has been sitting here since the restaurant opened for breakfast, pretending to be reading a very thick thriller, but in reality keeping watch for Gabriela and Beth. Meanwhile, Remedios Cienfuegos y Mendoza, having made certain that only one elevator is working, has been riding up and down in it for hours. It has been, to say the least, a long and

249

tedious morning. Otto's book, compared with his own experiences, is about as exciting as a cup of warm milk; and if there is anything more boring than silently and swiftly going up and down and down and up in a metal box, Remedios doesn't want to know what it is.

Nonetheless, they are both feeling confident as the breakfast hours pass and the time for the day's events draws nearer. There is no way today's plan can go wrong. Remedios has taken everything that might possibly go wrong into consideration and has prepared for every contingency. There are distractions that can be made; delays that can occur; diversions that can be created—should one of the girls make an appearance before the other comes downstairs. That is Otto's job. One way or another, Gabriela and Beth will find themselves in the same place at the same time. It won't take a second to switch them back, and the change should be complete even before they take their seats.

Remedios is almost wishing that she'd brought a newspaper with her so she'd have something to do, when the doors open and several chattering girls step in, among them Lucinda and her room-mate, almost glowing in the bright colours of their make-up and clothes. Remedios doesn't look at them, but keeps her head lowered so that no one sees her smile but the floor. At the next stop, Delila and her room-mate get in. Remedios can't believe her luck. This is going to be even easier than she'd hoped. Gabriela and Beth stand only inches away from Remedios—close enough to one another to touch, but not so much as giving each other a fleeting look. The elevator hits the ground like a feather falling on a cushion, and, in the instant before the doors swish open, Remedios lays a gentle hand on the girls in front of her. *Bingo!*

Otto peers over the top of his book as the elevator doors open. And nearly cries out loud. They're both inside! Standing next to each other. If he needed a signal that they're doing the right thing, then this is it. He leans back with a sigh of relief, and watches the girls walk out, hurrying towards the calendar of the day's events. The last person out of the elevator is Remedios, a smile on her face like a sunny day.

'Holy Hosanna!' says Otto as Remedios fairly floats towards him. 'You did it!' But he wouldn't be Otto without a second thought. 'You did do it, didn't you?'

'Yes, of course I did. Beth's back in her body, and Gabriela's back in hers.' Remedios smiles condescendingly. 'Happy now?'

'Yes. Yes, I am happy.' Otto stands up, tucking his book under his arm. 'Let's go back to that taqueria for breakfast. We've got a couple of hours before the winners are announced. Celebrate with a burrito.'

Remedios, always a wing beat or two ahead of Otto Wasserbach, turns so she can see Beth and Gabriela walking along as if they know where they're going. She allows herself a small but satisfied smile, but it disappears almost immediately. It will take a minute or two before the switch back is completed and everything's normal again, and yet Gabriela sails along effortlessly in her platforms and holds a pair of glasses in one hand; and Beth wears her glasses pushed down her nose so that she's actually looking over them. And then Remedios realizes the horrible truth. Merciful

Michael, they've taken each others' places! Remedios turns back to Otto. 'You know, I think we better stay here.'

'Stay here? Why should we stay here?'

'I think that, perhaps, there's been a little complication,' says Remedios. 'But it isn't my fault.'

Otto closes his eyes and groans very softly. 'Oh, no, now what's gone wrong?'

*   *   *

Gabriela wears the smile of a winner—head held high, eyes as bright as Venus, so happy that it's all she can do not to laugh out loud. Oh, but it feels good to be wearing her own clothes again, even if she's not in her own body. To be attractive; visible as a gazelle on a golf course. To see the way people look at her as she struts along the corridor.

'Wait a minute.' Gabriela stops by the door of the women's room. 'I just want to check my make-up before we go in.'

'I thought we didn't want to attract attention by being late.' Lucinda points down the hall. A line of people, as glamorous as a diamond necklace, is slowly moving past the guards and into the Grace Kelly Room. 'Everybody's going in.'

'Two minutes,' promises Gabriela. 'Two minutes isn't going to make any difference.'

But Lucinda has had quite a weekend herself and isn't about to have her better judgement derailed now. 'I know your two minutes, Gab. You have a compact. Check your make-up here.'

Meanwhile, Beth and Delila walk slowly because Beth has to pause every so often to adjust her glasses to see where she is. Nevertheless, Beth, too, is about as happy as a bear at a dump to be back in her own persona, if not her own person. It makes her feel more positive about the future. Optimistic. Surely this is the solution to her and Gabriela's dilemma. It may take their family and friends a little while to get used to, but this is all they have to do; just change their styles. Even Lillian Beeby will have to accept that although her daughter is a little blonder, has 20/20 vision and can eat nuts, she is still her Beth. Isn't she the one who always says, 'It's what's inside that counts'? Yes, she very definitely is.

'Dang it, but this is going to be one giant of a story to tell our grandchildren,' Delila says as they come in sight of the Cary Grant Conference Hall. 'Can't you just picture their faces? Their eyes'll pop out.'

'Delila!' Beth stops suddenly. Her voice is low, but urgent and not particularly optimistic. 'Delila! Wait.'

Delila turns around. 'Uh-oh.' Delila has only been on two boats in her life: the Circle Line cruise around Manhattan and the Staten Island Ferry. In both cases, the day was clear and bright and the water was as calm as a garden pond. Delila, however, is not a sailor and might as well have been in a washbasin in the middle of the Atlantic during a hurricane. Beth looks the way those boat trips made her feel. 'What's wrong?'

'Delila?' The girl whose skin is suddenly tinged with green takes off Beth's glasses and looks down at her hands. The nails, though clean of polish, have been cut, not gnawed to nubs. The skin is lightly tanned. She moves her gaze to her chest. She no longer has the physique of a twelve-year-old boy. 'Oh my God,' breathes Gabriela. 'I'm *me*!'

Delila is now standing very close, staring into those dark blue eyes. 'When you say *me*, which me is it you mean?'

'Gabriela.' Her voice squeaks. 'I'm *me*, Gabriela.'

And it is at just about this same moment—as Delila groans and the girl who a minute ago was Beth Beeby blinks back a tear—that Gabriela snaps the compact shut and slips it back into her bag.

'Ready?' says Lucinda. 'Let's go,' and she starts off down the hall.

Gabriela doesn't follow. 'Lucinda?' she calls. 'Lucinda, I don't feel well.' Her voice wobbles, as do her legs. She leans against the wall. 'I'm kind of dizzy.' Beneath the foundation, blush and toners her skin is colourless. She tugs at her skirt, which suddenly seems to have shrunk. 'And I'm having trouble walking.'

Lucinda sighs, but turns round. 'For Pete's sake, Gab, it's just nerves. You'll be OK once we get inside.'

'I don't have butterflies. I feel weird.' She feels like a wet cotton ball. Boneless. Weightless. Her voice breaks as she mutters, 'Something's wrong.'

'Gabriela?' Lucinda walks back to her, very slowly. Paintings have atmospheres. Rooms have atmospheres. Cities have atmospheres. And people have atmospheres, too. Lucinda can feel that the atmosphere that is Gabriela Menz has suddenly changed. Again. 'Gabriela, is that you?'

'No,' says Beth, the wooziness passing. 'It's me.'

Delila and Gabriela are already hurrying towards them.

One of the differences between this morning

254

and yesterday morning is, of course, that this morning neither Gabriela nor Beth is alone. They have Lucinda and Delila; they have each other. Another difference is that this body swap, though unexpected, isn't quite the terrifying shock it was yesterday. And they've changed back to who they were, too, which should be good news.

'So there's no problem.' Lucinda looks from Gabriela to Beth to Delila. 'Right?'

'Right,' says Delila. 'Everything's back to normal.' At least, she thinks it is; it's getting hard to tell.

'Normal? You call this normal?' Gabriela doesn't share their cheerful smiles. 'How do you figure that?'

'What do you mean?' Delila's smile looks slightly less cheerful and her eyes dart to Lucinda for moral support. 'You're Gabriela, in Gabriela's body.' She nods to the girl across from her. 'And she's Beth, in Beth's body. That's called back to normal.'

'You're forgetting something.' Beth, also, looks less than joyous.

'And what's that?'

Beth opens her arms. *Tada!* 'I'm dressed as Gabriela.'

Gabriela makes a curtsey. 'And I'm dressed as Beth.'

And there isn't time to change; the doors of both rooms will be shut within minutes and no one else allowed in.

Delila shrugs. 'OK, so maybe it's not ideal, but for now you'll have to keep pretending to be each other.'

'It's only for a few more hours,' adds Lucinda. 'I mean, it's a bummer that you'll miss the show, Gab, but, you know, after everything that's happened . . . I mean, it's not really a big deal, right?'

'Wrong.' Gabriela isn't looking at any of them now, but at the entrance to the Grace Kelly Room. Another minute or two and she would've been in her seat. 'There's no way I'm missing the show.' Not after all she's been through. 'I'm going in.'

'But you can't,' bleats Lucinda.

'Why can't I?'

Lucinda throws a help-me look at Delila.

Which Delila obligingly catches. 'Because you look like Beth Beeby, that's why. They'd be nuts to let you in.'

'They have to let her in if she has a ticket.' Beth removes hers from her bag and hands it to Gabriela.

Delila moans. 'Oh, mama . . . Don't tell me you think *you're* going into the writers' gig dressed like a body-spray commercial?'

'I'd like somebody to try to stop me,' says Beth.

THE MOMENT THEY'VE BEEN WAITING FOR

The Cary Grant Conference Hall is, in fact, an auditorium with staggered rows of seats and a stage across the far wall. It is a windowless room, lit indirectly, climate controlled and acoustically advanced, so that pins can be heard to drop no matter where you sit and no one has to shout to be heard or tap the mic or blanch when the sound system shrieks. Its anodyne walls have been decorated for the occasion with large black-and-white photographs of famous writers (Hemingway with a dead animal, Tolstoy with a beard, Jane Austen with a cap on her head), creating an atmosphere that is at once exotic and intellectual.

Every English department in every college in the area has been invited to this landmark event, and almost every seat is taken. The finalists in the Tomorrow's Writers Today competition sit in the middle of the front row, ready to take their turns at the podium, flanked by the distinguished writers and academics who acted as judges. Professor Gryck (who will be giving the opening address) stands like a sentry on the bottom step of the stairs that lead to the right side of the stage.

Among her many skills and talents, Professor Gryck is a consummate multitasker. Although she is busier than a Viking raiding party this morning, she knows exactly who is seated and waiting for the ceremony to begin—and who isn't. Beth Beeby. Of course. Who else? Apparently Beth Beeby is, if not the Devil's spawn, at least a close relative, who for some reason is determined to undermine Professor Gryck every chance she gets and is doing a splendid, almost inspired, job of it—so splendid that not even two run-ins with the law have been enough to make her stop. Professor Gryck looks at her watch. And then back to the two empty seats in the front row. Where in the name of Snorri Sturluson is she?

Being the proactive kind of person that she is, Professor Gryck doesn't hover hopefully at the front of the stage waiting for something to happen. Smiling grimly, she marches up the aisle to see for herself if there's any sign of Beth. She reaches the door just as it opens and Delila Greaves and

257

some blonde walk in. Though, like the rest of us, she often hides the fact, Professor Gryck is not a stupid woman. For a few seconds, she's puzzled by the apparition in front of her—where did she come from? what is she doing here?—but then she realizes that the shining blonde in the aggressively trendy suit and cinderblock platforms hasn't stumbled in here by mistake; she is none other than the drab and colourless Beth Beeby herself. She can just make out the small, pinched features under the make-up and the tiny bat wings that have been glued to her lashes. Professor Gryck is not the sort of person to giggle, but the corners of her mouth do twitch. You almost have to admire the girl. What better way to damage her authority and the integrity of the event than to turn up looking like you're going to a party?

'You're late,' she says, her eyes on Delila. 'Go and sit down.'

Delila, who'd expected more resistance, scuttles forward with relief.

But when Beth starts to wobble after her, Professor Gryck puts out a hand to stop her. 'Where do you think you're going?'

Though Beth, of course, would have preferred to tiptoe to her seat without attracting the professor's attention, she doesn't yet realize that there's a problem.

'I'm going to sit down.'

'Sit down?' Professor Gryck looks at her as if she said she was going to get her camel. 'Oh, I don't think so.'

'Professor Gryck.' Beth moves her head forward and smiles. 'Professor Gryck, it's me. Beth. Beth Beeby.'

'I know who you are.' Arms folded, mouth set, Professor Gryck has become an immovable force. 'But you're not coming in here looking like that.'

Beth blinks. 'I'm not?'

'No, you're not.' She leans forward to speak directly into Beth's ear. 'I have worked very hard for this day, young lady, and neither you nor anyone else is going to ruin it for me.'

'I don't want to ruin it,' says Beth, with remarkable calm and reasonableness considering the morning she's had already. 'I just want to take part.'

'You listen to me.' Professor Gryck's words hit the air like hail hitting the ground. 'This is a literary consortium, not an audition for some Hollywood movie. I will not have it cheapened and debased by the likes of you.'

'Me?' If only Professor Gryck were as reasonable as Beth. 'But that's ridiculous. I'm *me*. I'm exactly the same person I was when you met me.'

'No, you're not. Then you were a serious, sensible young woman. Now, you're a . . . a party girl.'

'No, I'm not. I'm one of the finalists. You can't keep me out.'

'Oh, but that's where you're wrong. I don't know who you are. You are not the girl whose photo is in our brochure. If I asked any of the others to pick Beth Beeby out of a line-up, they wouldn't pick you, believe me.'

'Delila would.'

'That's one out of twenty.' None too gently, Professor Gryck takes hold of Beth and propels her into the hall. 'Let me assure you that if you try to get back in here, I'll call security and have you

259

forcibly removed.' She turns to the young woman from the hotel who's been given the job of keeping out latecomers. 'Did you hear that? If I see this girl inside again, you'll find yourself working in a motel in Nebraska.' With which pronouncement, the leading authority on the Norse sagas steps back into the auditorium and shuts the door behind her.

'She's bluffing.'

These words so exactly echo Beth's own thoughts, that for a second she thinks that she spoke them out loud. And then she realizes that it's the hotel clerk who spoke them out loud, though she doesn't realize that this is not the same clerk who let her and Delila in only minutes before.

'Excuse me?'

'She's bluffing. She can't have you forcibly removed.'

'You don't think so?'

'No way. And I have no intention of keeping you out. But I think you should ditch those shoes before you hurt yourself.' Remedios, who beat Otto sixteen rounds at jan-ken-pon to be the one to sit in on the writers' event, goes over to the door and cracks it open. 'She has her back to us,' she whispers. 'Come on.'

Two days ago, an invitation like this would have sent Beth running back to her room. Now, however, she merely nods and, holding the offending shoes, quickly follows the young woman inside. They've already slipped into two miraculously empty seats at the back, slouching so they can't be seen behind the heads of the people in front of them, when Professor Gryck takes the stage.

'Firstly, I have to say that it is an honour for me to welcome you all to the First Annual Tomorrow's

Writers Today Symposium on behalf of our generous sponsors . . .'

Remedios closes her eyes. 'Wake me up when it gets interesting,' she whispers.

*   *   *

The man at the door of the Grace Kelly Room (an actor who's played a CIA agent in several forgotten movies and was very good in the role) lets Gabriela in with a puzzled smile but with no argument. She does, after all, have a ticket, and she is with someone who isn't dressed like a pilgrim and obviously belongs. 'Enjoy yourselves,' he says, looking at Lucinda, and winks.

Nonetheless, it's just as well that Taffeta Mackenzie, though also good at multitasking, is not at all skilled at astral projection and can only be in one place at a time. At the moment, that place is in the makeshift 'dressing room' off the service corridor where the models are getting ready for the show.

At last, Gabriela has her wish: even dressed as Beth, people are looking at her. Though with curiosity, not envy, of course. *Who is that girl?* their eyes say. *What on Earth is she doing here?* Ignoring the looks, she and Lucinda hurry inside, choosing seats at the back next to a young man impeccably dressed in a retro-eighties way (bespoke, hand-stitched pinstripe suit set off by a plain navy T-shirt and sandals), who shows no surprise at the unlikely sight that is Gabriela but nods and smiles. Lucinda, unaware that she has seen this very handsome young man before, nudges Gabriela. They both smile back.

261

The lights dim. Taffeta slips into a seat at the front, next to the runway, surrounded by journalists and photographers. *So far, so good*, thinks Gabriela. By the time Taffeta sees Gabriela, the graduate show will be well underway—or possibly even over. This is a comforting thought. They may get through the entire collection and be ready to announce the winner of the contest by the time Taffeta spots her. What's Taffeta going to do then? She can't throw Gabriela out. Not in front of all these people. Not if she's the winner. Gabriela leans back in her seat to enjoy the show.

*   *   *

As we all know only too well by now, things don't always go the way they're planned. Which makes this day pretty special, because, at both of the events taking place at The Hotel Xanadu, everything sails along like a sloop with a good wind on a calm sea. No one falls on the runway; no one stumbles over his or her words. The distinguished writers and academics give short speeches about the role of books in the twenty-first century and how much they enjoyed judging the competition, and only two people doze through these speeches, one of whom is Remedios. Likewise, the designs on show are faultlessly presented and modelled, and greeted with 'oh's and 'ah's and bursts of applause. The work, the tears, the worries and tantrums were all worth it. Feelings of pride and triumph fill the air.

And then—finally—the moments that everyone's been waiting for arrive.

In the Cary Grant Conference Hall, Professor

Gryck introduces her surprise guest, who will present the winners and call them to the stage to receive their prizes and read their work.

'It is my great honour and pleasure,' says Professor Gryck, 'to welcome a writer who needs no introduction to any serious reader of contemporary literature. JC Ferryman is one of the most respected, influential and admired writers of the last forty years . . . '

Beth gives Remedios a nudge. 'It's starting to get interesting,' she whispers, as Professor Gryck continues in her praise—detailing into how many languages JC Ferryman's work has been translated, how many universities and colleges teach it and how many awards it has won. 'They're about to announce the winners.'

In the Grace Kelly Room, the graduate show has ended and, as the presenter prepares for the showing of the clothes made by the finalists in The City of Angels College of Fashion and Design's annual contest, Taffeta Mackenzie scans the room to see where everyone's sitting.

'Holy Mother,' she mutters, when her eyes fall on Lucinda and the girl sitting beside her. Having been a model herself, Taffeta is a master of disguise, who can change her look at the drop of a false nail. Despite the clothes, the hair and the glasses, she recognizes Gabriela immediately. 'What in the name of haute couture is she doing?' Maybe Gabriela Menz is having a breakdown. She's certainly been acting as if she's having a breakdown. Some people can't hack this business, that's all there is to it. Or maybe she's been hired by a rival to sabotage Taffeta Mackenzie and her school. The duplicitous witch.

Smiling as if life is nothing but good news, Taffeta unobtrusively leaves her seat.

But she isn't smiling as she comes up behind Gabriela; she looks as if she's about to spit pins. Leaning over her she says, very clearly and far from softly, enunciating every syllable, 'Get out of here, Miss Menz. Get out of here right now.'

Gabriela, Lucinda and even Otto have been watching the show with trance-like attention and never saw Taffeta leave her seat. Startled, the three of them turn.

'Did you hear me, Miss Menz?' Taffeta demands. 'I want you to get out of this room this very minute.'

'What?' says Gabriela

'You heard me. I've had all of you I'm going to take. I don't know if you think you're being funny or if you're wilfully trying to humiliate me or what, but I am not going to let you ruin this day for me.'

'But what about my dress?' Gabriela looks from Taffeta Mackenzie's angry face to the runway. 'Bring on Tomorrow' has begun to play; the show is about to start. 'Why should I leave?'

'Why?' Taffeta glares down at her. *My God, she's actually wearing tights!* 'Because you look like you have as much interest in fashion as a raccoon, that's why. You standing up there and taking credit for the angel dress would be like a monkey getting up and taking credit for Dior's spring collection.'

'But that's ridiculous,' Gabriela protests. 'The angel dress is my design. What does it matter what I'm wearing?'

'Out.' Taffeta nods towards the man standing at the entrance as though he's waiting for an emergency. 'Or I'll have you thrown out.'

The fact that Otto doesn't believe in the kind of interference practised by Remedios doesn't mean that he doesn't believe in any interference at all.

He leans across Lucinda to say to Gabriela, 'Stay right where you are. You're not going anywhere, except up to the runway to receive your prize.'

Taffeta's head appears over Gabriela's shoulder. 'And who in God's name are *you*?'

'Ah . . .' says Otto. 'That's it, precisely.'

* * *

JC Ferryman walks slowly onto the stage, leaning on a walking stick topped with a silver ball. He wears a rumpled suit that he bought twenty years ago for occasions such as this, and he is the other member of the audience who found it hard to stay awake during the speeches. Much to Professor Gryck's disappointment, he wastes no time giving a speech of his own, but mumbles a few words of greeting and rips open the first envelope.

'In third place . . .' A small smile flickers across his face '. . . is Ms Elizabeth Beeby.' In the wings, Professor Gryck gives a gasp of surprise. Beth has been such an annoyance that she forgot that she might actually win something. JC Ferryman glances at the front row. 'For her short story, A—'

'Oh, I'm so sorry.' Professor Gryck lands beside the great writer so suddenly that he teeters. She puts one hand over the mic. 'Mea culpa, I should have said that I'm afraid Ms Beeby isn't able to be with us this morning.'

JC Ferryman looks almost disappointed. 'She's not here?'

Professor Gryck shakes her head. Sadly. 'I'm

265

afraid not.'

'Yes, I am! Here I am! I'm right here!'

Though she doesn't actually remember leaving her seat, Beth is walking down the centre aisle, sure and steady in her stockinged feet. And suddenly, though she has no idea how, she knows for certain that JC Ferryman is Joe. Joe, the man who sprained his ankle. The man Delila and Gabriela helped home.

'Look at her!' hisses Professor Gryck. 'That is not Beth Beeby.'

Delila hears her. 'Yes, it is!' She is on her feet. 'Joe!' she calls. 'Joe, it's me, Delila. Don't you remember me and Beth?'

'Of course I remember you,' he says, but he is squinting at the figure marching towards him, looking confused. 'What have you done to your hair? You look a little different . . . '

'Joe!' Beth waves. 'Joe! I see the peas worked.'

And JC Ferryman, whose reputation as a curmudgeon is perhaps slightly exaggerated, smiles. 'Like a regular miracle,' he says.

THINGS GO BACK TO NORMAL—MORE OR LESS

There have been several historic firsts in the lives of Beth Beeby and Gabriela Menz in the last few days, and now here is another one. On Monday morning, they walk to school together. There's nothing like shaving someone else's legs and dressing someone else's body to forge a bond.

'It still seems like some kind of dream, doesn't

266

it?' says Gabriela as they mooch along.

'I know what you mean,' says Beth. 'I was sitting on the couch with my mother last night and it was so normal I thought I must've hallucinated the whole weekend.'

'Me, too.' Gabriela laughs. 'Even this morning. There were a couple of seconds when I woke up when I really thought I had been dreaming.' Till she checked in the mirror and saw that her hair was still short and brown.

'But it did happen.' Beth sighs. 'And we'll never know why.' They've been over the events of the weekend several times—at the airport, on the plane and over the phone late into the night—but there is, of course, no reasonable explanation. Not in this world. 'I guess we should just be grateful that everything turned out OK.'

'Better than OK.' Despite the fact that she looked as if she belonged to some weird religious cult, Gabriela and her angel dress received a standing ovation at the fashion show. They loved her design. And they loved her. She was different; unique; a breath of extraordinarily fresh air. As one journalist put it: 'If you think fashion is a dog that chases its own tail, you haven't met Gabriela Menz'. 'It was like a miracle. Taffeta was really going to kick me out, but that guy sitting next to us just looked at her and she totally backed down. It was awesome. Like he had magic powers. And now she thinks I'm the best thing since the electric sewing machine.'

'The miracle was that you and Delila rescued JC Ferryman when he hurt his ankle,' says Beth. 'That was the miracle.' Who knows what would have happened if they hadn't. It's certainly unlikely that Professor Gryck would have had a change of heart about Beth if it hadn't been for him. 'He only came because of you two.' It seems that Mr Ferryman, who in spite of twisting his ankle had had a more enjoyable afternoon than usual, didn't feel he could leave two such spirited young writers to the ponderous care of his sister-in-law, Professor Gryck. 'And then there's that woman who snuck me back in. I don't think I would've had the nerve without her.'

Gabriela looks over at her. 'You don't think that our guy and your woman could've had something to do with the—' Somehow, in the bright light of a spring morning, on a familiar road in their quiet town, it's hard for Gabriela to actually say the words *body swap*. 'You know.'

'A hotel clerk and a fashion hound?' Beth shakes her head. 'No way. It was just a lucky coincidence.'

Still mulling over the last two days, they turn into the school grounds.

'Gabriela!' Mr Sturgess, in his usual unironed corduroys and throwback tweed jacket, his old beat-up briefcase in one hand and a thermal cup in the other, lopes towards them across the parking lot.

'Hi, Mr Sturgess!' In another break with tradition, Gabriela doesn't think how much she'd like to take him shopping, but that she'd probably find his class really interesting if she tried a little harder. Which she just might do.

He catches up with them with a smile. 'How was your weekend?'

'It was cool,' says Gabriela as he falls into step beside them. 'I won the contest. Isn't that awesome? And guess what else?'

'You met a movie star?'

Gabriela laughs. 'Not a movie star.'

'I give up.' He wouldn't guess this if he had a million years.

'I met this really famous writer.'

Mr Sturgess half smiles. 'At the fashion show?'

'No . . . in the Hills. Me and my friend got lost in the Hollywood Hills? And we met JC Ferryman. You've heard of him, right?'

Edward Sturgess nods. Slowly. The wonder is that Gabriela's heard of him. 'Yeah. Yeah, of course. I'm more than familiar with his work.'

'He's supposed to be a really good writer.'

The teacher nods again. 'He is. He's very good. One of the best.'

'Right. So I was thinking . . . You know our big book report for the term? I figure maybe I'll do one of his novels for it.'

'Really? One of his?' He tries not to sound discouraging. 'They're pretty com—they're pretty long, you know.'

'Oh, I know,' says Gabriela breezily. 'They had a couple at the airport.'

It is only now, as they approach the main entrance, that Mr Sturgess realizes that the girl walking with them is Beth Beeby. Gabriela's always doing things to change her looks, but Beth always looks exactly the same. Until today. 'I'm so sorry, Beth. I didn't recognize you.' He gives her a bemused smile. 'You seem different.'

'My hair's lighter.'

He shakes his head. 'No . . . No . . . It's something else.' He's often felt that Beth is never completely present; but she's very present today. Taller. Straighter. Unworried. 'So did you have a

269

good weekend, too?'

'It was great. I had a lot of fun.' And though she usually keeps her sentences short and infrequent, Beth goes on, 'Plus, I came third in the competition.'

He glances over at her. Third and she's smiling? 'I hope you weren't too disappointed.'

Beth shakes her head. 'No. I think third place is really good. Besides, what's important is that I enjoyed writing that story. That's what really matters, isn't it?'

'Yeah.' He nods. 'Yeah, I'd say so.'

'And I met JC Ferryman, too, which is something I never dreamed would happen. He was amazing, Mr Sturgess. Not like you'd think a famous writer would be. He said next time I go to LA I should call him. My mother and I are going to have dinner with him and his wife.'

'Well, well . . .' says Edward Sturgess. Beth Beeby and her mother sitting down to dinner with JC Ferryman. Apparently he missed the blue moon on the weekend. 'What do you know about that.'

He watches the girls walk off to their lockers, their heads together in earnest conversation.

That must have been one hell of a weekend.

*   *   *

Otto is glad to be back in Jeremiah. The weekend wasn't all bad—he's definitely developed a taste for both black-bean burritos and convertible sports cars—but it was draining. He can't help thinking that it would be a lot less stressful to guard Heaven's Gate with a flaming sword than face down Taffeta Mackenzie (though he did it well, and with considerable panache). At the moment, he and Remedios are sitting on the south lawn of the high school, covered in sunshine and surrounded by students on their lunch breaks. Some of the students are talking excitedly; some are texting; some are playing games; a few have their heads bent over a book. Remedios and Otto are bickering.

'Did I say that we weren't successful?' He shakes his head. Very firmly. 'No, I never said that, Remedios.' He didn't. Even Otto has had to admit that, despite the problems and complications and difficult personalities of Ms Mackenzie and Professor Gryck, he and Remedios did a very good job. Not only did Beth and Gabriela do well in their respective contests, but there's no doubt that they both changed for the better. Beth has started thinking of life as an adventure rather than a competition, and Gabriela is knocking down the walls of the closet that is her mind and putting much more in it than she did before. 'What I said is that next time we might not be so lucky. That's what I said.'

'Luck, schmuck,' says Remedios. 'I knew what I was doing. *I* never doubted for a second that everything would turn out fine. I planned the whole thing.'

'Of course you did,' says Otto. 'And where were you when that dragon—what's her name? Organza . . .'

'Taffeta.'

'When she tried to throw Gabriela out of the show and do her out of first prize? Was that also part of your plan?'

'I was taking care of the other dragon, the one

271

with the doctorate, that's where I was.' Remedios pulls a blade of grass from the lawn. 'And besides, I knew you could handle the situation.'

'And what if I hadn't?' Otto persists. 'You would've ruined poor Gabriela's life for nothing.'

'But you did handle it.' She slips the leaf of grass between her thumbs. 'I never had any doubts about that, either.'

'Remedios . . .' He's getting that earnest, schoolmaster tone in his voice. Her eyes wander across the quad. 'I know things turned out well, but what I'm saying is that they might not have. The risks were more than equal to the rewards.'

This isn't true, and he knows it.

'What are you saying, Otto? That people should just spend their lives sitting in one place? That they should look at the world through a pinhole in a wall and not experience life? What are they, prisoners?'

'That's not what I'm saying. You're always twisting my words. I'm just trying to get you to admit that you went over the top this time. And to promise that you won't do it again.'

She looks from one group of students to another, picking up snatches of conversation, snatches of thought, shadows of dreams.

'Remedios? Did you hear me?'

Seeing things that aren't there.

'Yes,' she says, 'I heard you.'

'And you promise? You won't get me involved in another hare-brained scheme like that again?'

'Of course not,' says Remedios. And she raises her hands to her mouth and blows on the grass as if it's a very small trumpet.

This time Otto definitely catches a shimmer.

272